James A. Hunter

Strange Magic

J. A. Hunter

Dedication

For my Pop, the truest Rambler I know …

ONE

The Big Easy

The piano keys bobbed and danced under the pressure of my fingers. Music—low, slow, and soulful—drifted through the club, merging and twirling with wandering clouds of blue-gray smoke. So many places have no-smoking laws these days, it seems like there's nowhere in the country where a guy can take a drag from a cigarette in peace. Everyone is so worried about *their* health, they make damn sure you stay healthy by proxy.

Not Nick's Smoke House, though. Nick's—like some rare, near extinct animal—is the kind of bar where you can die unmolested by laws or ordinances. You can burn yourself up with cancer, drown yourself into liver failure, or binge on a plate of ribs until a heart attack takes you cold, and no one will say boo. And you can die to music here: the beautiful, lonely, brassy beats, of the like only ever found in New Orleans.

The house band was on a break, so I sat thumping out an old Ray Charles tune in the interim while I watched the man standing off stage in a pool of inky shadow.

I'd never met the guy before, but I instinctively knew he was looking for me, or rather *The Fixer*—a shitty alias I've been trying to ditch for years. It was in the way he stood: chest forward, back straight, arms crossed, chin outthrust. He was a man used to intimidating others, used to being obeyed. In short, he was a thug. A thug sporting an expensive suit, a three-thousand dollar watch, and a pair of loafers that probably cost more than most people paid on rent. At the end of the day though, he was still just a thug—somebody else's trained pit-bull.

I don't know why, but thugs are always looking for The Fixer. Either they got something that needs fixing or they're looking to fix me. I didn't know whether this guy wanted option A or option B, but I figured he'd get around to it in his own sweet time. So, instead of tipping my hand prematurely, I continued to pound out melodies on the black and whites. My Ray Charles faded out and I started up a gritty, ambling, version of Meade "Lux" Lewis' famous "Honky Tonk Train Blues."

My left hand hammered out the thudding, rhythmic, rock-steady pulse of a driving train, pushing its bulk across the rolling open space of some forgotten Midwest wilderness; the bass notes offered a mimicry of the ebb and flow of pumping gears. My right hand flitted across the keys, touching down here and there, sending up a rusty whistle blowing in the night. The dusty clatter of track switches being thrown. The braying of hounds, while bullyboys searched for stowaways. If there was ever a song to make a man dance his way onto the box car of a rolling train it was this funky ol' honkytonk rhythm.

I let the beat roll on, hoping the thug would hop and jive his way right out of Nick's Smoke House and out of my life, no harm, no foul. Though a whole helluva lot a people think of me as The Fixer, really I'm just an old rambler trying to get by and enjoy the time I have on this spinning little mud ball. All I wanted was for this overdressed clown to walk away and leave me be.

The man in the black suit just glared at me like I'd offered him an insult, and I knew then things would not end well between us. Still, I mostly ignored him. I should've been worried, but I wasn't.

I've been around for a good long while and I don't scare easy.

After what felt like an age, the hulking suit stepped up to the stage and into a pool of soft amber light, illuminating his features for the first time. He was enormous, six and a half feet of pro-wrestling muscle, with a pushed-in nose, and military cropped blond hair. His face was a mosaic of scars, though the thick tissue on his knuckles put them all to shame. One meaty paw lifted back a coat lapel, revealing the glint of chromed metal: a Colt 1911.

A Colt 1911 is a *big* gun, not the kind of thing a person normally chooses as a concealed carry. The things are too large to conceal easily and they can be awkward to draw on the fly, so he probably wasn't here to assassinate me. A pro-assassin would never have used something as ostentatious and conspicuous as this McGoon's 1911. A hitter would've chosen a sleek, nondescript .22. The kind of gun that's easy to hide, would go off unnoticed, get the job done without much mess, and could be disposed of in a dumpster somewhere. This guy's choice of weapon told me he was intimidating muscle, but likely better with his fists than with his piece.

"Yancy Lazarus?" he asked with a low voice like grating cement, "you the guy who fixes things?"

Yep, a thug.

I could've denied it, but the guy had found me fair and square, so it was safe to assume he already knew the answer. I nodded my head a fraction of an inch. That was all. I went right on playing as though I hadn't noticed his veiled threat or didn't care. Now don't get me wrong, I'm not suicidal and I'm not a pompous jackass—at least that's not how I see myself—but I knew I could take this guy. I had an edge, although Macho Man Hulk in the other corner didn't know it.

I can do magic and not the cheap kind of stuff you see in Vegas—with flowers, or floating cards, or disappearing stagehands. People, like me, who can touch the Vis can do real magic. Although magic isn't the right word: magic is a Rube word, for those not in the know, which is precisely why we who practice call it the Vis in the first place. *Vis*, is an old Latin word meaning *force* or energy, nothing fancy about it.

There are energies out there, underlying matter, existence, and in fact, all Creation. As it happens, I can manipulate that energy. Period. End of story.

It's a hard line to swallow, I know, but there it is. Big part of me wishes it wasn't true. Would probably make things easier for me in the long run.

One truism I've discovered in my sixty-five-years of life, however, is this: you can't always get what you want. Mick Jagger taught me that when I was still a young buck and it's as true today as it was when he first uttered those sage words. I never wanted to get mixed up with the supernatural or end up consorting with people like McGoon, standing off stage. But, let me say it again, *you can't always get what you want*, and furthermore, shit happens—I think we can safely give Forest Gump the credit for that one. Sometimes gun-wielding, pro-wrestling, goons are going to pop up in your life and complicate things.

The blond-headed giant flashed me the kind of grin that makes you want to cross the street. "It's time to leave," he said. "Time for you to get up, nice and slow, and walk out of here with me."

"And if I decide I'd rather stay?" I asked, as though such a thing was actually an option.

He shrugged meaty shoulders as large as a half side of beef. "Bad things are going to happen." He glanced left and right at the people filling the bar. "Doesn't have to be that way though, Mr. Lazarus. I'm not here to hurt you, I'm just here to escort you."

I looked around at the crowded bar, surveying the rough splattering of men and women who would be injured, maybe killed, if I let something go down in here. That wasn't something I wanted. I'm not a perfect human—I drink, smoke, and gamble in amounts *a few* might consider excessive. I may not be the most positive role model for your kids, but I don't like folks getting hurt either.

Usually, if I see some supernatural shenanigans going down, I'll put the kibosh on that shit. That's why people call me The Fixer. Stupid nickname—all because my stupid bleeding heart doesn't know when to say no.

"It's time to leave," he repeated, this time in the tone of voice that told me he was getting impatient, perhaps close to violence. But hey, let's face it, guys like this are almost always close to violence. It's like they carry a pocket flask of pent up anger and rage, taking little nips to keep 'em ready and steady.

I let out a colossal sigh—definitely going to be one of *those* days—and got up from the piano, careful to move slowly, deliberately, with my hands highly visible. Thugs, like this guy, can be a little paranoid and trigger happy, which makes sense considering the risky line of work they're in. Even though I can be hell on wheels when it comes to smashing, shooting, or otherwise blowing things up, I *am* still human. If Macho Man Hulk decided to put one in the back of my head from pointblank range I would die like anyone else.

So, I played along.

Once we got clear of bystanders I'd be at a greater advantage—able to move, find cover, toss a little lead and energy around without so many worries.

We weaved through the couples on the dance floor, dodged a few tables—obscured by drifting clouds of smoke—and then bee-lined for the back exit, which let out to the alley. I cannot tell you the number of fights that start and end in back alleys. Tip: if you find yourself in a bar and about to walk into a dark alley with a guy who would like to do you violence, don't. Just don't do it. Not ever. Not even if there's a woman to impress or friends to show off for.

Let your pride take one on the chin, instead of actually taking one of the chin. Usually, your pride will heal faster than a smashed jaw. Trust me, drinking a cheeseburger through a straw is an experience to avoid if at all possible.

Nick, the bartender and proprietor, shot me a look that said, *should I call the cops or get the shotgun?* Nick and I weren't close exactly but we were more than passing acquaintances and he was a good guy who *would* give me a hand if I needed it. I wasn't about to involve him in this trouble. Even if he didn't get hurt, he might find himself with a powerful enemy who could make things bad for him in the future.

It wouldn't be fair to do that to anyone, especially not a good guy like Nick. So instead, I gave a slight shake of my head and stepped out into an alley with rent-a-goon trailing on my heels.

Here's another tip: sometimes, bad choices are the only ones available.

The alley was not nearly as slummy as you might think. Usually in movies or books, alleyways are shadowy foreboding places: the den of seedy things like gangs, pimps, or mysterious and otherwise undefined beings of an even more unsavory nature. Maybe vampires, werewolves, or worse … In movies, the air is always resounding with the crack of gunshots or the ferocious hollering of domestic violence. Oh, and there's always some heavily muscled thug with shifty eyes, leaning a little *too* casually against the wall, smoking a cigarette, and you just know he is up to no good.

The reality is that most alleys aren't like that at all, this one included. Yes, this alley was dark, and the slightly sour stink of old garbage hung on the air, but it wasn't bursting with scores of winos roasting hot dogs over an open bonfire. It was just an alley, not super disheveled or dirty, though one I wasn't too keen to be in. That's life though, and hopefully if this was the night my ticket got punched—well, at least my body would get pitched into a relatively clean dumpster.

You have to celebrate the small things.

The bar door clicked shut. McGoon, the thug, had exited behind me so I was unable to see him pull the Colt. That in no way impeded me from hearing the soft rasp of the gun leaving its holster or the metallic click of the safety disengaging.

Well, there went the small margin of hope that things would turn out okay tonight. Not a terribly shocking fact, as things go.

A black Benz with heavy tints loitered at the end of the alley, its engine purring softly as the car idled. I was sure the car was waiting for me. That meant I had at least a few moments to think before the shooting began. Another piece of advice, compliments of your friendly, though slightly shady, rambler: do not get into mysterious cars parked suspiciously at the end of dark alleys. This is especially true if there is a man pointing a gun at you. Once you get into a car, you are more or less at the mercy of your assailant. Cars are private places where bad things can happen unobserved, and it is extraordinarily hard to dodge a bullet at pointblank range in a small, confined space.

It's always better to duke it out in the open—even if your odds aren't great—than to throw yourself on the mercy of a bad villain in a pimped out Benz. You *might* die in a firefight in the open, but hey, you might also come out on top. If, however, you get into a car with some smug, gun-toting, behemoth and he decides your time is up … well, your effective survivability rate drops to a big fat *zero*. This goes double for us mage types.

I tend to rely heavily on a hard-hitting offense and in the constricted space of a car interior I can't throw around much power without the risk of blowing myself up too. Once the Vis is conjured into the physical realm of existence, the laws of physics begin to apply. A fire construct, summoned from the Vis, will act like regular fire. Namely, it will burn the cow-farting-crap out of me just as well as the bad guys.

The car door opened ominously. Yes *ominously*—if there are dark alleys *and* guns involved, then things become ominous— and the big man behind me prodded me onward with his gun.

"Let's go for a ride," he grunted with the linguistic grace of a large boulder.

"Not gonna happen," I protested loudly enough for whoever was in the car to hear. "This is the way a lot of bad movies start—if you guys want to talk, we're gonna do it out here in the open. Or even better yet, we could go back into the bar and have a conversation over a pitcher of beer like normal people. No guns or threats." A soft chuckle drifted from the car, followed by a dumpy, thin, balding man from the backseat.

The guy reminded me more of an overworked accountant at H & R Block than some sort of Mafioso-type lieutenant. Wispy hair jutted up from the sides of his pate, a slight double chin rested against his throat, circular wire-rimmed glasses adorned his otherwise unremarkable face. If I were judging on appearances alone, I would surmise that his college counselor may have steered him into a very poorly matched career field.

But hey, who am I to judge? I look about forty—even though I'm actually in my mid-sixties—keep my hair short, and stand at 5' 10". Slightly built and in good shape, but not impressively so. I usually sport a pair of blue jeans, a T-shirt, some old boots, and my black leather coat. Pretty, unremarkable. You definitely wouldn't think scary mage or fix-it man by the looks of me.

"I've heard you have quite the sense of humor, Mr. Lazarus," the man said. "Sadly, my employer does not—its company policy that none of us underlings engage in witty or humorous banter." Hilarious, except that his perfectly deadpan delivery made me think he might not be kidding.

"This needn't take long," he said. "I suspect you already know why my associate and I are here."

"Enlighten me," I replied. As a rule of thumb, it's always good to pump enemies for info; assumptions can lead to all kinds of silly mistakes, particularly if thugs and automatic weapons are involved. That old adage, 'shoot first and ask questions later' can get real messy, real fast. A little patience, by contrast, sure goes a long way and can save a whole lot of pain—for example, the pain of getting shot in the face.

"We know you received a call earlier today, Mr. Lazarus. My associate and I are here to persuade you to stay out of that bit of business—to turn down the contract, and walk away. My employer has even authorized me to compensate you handsomely for your compliance. The price of your contract plus ten-thousand, no other strings attached."

"Gosh, that's a sweet offer." I rubbed my chin thoughtfully, even though I had no clue what in the hell he was talking about. I *had* received a call from an old friend out in California, but I hadn't taken on any kind of contract. My buddy told me there was some bad shit coming down the pipe—I had reluctantly agreed to go out and take a looksee. That was it. "Do you guys validate parking too? 'Cause that might be a deal breaker."

Silence filled the air, uncomfortable and telling.

"And if I say no?" I asked

"My associate," Mr. H & R said, nodding toward Thugzilla behind me, "will shoot you in the head and dump your body in the swamp where you will be eaten by alligators. It is highly unlikely you will ever be found given both the high rate of disappearances here in New Orleans and the transient nature of your lifestyle."

Huh. Damn good plan as such things go. Quick, efficient, brutal, and highly practical. Apparently, Mr. H & R was the Sith Lord of Mafioso bureaucrats. Lots of people *do* go missing down in the Big Easy. New Orleans is a huge city with the problems that go along with any big city, only worse. Take the problems of most major-metropolitan centers and then introduce those problems to crack, and you have New Orleans. The violent crime rate here is twice the national average and the murder rate is nearly ten times higher. Absolutely no better place in America to make a man go missing.

"You're a man of considerable talents," H & R continued, "with many connected friends. We would much rather prefer you take us up on our offer, but if your convictions compel you to say no ... business is business." He shrugged.

"Thanks, but no than—" The world exploded with sound as the Colt aimed at my head belched an unbelievable roar.

TWO:

Gun Fight

Gunshots are really, really loud, even if you are well acquainted with firearms. There are, of course, a few exceptions—little .22 caliber handguns for instance—but the Colt 1911 is *not* one of them. The abrupt and startling crash of noise was more painful than the shot. I'd prepared for the ambush shooting, of course, but I had failed miserably to account for the damn gun going off half-a-foot from my ear. At least I wasn't dead. Like I said, I have the Vis, and that gives me a tremendous hand up over most folks, even professional thugs who are clued into the supernatural side of things.

Also, this is not the first time someone has tried to shoot me in the head. Surprising, I know, considering my overwhelming tack and agreeable personality.

I'd been preparing my minor deflection construct from the moment we stepped out into the alley. Though it's not terribly difficult to stop incoming bullets outright, it is difficult to do from such close range. So instead of conjuring up some gaudy and overt construct, I created a thin invisible barrier between Rent-a-Thug and myself; a barrier which absorbed the kinetic energy from the bullet and redirected it, causing the round to career passed my face and into the wall on my right.

Thankfully, the walls of the bar were thick slabs of concrete and brick, which stopped the round cold without any further ricochets.

Man, I wish I had a Polaroid of the shooter's face. It's not every day that a pro thug misses a shot from so close. I bet he looked like a bully who had some bigger bully steal his lunch money. Classic.

I turned and rolled out left, not expecting the shock of missing to last long. In short order, the Colt would fire again and I wanted to make my move before the shooter got his bearing or his chance. I came up in a crouch and took a slow, measured breath, drawing deeply from the Vis. I could feel energy course into me, thrumming and pulsing in time to the beat of my heart. I was afraid, but that was no good right now. I needed stillness and focus to work. So I breathed *out*, expelling my fear, anxiety, and anger in that short pause—those were things for later, acquaintances I couldn't afford right now. I inhaled power, force, raw life. Time slowed, taking a deep breath all its own, as my body tightened like coiled steel.

I lashed out, left hand forward, palm open, a snarl curling the edges of my lips.

Air and spirit, intertwined into a complex weave of force, filled the space around me like a tightly compressed pocket of fluid. In one instant, I could feel the weight of all that accumulated air and in the next instant it rolled out like a crushing tsunami of force, spirit, and wind.

A javelin thrust of power picked up the thug in the nice suit and sent him sprawling high into the air. The thug flipped head over heels, cartwheeling through the evening sky, a string of shocked and panicked curses filling the night. He sailed over the nearest dumpster—a well-aimed golf-ball headed for the green—before colliding with a sickening crack against the building wall.

Simultaneously, a serpentine wave of hurricane wind surged out from me, eating up ground as it hurtled toward the Benz—an ethereal onslaught of silvered force rolling and bubbling like a fast moving mist. In seconds the mist enveloped the tricked out ride, obscuring the vehicle and bleeding over onto the street beyond. There was a swirling rush of movement within the opaque haze as the Benz jolted violently into the air, casually flipping onto its roof as though swatted by some enormous, unseen hand.

The car landed with a crash of shrieking metal and crunching glass, a mammoth clamor, though softly muted by the constructed force fog, which easily concealed the sharp report of my behemoth pistol firing into the night.

15

Now, I can sling some energy with the best of 'em, but I also carry a single, heavy-duty pistol as backup. My gun is a specialty item, hand crafted by the *Dökkálfar*, and acid etched with runes of power—think the ill-behaved-Frankenstein-spawn of Dirty Harry's .44 Magnum Smith & Wesson. Most handguns don't do diddly against preternatural players, besides annoy the crap out of them, but my piece inflicts lots and lots of damage on *anything* unfortunate enough to be in my way. I'm talking colossal, scorched earth, damage. Also, it's quiet, supernaturally tempered to be so— the Vis equivalent of a silencer.

But wait, there's more … the damn thing also weighs about a million friggin' pounds and makes a great paperweight. Doesn't get any better than that.

I spun, pistol drawn and level, ready to fill the thug from the bar with about a pound of lead, but he was already sprawled up against the wall in a heap, blood oozing from his scalp and face. I should have killed him, if I left him alive and at my back, he could wake up and finish me. My finger was on the trigger, squeezing ever so slightly.

Shit. I couldn't kill him lying there as defenseless as some ugly, genetically altered gorilla. Killing him was the smart choice, but I've never been terribly bright. Killing a man in self-defense is one thing, but that guy was out like a busted light bulb and I couldn't off him.

I swiveled back to the front, scanning the upended Benz for any potential threat.

The *rapt-tat-tat*, of semi-automatic assault rifle fire filled my ears. It took me only a moment to locate the source of the heavy weapon blast. The driver of the Benz had crawled loose of the twisted wreckage and was placing precise and even bursts of fire at me. This was not pray and spray shooting either, this was the measured fire separation of someone with tactical training— either former military or police. The alley left me little room to maneuver and few obstacles to seek cover behind.

I gathered my will once more, drawing in compressed air and thin strains of radiant heat, intertwining them with spirit and will into a vaguely shimmering mist of reddish-light. The shield wasn't intended to stop the bullets outright—physics are an issue even when using the Vis, and stopping something so small, moving with such tremendous force takes a proportionally greater degree of energy. Instead, I created a superheated friction barrier which dissolved the incoming rounds into a fine spray of slow moving and harmless powder.

The shooter's bullets continued to plow uselessly into my friction shield, while I lined up my shot. He was in the prone, forty-yards out, and partially concealed by the hulking wreckage of the toppled Benz, not an easy shot. It's the kind of shot people don't make in real life, not with a handgun and definitely not in a combat situation.

I'm a good shot. My pistol's imbued by the Vis and responds, at least in part, to my will, which grants me a far greater degree of accuracy than most other shooters. I fired two shots in rapid succession on the exhale, surrounding my rounds in a small pocket of air, allowing them to pass unmolested through my glowing shield. The first shot crunched into metal frame some three inches or so from the shooter's head. Here I am talking about what an exceptional marksman I am. *Jeez.*

The second shot punched a gaping hole in his head, above his left eyebrow.

The resultant mess was not pretty. I know, such senseless violence doesn't befit a hero. I'm not a hero. A hero might fire to disable, a hero might try to save the hapless goon, a hero might do any number of improbable and idiotic things. I'm not that guy.

In my book, when people try to kill me, it's my policy to kill them first and to do a damn thorough job of it. I don't go around shooting people all willy-nilly, now, but if someone intends to harm me or mine … I hope their life insurance is paid in full.

THREE

Answers

Now, someone might ask why I carry a gun at all, especially when creating constructs from the Vis can be so much more efficient. There are a couple of things to remember. First, those flashy constructs—badass as they may be—take a veritable truck-load of work and energy. It's like lifting weights, every rep takes a little bit out, and over time those reps add up. A good bit of that energy comes from the environment itself. In fact, most constructs are a combination of elemental forces derived from whatever is near at hand—water, air, heat, magnetic force.

But a healthy chunk of that power also comes from inside the practitioner. Tapping into the Vis is kind of like trying to light a candle with a friggin' volcano—one misstep, one lax moment, and your ass will be up a fiery-stream of doom. An irresponsible mage can easily draw in too much Vis, become overtaxed in the process, and permanently lose the ability to touch the source at all. Burn out happens all the time.

Shooting, on the other hand, takes almost no effort whatsoever. It's fast, ugly, and brutal, sure—but as long as you have enough rounds, and the stomach for it, you can go all day. Precisely why I carry the gun in the first place, it offers me portfolio diversity. Flipping over cars isn't easy lifting, let me tell you, so whenever I can rely on my good ole fashion bang-bang machine, I do. Waste not, want not, my granddad use to say—though I doubt he was talking about shooting people.

I let the reddish mist disperse, though I kept myself open to the Vis, ready to recall the shield in an instant. I felt fairly certain that the thug and the driver were the only muscle, but it was possible that the unassuming accountant was packing too. I made my way to the wreckage and found the little man slumped on the other side of the vehicle, wounded. A bleeding gash marred his right arm; his right foot was pinned under the roof of the Benz. He was passed out but breathing steadily.

Average police response time for a neighborhood like this was about eight minutes, which meant I had maybe six minutes to pump the guy for information. Drawing upon the source, I gathered microscopic particles of humid water vapor from the air, condensing those bits and pieces until a basketball-size glob of water floated above my palm. Then I dumped that water right into H & R's face.

He awakened with a satisfying sputter and a gasp.

"Alright, you need to tell me what in the hell you're talking about. I want to know who your employer is and I want to know what contract I am supposed to walk away from. Easy peasy, bud."

"The cops will be here soon," the little man said, a groggy slur to his speech, "and I assume there are a couple of dead men here—this could get messy for you. You are a wanted man, Mr. Lazarus, and I shouldn't think the justice system will afford you another chance at escape—not after you slipped away from those FBI agents in Memphis. I'm sure they will take ample care to ensure you are well restrained, perhaps sedation ..." He smiled, smug and full of himself.

Err right, I also travel around because I'm sort of a wanted fugitive. The FBI has a longstanding *BOLO* out on me—I'm wanted for murder, aiding and abetting, acts of domestic terrorism and sedition, tax-evasion ... blah, blah, blah. You get the drift, though I really feel like my record has been blown hugely out of proportion. I'm not a terrorist that's for sure as shit. And sedition? I fought for this country, lost friends for this country. Tax evasion? Well, maybe I'm behind on a few taxes. And technically, I guess they were right about the murder wrap, but the vast majority of the things I've killed over the years weren't human, contrary to appearances.

"Precisely why we don't have time for this shit," I replied. "Who's your boss and what contract are you talking about?"

"Like you don't know," he said, which pissed me off because I *really* didn't know. My friend out west had asked me to come and take a look—said he would count it as a personal favor. I didn't know anything though; I didn't know who this guy's boss was, nor had I been contracted out for any kind of job. This was pro bono work I tell you. I was only being a Good Samaritan!

I could hear the distant warble of a police siren. My first inclination was to drop a compulsion glamour on his ass to elicit the information I needed, but that's some gray area shit. The mage ruling body, The Guild of the Staff, looks down on that sort of thing. I couldn't afford another misstep with them.

So instead, I settled for good ol' physical torture, which—believe it or not—was the more merciful option. I focused my will and energy on the moisture in his eyes.

"You feel that?" I whispered.

He groaned in response.

"That's the intraocular fluid in your pupils freezing. Hurts like a real son of a bitch, I know from experience. Pretty soon—I'd say maybe thirty seconds—ice crystals will form. It's gonna hurt worse than a bad divorce and leave you with irreversible blindness. All I want to know is who your boss is, and what contract you think I've taken. This is information you already assume I have, so please cooperate—you're not betraying anyone with that info."

He let out another soft moan as miniscule ice-chips occluded his vision. The guy made it thirteen seconds before he caved. Impressive.

"Yraeta. Cesar Yraeta ..." he said through clenched lips. "Reliable sources have informed us that you have been contracted to make a series of retaliation hits on our organization."

Well flaming-dog-poo-in-a-bag. That was a curveball I hadn't seen coming, a real kick in the groin. I released my effort of will, the ice crystals immediately dissipated.

"I *am* going out to California," I said, "but I have no contract and I intend to perform no retaliation hits—clear? I may be a lot of things, but hit man is not one of them. Not anymore." I turned and walked away as a black and white tore ass around the street end, its sirens issuing loud squawks, while its flashers tattooed the surrounding buildings with splashes of red and blue. More marked cruisers followed, but I wasn't worried. Now, there would be more cops flooding in, and those cops would undoubtedly be on the lookout for suspicious characters fleeing the scene.

As it happens I am a suspicious character, and, as it happens, I was also leaving the scene. But, I was still certain I would pass by unnoticed and untroubled. I'm a wanted man, but I'm also as tricky as a chameleon to find. I was not fleeing, for one, I was walking quickly—not nearly as suspicious. More to the point though, my black leather jacket is also a specialty item, which offers a wide array of impressive survival features. My jacket is flame retardant—not the same thing as flame *proof*, believe you me—and lined with ultralight Kevlar and slash-resistant fabric, which means it'll stop small caliber bullets and knives. Covert, modern day, body armor. An absolute essential in this uncertain day and age.

It also maintains a subtle glamour, making the wearer, me, more innocuous. It doesn't make me invisible, which is possible but tremendously more difficult, but rather makes me boring— Alan Greenspan giving a lecture on market fluctuations, boring. Unless someone is looking for me specifically, their eyes will slip around me as though I am nothing more than an extra on a movie set. The Vis does have its perks: you can *literally* make yourself duller than drying paint, which is awesome I guess … unless you're trying to pick up women.

I strolled around the corner as another patrol car sped by. They didn't even slow down.

I probably could have loitered around a little longer, but I figured it was time to get out of town, time to get west and find some answers.

FOUR:

Going West

The drive from New Orleans to Los Angeles is not a short one, though there are longer trips. The journey is about 2,000 miles of open roadway and rolling strips of empty desert wilderness. You have to drive across the entire state of Texas, which ought to tell you something since Texas is larger than many modern nations. The drive takes a little under thirty hours to make and that's if you're one of those ultra-committed, no-nonsense types who only stop for fill-ups. Oh, and if you don't mind having your ass glued to a seat for thirty-friggin'-hours straight.

I am not on ones those types of people.

I love being on the open road. For all intents and purposes, I basically live on the open road. I am technically homeless, as in I have no house, apartment, or condo to call my own (glamorous, I know). Please understand that I choose to exist this way. I am not a bum or a panhandler. I don't beg to make a living. I am gainfully employed … admittedly, my line of work consists mostly of playing blues for beer and gambling for groceries.

Say what you will, employment is still employment.

Now, I may not have a home, but I do have a car: a midnight blue '86 El Camino with a high-gloss, black camper shell attached to the back of the truck bed. Yeah, you heard that right— an El Camino with a camper shell. That's what's up. At first it might sound a little funky, but it's one sweet ride and it's about a gajillion times cooler than having a stupid apartment. The camper shell doesn't have a shower or toilet, so it doesn't make a proper home, but it does give me a nice little nook to keep my gear and catch a long blink once in a while.

And the Camino is also one souped-up mutha—I'm talking a 355 Chevy small block, turbo 350 transmission, posi-track rear differential. In short, my home is fast, mobile, badass-squared and can take me pretty much anywhere I please, which is not a bad way to live even if it's not exactly the way most people live. I'd also bet dollars to donuts that my home can beat your home in a car-race any day of the week.

With all of that said, thirty hours of straight driving through southern desert still sucks—you need to be damn near inhuman to drive for thirty hours. We magi are human and only slightly less physically fragile than most regular, Joe-blow, mortals. Tapping into the Vis does grant us a certain edge: we move faster, can lift a little more, heal injuries quicker and live *much* longer. But aside from longevity, the Vis only grants slight improvements in most areas.

I could have pushed myself to make the trip in a single go, but then I would show up with a terrible caffeine headache, nearly zombified from exhaustion, and there would probably be a goon convention in town, expecting me as the keynote speaker. So instead, I settled down in Las Cruces, New Mexico after a grueling fifteen hour slog filled with lots of Zeppelin, Bob Dylan, Ray Charles, Little Sammy Davis, and Muddy Waters. Oh, and also about a cooler full of energy drinks and a bathtub worth of gas station coffee.

Plus, giving myself a little extra space and time was good and necessary for my soul. I'd killed a man back in New Orleans. It had been the right decision and I would take the same shot again. But still. I killed a man.

In action flicks, the hero can murder a football stadium full of bad guys and never even blink. That's not the way it is in real life though, or at least it shouldn't be. When the firefight is on, it's important to push your emotions into the background. Feeling all soft-hearted and conflicted instead of pulling the trigger *will* get you killed. Eventually, the firefight ends. Eventually, those emotions come roaring back like a crazy ex, and that crazy metaphorical ex will toss all of your emotional furniture right off the balcony and into the pool.

Killing someone is not glorious. I've killed a good number of people and each one has taken a toll and left a mark. The guy I shot back in the alley would never go to another movie. He would never eat out at a nice restaurant with his significant other. He would never pray or laugh or cry again. Whatever bad or good he might have gone on to do—he wouldn't. A life, full of possibility, snuffed out. It hurt.

He shouldn't have tried to kill me.

Still, I would carry his memory.

I was glad for the ride, it gave me the space I needed to vent and grieve, to decompress and deal with all the shit.

I could have camped out in the Camino, but I wanted a shower, and having four walls around me also seemed like a good idea.

The motel I pulled into was called the Ranger, a cheap and dirty off brand place, which proudly displayed a gaudy red-neon sign boasting both *vacancies* and—I kid you not—'*Color TV.*' Seriously, what century do we live in? There were two other cars loitering in the pothole-filled lot, but it looked like everyone was in for the night, not surprising since it was well after eleven. The building was small and made of cheap motel stucco—typical for the southwest—and sat in an L-shape. The renting office was at the front of the L with fifteen or so rooms jutting off and to the right on both floors.

I made my way into the renting office, a small bell above the door gave out a little tinkle. The room was devoid of life, the only occupant was a small flyer rack against the far wall, littered with pamphlets which proclaimed all the wonderful attractions Las Cruces had to offer. The room smelled of stale coffee and stale air, a harsh piney odor hung in the room like a haze trying to cover the scent of poor maintenance—you can only polish a turd so much.

After a few moments, a moderately overweight man of maybe fifty, with gray swoops at either temple, appeared behind a small, wood-paneled desk housing an antique computer and a host of loose-leaf papers.

"Evenin' Sir, what can I do for ya' tonight?" The man's accent was thick with the twang of the country, his drawl, slow but pleasant.

"Good evening," I said, stifling an abrupt yawn with my fist. "Been one heck of a long day, I need a room for the night. A bottom unit." Under normal circumstances, the clerk might have been suspicious—it was late and it looked like I had been in a helluva scrap, which was true. My glamourous jacket though, ensured a bored and slightly annoyed look never left his face.

Even without the jacket, though, he probably wouldn't have taken too much note of me. I cultivate the unremarkable, it's one of my minor hobbies. Oh, and it helps me not to die. The ability to fly under the radar is crucial to creating a certain degree of safety for myself—it makes me harder to find and harder to follow, both important things when you have as many enemies as I do.

"Well 'at shouldn't be a problem," the clerk said after a moment, "we're nearly empty on the bottom, so you can have your pick. It's gonna run you forty-five fifty for the night, and you're free to stop by in the morning and grab a complimentary coffee. Check out time's at eleven—if you steal the towels we'll charge your card for them. I'll need an ID and a credit card."

I pulled both from my wallet, the license and credit card read Rick Daily and both were fakes, good fakes. I have about twenty other aliases that I go by, each has his own set of ID's (including passports), credit cards, and bank accounts. Only a few people in the world know more than a handful of those names, and none know all of them. Anonymity is king.

I grabbed my rucksack from the camper and headed over to my room. I've stayed in a lot of hotels in my time, you might say I am something of a connoisseur. The room concealed behind door 7 was exactly as I had envisioned it. Only dirtier, which is saying something rather significant. A full bed covered with a worn motel comforter of blues and grays sat against the left wall, a chipped nightstand was snuggled cozily against the right side of the bed. A TV, straight out of the 1950s, sat on the opposite wall. The white walls of the room had been stained a sickening yellowish color from years of accumulated tobacco smoke. The smell was pungent—and I smoke like a chimney.

All I wanted was sleep, but in my line of work it's always better to play things safe. It was especially wise to take precautions tonight, considering I knew there were bad people actively gunning for me. It was unlikely that anyone would've been able to track me, but not outside the realm of possibility. I mean, it had only taken those yahoos at the bar about twelve hours to find me.

Against my better judgment, I placed a call to my friend out west to let him know where I was and filled him in about the attack outside the bar; then I went about setting up my defensive wards for the evening.

It's hard to create defensive wards for a motel room because they lack the foundational *domicilium seal*, which is optimal for creating a Vis barrier. A domicilium seal surrounds most proper homes, or really any place where human beings live for any extended period of time. It's a barrier of sorts, a super-real energy field, more solidly grounded in material reality than just about anything. They accumulate a certain energy from the ordinary, the mundane, the routine affairs of everyday human life.

That energy is kind of like a static charge: it builds and builds and builds as mortals shuffle their way across the carpet of life, and overtime that charge can become damn potent. It does take time—a seal won't pop up overnight—but eventually that invested static life force, Vim, will create a barrier which is too real for most beings of Spirit to cross over without invitation. Precisely the reason a dirty Vamp can't enter your home without permission. Though seals are not impenetrable to supernatural beings, they're damned close even without wards.

Four walls and a roof does not a home make, however. Hotels, like the Ranger, didn't have any such seal—they're full of people in transition and thus lack the necessary stability for creating a solid barrier. This is the only part about being a drifter that sucks. I've lived this way for a long time though, and have managed to create some defensive wards despite my limitations. Improvise, adapt, and overcome I say.

I salted the door and window with grocery-store rock salt, which is hell on wheels against beings of pure spirit, like ghosts or poltergeists. Then I placed a charm bag—a small burlap sack filled with ritual ingredients and infused with a small measure of power—underneath my pillow, meant to help hide me from supernatural predators.

Finally, I rummaged around in my rucksack until I found my pack of sticky note wards. Yes, sticky notes—little yellow ones. When a guy's on the move and without the protection of a permanent home, it's good to have a backup plan; the sticky notes are my plan and they work well, thank you very much. Each one has been inscribed (by a *magic* marker—magic, get it) with various names and symbols of power, and then invested with a slight amount of latent energy, which is stored in the sigils. The notes don't last long—they degrade and lose their potency after a month or so—but that means I only need to create a new batch twelve times a year. Work smarter not harder, right?

I pulled off the top sheet, covered front and back with writing, and affixed it to the door. The sticky note would wake me up if any supernatural predator stopped by, and it also had a viscous surprise for anything that tried to force the door open.

With my dirty and nicotine stained room as warded as I could manage, I washed up, stripped down to my jeans, and hit the rack. It would be an early day and I deserved a little undisturbed shut-eye.

FIVE:

The Ranger

They say there's no rest for the wicked, which I guess is true since I woke up after only two hours of sleep. Something was in the parking lot—I had no idea what, but the sticky note had given me a heads up—and I was positive of two things: one, whatever was out there was bad news, like uber-smart-gun-wielding-bears bad news. Two, whatever was out there was about to make my evening absolutely craptastic.

I had enough time to get my shirt, jacket, and boots on before the thing in the parking lot opened up on my room with a spray of automatic machine gun fire. I leapt behind the bed—a thin and feeble shelter against machine gun rounds—and curled into a tight ball, back exposed to the front wall but covered by my Kevlar strength coat. Most of the rounds went wide or remained at thigh level, well above my heroic, and not at all cowardly, fetal position on the floor. A few strays passed through the mattress and smacked me square in the lower back. The jacket prevented the lead from penetrating, but my kidneys still felt like they'd been worked over by Mighty Mouse. When the firing finally let up, I rolled over with a grunt, and fetched my gun from the nightstand.

I moved into a low crouch and took a quick looksee over the edge of the bed. The nightstand, walls, and TV were riddled with wounds—chunks of wood and shattered glass decorated the floor. The guest phone lay devastated near the window, its electronic guts spilled out in a heap. The damage was intense yet, surprisingly, the room didn't look that much worse than when I had checked in. Before, the room had been a real P.O.S.—now it was a real P.O.S. sporting a few holes. Not a huge loss. The damage might even motivate the owner to consider some renovations. There's always a silver lining.

I dropped back into the prone, my head on the floor, in case the gunman decided to indulge in another round of target practice. I stared at the entryway from beneath the bed, gun fixed at ankle level. The door handle rattled. Then, after a moment, *click*. The cheap hotel door exploded outward in a shower of brilliant light and wood-turned-shrapnel pieces. Apparently, my sticky note construct had survived the initial wave of gunfire.

Good for me, something actually worked right.

I cautiously moved back into a crouch, taking advantage of the few seconds I had to ready myself for another onslaught. I held my pistol with my right hand, my left was empty and palm open, holding the weaves for either a defensive air shield or a lance of fire.

The tip of a gun barrel popped through the smashed doorframe, followed by a gunman peeking around the corner. I let loose a javelin of red-white flame, thick as my wrist. With a whip-like *crack*, it tore the gun from the assailant's hand and sent it clattering onto the parking lot asphalt. A vaguely humanoid thing, wearing black fatigue bottoms, blurred through the door toward me.

It was all long arms, crushing teeth, and gray, flabby flesh interspersed with ragged tuffs of yellow fur. Its visage was vaguely reminiscent of a feral hyena: elongated muzzle filled with vicious shark teeth, a punched in snout, and beady, deep-set eyes, all framed by a cropped mane of spotted golden fur. It scared the living bejesus out of me.

The monster surged forward in a rolling gorilla-like gait, quickly eating the distance between us.

"Well crap," I said to no one in particular.

The thing cannonballing toward me like death on roller-skates was a Rakshasa—a filthy scavenger dredged up from the lowest pit of creation. The things aren't a common sight, particularly outside of India where ancestral ties and totems of power invest them with minor deity-like power. And usually when they are running around, they hide behind human flesh masks, all the better to avoid detection and hunt their prey.

I unleashed another spear of angry heat on instinct, but I might as well have shot the shit-eating thing with a squirt gun for all the good it did. Rakshasa have a notorious reputation as mage killers because of their natural resistance to all things Vis. The flame rolled around the Rakshasa's charging form in a flare of light, setting the curtains ablaze, but leaving the creature intact. Man, the owner of the hotel was going to charge my credit card for sure.

I opened up with my revolver, pulling the trigger twice in rapid succession.

The creature flowed around those first two shots, it limbs moving as though the bones beneath were gelatinous. My third, more carefully aimed shot, clipped the thing in its ankle, gauging out a fist-sized chunk of loose, gray flesh. Black blood, like tar, sprayed the carpet in a shower of gore—the Rakshasa pulsed forward, unfazed. I took aim at its knee, hoping to hobble the bastard, but before I could pull the trigger, the creature hurled itself onto the ceiling—yes the ceiling—and scampered toward me. I stared on in slack-jawed surprise.

Hadn't seen that coming.

I dropped and rolled onto my back, tracking its progress across the ceiling, hoping to get another shot off before the mauling began.

I felt supremely outclassed as the beast launched itself at me from overhead, crashing into me like a semi-truck. Pain exploded through my ribs, back, and neck as it pinned me to the floor, the wind gone from my lungs as the Rakshasa's immense weight pressed in on me. The reek coming off the creature was almost enough to push me into delirium: an awful stench of old meat, soured garbage, and musky, unwashed animal. The texture of its saggy flesh was like an old, rubbery boot and it let off heat like a personal furnace.

God, my life supremely sucks sometimes.

I had, by some magnificent stroke of good fortune, managed to interpose my revolver between myself and the Rakshasa's formidable, though saggy, body. I pulled the trigger three times in quick succession. The detonation reverberated in my chest and a flood of warm viscous liquid ran over my gun hand.

Gross, but oddly satisfying.

The creature let out a yowl of frustrated pain and rage as it pulled away. Crushing pressure engulfed my arm. The world rattled at the edges. My body jerked up and out, and just like that, I was sailing toward the large front window; another bit of good fortune, since I probably would've broken my back had I collided with the wall.

Right through the window I went. Most of the glass had broken out during the first spray of gunfire, saving me from a myriad of minor lacerations. I landed a full ten feet out on the rough parking lot blacktop. The son of a bitch had a heck of an arm, I'll give it that much.

I rolled into the fall, robbing the impact of its full and devastating effect, but the pain was still significant. My rotator cuff shrieked its protest while my back and knees joined in the impromptu rally. In movies, action heroes regularly get up from this kind of thing, but let me tell you something: that's a bunch of bullshit. I'm raising the flag here.

All across the country, people sustain serious injuries from slipping on ice. To offer some perspective here, the second leading cause of accidental death in the world is *falling*. Seriously, falling. Getting tossed twenty feet is much worse than slipping on ice by an order of magnitude that's hard to calculate. Even still, this was the best possible thing that could've happened to me. At least with some distance between us, I would be able to do something.

Yes, getting my ass hurled through a window and into the parking lot was good news—I know, I know, my life *is* amazing.

My revolver was out of rounds and I didn't have time for a reload, so that option was out. But the Rakshasa's boxy little automatic—it looked like a PP-19 Bizon—wasn't far off. With a grunt of effort, I flipped onto my belly and started crawling for it. The gun couldn't have been more than two feet away when a hail of ninja kunai knives soared through the open window in my direction.

Not only was my assailant almost physically unstoppable, supernaturally resistant to the Vis, and military trained—it was an honest-to-goodness ninja. A ninja. In what world is that fair or okay? If you ever have to say that you've been assaulted by a supernatural, man-eating, hyena-ninja, it is a sure sign that your life has gone terribly, terribly wrong somewhere.

Most of the blades were hastily thrown and went wide, but one of the sharp matte-black razors grazed my outstretched arm, leaving a flare of bright crimson pain in its wake. The Rakshasa hurtled through the broken window like an Olympic athlete—never mind that it had most of one foot missing and several fist-sized holes in its torso—before launching itself at me.

That was exactly the kind of mistake I needed.

I couldn't stop it outright with the Vis and its mass was far too great to halt with raw force, but I had a plan. I reached into the well of magma-hot power, drawing forth energy deep within the dusty New Mexico soil. Fine flows of fire, air, and earth sprouted to life from the ground before me.

With a great *crack-thud*, a chunk of concrete and asphalt big as a car tore itself free from the parking lot and whipped at the incoming Rakshasa. A stone hurled from some giant and magnificent sling. This was my version of David and Goliath. Now, the Rakshasa may have been big, and it may have been immune to direct Vis constructs, but it was not a being of pure spirit—like a ghost or poltergeist. Therefore, in the real world at least, it was still constrained by the laws of physics. While suspended in the air, it was on a fixed and unalterable trajectory.

The enormous chunk of rock sideswiped the Rakshasa like a NFL linebacker and the creature was as susceptible to the impact as any other material object would have been. Even though the beast was heavy, the rock was heavier and moving at a greater rate of speed—force equals mass times acceleration. The rock won the math equation. My high school physics teacher was right, math *is* applicable to real, everyday life.

The Rakshasa crashed into a parked car about thirty feet away, sandwiched between the now twisted steel frame of the car and the enormous boulder.

The rock had smashed up a large portion of the Rakshasa's jaw, one of its lank and disproportionate arms hung limply down the side of its body. It tried moving forward, but couldn't. I hadn't just hit the beast with a big rock—I'd hit it with a big rock made of asphalt, superheated with weaves of intense thermal energy. The tar melted into hot black sludge, which clung to the Rakshasa's form, impeding its movements, even if not stopping them completely.

That rock trick had been a spectacular construct—a real bit of metaphysical heavy lifting and I didn't want to risk trying the same thing again. The Rakshasa's boxy little gun was my best choice. I staggered to my feet with a grunt and a tremendous effort of will. I reached the gun well before the Rakshasa could get its shit together and get moving.

I knew what the weapon was, but I hadn't fired anything like it before. If I had needed to reload—or even turn off the safety—I probably would have been shit outta luck. The gun was ready to go though, so I tucked the butt-stock into my shoulder and cut loose like a college kid on his first binger.

The trigger was light under my finger and the gun responded quickly and with surprisingly little recoil. Angry noise and pinprick flashes of light cut into the night as the gun spat out round after round. Though a few regular rounds probably wouldn't have done much to the Rakshasa under normal circumstances, there were way more than a *few* rounds and these were anything but normal circumstances.

Within seconds, thirty-rounds chewed into the horror, leaving a score of gaping and bloodied wounds. Such injuries may have been small beans and bee stings to the Rakshasa, but enough bee stings can kill a man. My efforts still weren't enough to put the Rakshasa down for good. It was enough motivation, however, to cause the thing to turn tail and hobble slowly into the night with another yowl of anger. It was moving pretty slow with all that tar stuck in its nasty-ass fur, but I couldn't have given chase even had I wanted too.

So, I flipped it the bird—not terribly helpful, but very cathartic—and wobbled back toward my room, pulling in labored and painful gulps of air.

I needed to move quickly before the authorities got involved, so I made a sweep of the room. All I had to do was grab my bag and hit the road. My rucksack was shoved down between the bed and the wall. Close by, and slightly under the mattress, lay a cheap, black, disposable cell phone—the kind a hired assassin might use to contact an employer. I stuffed it in my jeans, slung my pack across my shoulder—sending a renewed wave of pain along my spine—and limped out to the Camino.

At least my wheels hadn't been mistreated by the Rakshasa. Had the creature hurt my baby ... well, let's just say that would've made things personal. Shoot at me, okay. Throw me through a window, maybe we can work things out. But mess with the Camino? I don't put up with that kind of shit. No one messes with the Camino.

I slid into the driver's seat, started the engine, and puttered onto the road, driving away slowly in a deliberate effort to draw no unwanted attention my way.

After a minute or two, I dug the cell phone from my front pocket and checked the contact list. There was a single California number listed under Gavin Morse.

Progress—I had a lead.

SIX

Stitches

"Twice, Greg," I told the stocky man sitting next to me at the little kitchen table. "Twice, people have showed up trying to sell me the farm, and all because I agreed to do you one miserable little favor."

"Shut up and stop fidgeting," Greg grunted curtly as he threaded a curved needle through the gash in my arm, compliments of the Rakshasa's kunai knives. Greg was a black guy, in good shape, sporting a military grade haircut, and a close-cropped beard speckled with more gray than black. A real sparkplug.

"We'll talk when I'm finished," he grunted again. "Until then, hold your belly-aching." I sat in sullen silence—this was his fault. The least he could do was endure my good-natured, and totally reasonable, complaining. Sure, maybe complaining didn't change anything, but it's still the sacred right of the suffering. Sacred right, dammit.

Greg Chandler was a good and solid man, but he had never been the type to suffer complainers easily or lightly. We had both been Lance Corporals during Nam, did a rough tour together, and the rest was history. Never mind that he had been a Marine-Corp-lifer from the get go and I had been, at best, a reluctant and occasionally whiney recruit. We had parted ways years ago—he to a lifetime of military duty, and I to a life of rambling, blues, and beer—but we had stayed in touch.

Generally, a friend made in a fighting position—never a foxhole, for Marines—was a friend for life.

"Alright." He tied off my final stitch and cut the thread. "You look like twenty pounds of shit crammed into a ten pound bag—bruises, lacerations, and I think you may have had an arm underneath this purple sausage attached to your torso." He cast a suspicious look at my gun arm. "Better tell me everything."

"Thank you for your overwhelming compassion, Greg. It's moving, really."

"Boo-hoo," he said, "Tears later, talk now."

With a sigh, I told him about the scuffle outside the club, the mild-mannered H & R Block lieutenant, the Rakshasa, and the name in the fumbled cell phone.

Greg may've moved into a quaint ranch-style home in an upscale LA suburb after retiring from the Corps, but his life wasn't all solitude, tranquil gardening, or paint-by-number landscapes. He'd taken up with the Lucis Venántium, a secret order devoted to hunting and killing anything that dared to prey on hapless mortals.

It sounds fake, I know, like some kind of cheesy TV show or something, but someone *does* need to keep a check on all the Outworld things lurking under bridges and down dark alleys. The Hunters of the Venántium are kind of like the mortal police, only for all the things—both malicious and benign—which are untouchable through regular channels.

You can't call the cops on an angry spirit or rogue vampire.

"Hmph," he said. Classic Greg, let me tell you.

"Hmph," I repeated, "that's what you got for me? Greg, I'm good but I'm not a phone-line physic. You're going to have to give me a little more to go on, bud."

He paused, not saying anything, a far off look in his eyes. I knew the look. He was going through the story again, adding up the pieces, trying to fit the details into a bigger picture.

"Well this whole thing stinks to dagon hell," he finally said, "and it doesn't cast me in a fair light—if our roles were reversed, I'd be takin' a hard look at me right about now ..." He let the sentence drag into an uncomfortable silence. He was right, of course, this whole thing did make him out to be a likely villain and my natural number one suspect.

He started this colossal shit-storm by calling me in the first place. He'd known my location in New Orleans, and he'd been the only one clued in to my location in Las Cruces. True, there were some freaky-deaky types that could've gotten the info through the mystic pipeline, but there weren't a lot of them. Now, Greg didn't have a motive for the hit, but the facts were still rather unflattering.

I didn't suspect him though. He was Greg, and Greg wouldn't sell me out, no matter how the stats stood at the moment.

I lit a cigarette, earning a glare of disapproval, but no comment. He was the health conscious sort.

"Greg, we go back an awfully long way." I took a few drags, letting the smoke linger between us. "And I guess I'd be lying if I said that I wasn't wondering how all the bad guys happened to know where I was … but when it comes down to it, I trust you, brother. Something *is* going on here, but I know you wouldn't give me up like that. I came to you wounded and damn-near defenseless." I waved my sausage arm in his direction. "Wouldn't have done that if I didn't think you were on the level with me. But maybe it's time you told me what's going on here— I'm tired of having people take shots at me without at least knowing why."

"Fair 'nough." He rubbed at his chin for a moment, lightly scratching at his beard. "Fair 'nough. This whole thing started 'bout a month ago," he said. "There were some gangland hits that looked like they might've belonged in our end of the pool. I always keep my ear out for that kind of thing, and when I saw these hits on the police blotter, I knew it was worth pursuing. Plus, the lead agent is a buddy of mine, Alan Harley, so I thought it would be safe to take a look. Al's a detective with the Criminal Gang and Homicide Division—he's been on the job a long time, seen some strange shit. Usually, he comes to me when he thinks it's something the LAPD won't be able to handle."

"Okay, so he came to you with it?" I asked.

"No. I went to him."

"Well, why didn't he come to you? Are you sure you can trust the guy?"

"We're not exactly regular drinkin' buddies, but we've worked together a handful of times and he seems like an all right fella. I've taken a look at him, and he seems clean. Internal Affairs investigated him once upon a time—some suspicion that he might be an on-again-off-again informant for a few gangs, but IA cleared him. Hell, even if he is a little dirty, that's none of my business anyways. Other than that—pretty vanilla. Has a wife named Judy. Lives in Burbank."

"All right." I tried laying it all out in my mind. "So you approach Detective Al with your hunch and you guys have been working the case, but why drag me into it—gang violence isn't up my alley."

"Good grief, Yancy, I'm gettin' to it—hold your horses— you'd think you'd have learned some patience by now."

I took my last drag and snubbed my cigarette in the ashtray—the one Greg only ever uses when I visit—and gave him my most patient and winning smile. He didn't look all that impressed, but hey, it's all I've got to work with.

"Now, like I was saying," he continued, "I went to Al and we took a hard look together. There were a bunch of gang-related murders, mostly aimed at street level lieutenants in Gavin Morse's organization. Morse is a relative small-timer who presides over a motorcycle club called the Saints of Chaos—runs some drugs and guns, has a hand in a few protection rackets. Still a small fry. His name is also the one in that cell phone you found."

"What about the hits, Greg? Why'd you call me in?"

"Right, the hits. They were bad and they were excessive. Wives, children, family pets—scorched earth, no survivors excessive. Bodies ripped apart, charred, tortured. Enough blood to paint a house red."

"These attacks were literally inhuman," he continued. "My guess is some kinda conjured demon or greater dark spirit. I wasn't so worried about whatever was doin' the killin', but I was sure as hell worried about whoever was conjuring the thing. I can handle some small time hoodoo, maybe even a lesser familiar. Whoever conjured this thing, though, has serious chops—big-timer for sure. I don't do big-timers. That's for you and The Guild to take care of."

Greg was right, conjuring up a major demonic being or minor dark godling takes real power—even if you have a serious old-timey ritual construct to work with. In order to smuggle something into our reality, the mage, or practitioner, needs to create a bridge between our world and another disconnected dimension, then punch a friggin' hole into the fabric of material existence. It's not easy to do and if you do it wrong, there's a good chance you'll kill yourself in the process. Whoever was doing this had some serious chops all right.

"So any ideas on the identity of the asshole calling up the demon?" I asked.

"No. But I hear that whoever the Conjurer is, they were contracted to perform the hits by another outfit—Cesar Yraeta's guys. Yraeta runs a powerful Mexican syndicate, called the 16th Street Kings. The Kings are into all kinds of shit: guns, drugs, prostitution—damn-near untouchable—they're even connected with the De La Llave Cartel down south and the Cosa Nostra. Bad folks and bad business."

"The Kings started out as small-timers over in Oakland, but Yraeta came up through the ranks and turned the whole organization into a national corporation. That would be the same Cesar Yraeta who sent goons to take a poke at you down in New Orleans. Based on what you've told me, it sounds like Yraeta has the distinct impression that *you* have been contracted by Morse to make a retaliation hit."

"Wish someone would tell Morse and his Rakshasa that," I said. Oh the joys of being a rambling, bluesman-turned-mage who's too dumb to keep his fat nose out of other people's business. Stupid moral compass. Sometimes I wish I could aim my iron at the pesky little Jiminy Cricket perched on my shoulder—that S.O.B. sure does have a penchant for getting me into heaps of unnecessary trouble.

"There's more bad news, Yancy. Word's also gotten around that you might be the Conjurer. It would explain why Morse would be gunning for you."

"So," I said, "both sides are trying to sink my battleship. Awesome. That sure is a great big pile of crap to sort through—and I still don't have any idea why my name keeps getting thrown around. What about the murders themselves? Is it likely that Yraeta *is* somehow responsible for the hits?"

"I don't know," Greg said. "Based on the evidence the LAPD has collected, it looks like there's a compelling case against the Kings—Yraeta looks good for it, though the case wouldn't ever stand up in trial. Inexplicable monster attacks and all."

"What about a timeline? Something this big probably requires a ritual, so there should be a fairly clear pattern to track."

"Yeah," Greg replied. "The pattern's as clear as True Kentucky Shine: four separate attacks, each on Saturday shortly after sunset. Gives us about twenty-four hours before this thing hits again. So we have a time, but no target or location. Still better than nothin' I suppose."

"It's a place to start." I ran a hand through my hair. It was a place but not a good one, and there was still the question of how these gangland goons got a hold of my name in the first place. Plus, there was a friggin' murderous demon to consider, not to mention the colossal frame job going on. I was starting to feel a lot like Roger Rabbit; at least I had Greg to play the part of Eddie Valiant.

"I have a PI back east who I trust," I continued after a time, "I'll have him take a hard look at your detective friend Al. See if maybe he isn't as squeaky clean as he appears." Since this guy Al was working the case, it was likely that he knew about my involvement, which bumped him right up to my number one suspect spot, even if I couldn't pin a motive on him yet.

"Can you run down any contacts you might have to see whether Yraeta is behind the attacks?" I asked. "Go deep—I mean cavity-search-to-the-elbow deep—official channels, street informants, Venántium files. Shit, even friendly spirits who might owe you a favor?"

"Yeah, okay. I can do it." Greg sighed, "but if I'm doin' all the hard work, what are you gonna do?"

"I'm going to try to get a bead on Morse. Pump him for info, see if I might find out likely targets for the next attack."

"I can help you out there." He drummed his fingers thoughtfully on the white linoleum tabletop. "Something that might be right up your alley. Morse is a card shark, plays high stakes poker at a joint in the city on Fridays, called The Full House—the bar's owned and operated by the M.C. The buy-in for the game is high—maybe ten thousand, could be more—but it might offer a less violent approach. I know you tend to channel the spirit of the Incredible Hulk, but maybe James Bond would suit you better for the night."

A card game. Now that was something I could get behind. Despite Greg's insistence that I like smashing things, I don't. Sure, when I get involved in a case things usually get both bad and bloody—sometimes people die, and things do often get smashed up real good. So, I suppose from a certain angle I might seem a little Hulk-ish, but it isn't me. Honest. I'll take a smoky pool hall with some good music and a shady card game over a firefight any day of the week.

"Awesome," I said and meant it. "Sounds fine to me. But before I double-o-seven my way into see Morse, I could use a few hours of shuteye."

"Sticking me with all the leg work while you lounge around and sleep," he said. "Your room's at the end of the hall, princess."

"Once again, I am moved by your overwhelming compassion and understanding," I replied. "And you're damn right I'm going to catch a little shuteye. I've been up for twenty hours, I need some time to recharge if I'm going to be at my peak."

"You always were a real beauty queen," Greg grumbled as he got up from the table, grabbing car keys off a wooden key shaped plaque near the back door. "I'll leave the address for the club on the coffee table. Be careful."

J. A. Hunter

The Full House

I found myself outside The Full House at eight o'clock, mostly rested, showered, and roughly resembling a normal human being. After taking one look at The Full House, I sort of regretted not keeping the rumpled, blood-stained look—I probably would've attracted far less attention. The bar was a dive and not in the cool, gritty, American-dive-bar-scene way. This place was a genuine shithole: dark, dirty—broken beer bottles and old vomit littered the sidewalk out front—and supremely suspicious. Pretty sure there was a blood stain on the exterior wall. I should've gone in for a tetanus booster just from looking at the place.

The building was a box: dull gray concrete, offset by a small swath of red brick lattice near the entrance. A few narrow windows adorned the front wall, covered with thick rebar, which screamed *turn around and go away*. A long row of Harleys filled the parking lot to the right, each gleaming in the sterile florescent lighting provided by a single light post. It was the kind of members only bar that didn't advertise and didn't want your business—it was a place you came to only if you had a good reason and an invitation.

I had neither, but wasn't too worried—places like this are my natural habitat. I take to slummy bars and sheisty gambling halls like a proud lion to the rolling grassy plains of the savannah. Well acquainted, am I, with the various beasts of the beer-tavern. The cackling hyena pool players—scavengers, lurking in the shadows, waiting to prey upon the unwary sucker. The sports-betting meerkat folk who poke heads out of their beer mug homes only long enough to check scores, before ducking back down in a bid to avoid the larger predators. The aloof but noble bartender baboon, dispensing suds and bar room wisdom in equal portions—kind of like Rafiki from the *Lion King*, sans the beer-thing.

Though I like to keep my head down, make no mistake, I am the lion of the dive: at the end of the day everyone gets out of the way for me. I'm not bragging either, just the facts, ma'am. People subconsciously recognize power and danger when they see it, and those are things they avoid—an instinct left over from the survivalist-reptilian part of our brain.

Tonight, however, I was going incognito. First, the subtle glamour on my jacket would make me more like a piece of furniture than a person—easy to ignore and fairly inoffensive. Second, I had taken the time to weave a complex illusion of spirit, fire, and air. The working was a veil, one which gave me the appearance of a rough and tumble old-timer with wrinkled skin, some bitchin' scars, and a wispy white beard.

Though Morse and his crew would surely be on the lookout for me, they'd never see through my conjured mask. The working had taken me half-an-hour of concerted effort to mold into place, and it took a good chunk of energy to maintain, but it was worth the effort. Instead of a lion, I was going disguised as a tired, old water buffalo—just another harmless herd animal, hardly worth a second glance.

I steeled myself for whatever might come next, and went into The Full House.

The fragrant haze of thick tobacco smoke—mingled with the underlying pungent scent of pot and stale beer—hit my nostrils. Pool and card tables filled most of the floor space, each illuminated in a small puddle of amber light which only served to emphasize the oceans of darkness between them. The men and women filling the joint were hard looking types: lots of leather, metal, tattoos, and beards. My God, but there were some truly magnificent beards.

Shinedown's acoustic version of "Simple Man" blared through the air. Great tune. For the first time since getting caught up in this shit, I felt *good*. Most of these people would probably kill me if they knew who I was, but in-spite of that, these people were my people. Fellow wanderers, gamblers, drunkards, ink-covered hard-cases. They were also more than those stereotypes, too. They were people, complex beings who were fathers and friends, wives and advocates, lovers and parents. Many of these people weren't good people—probably gunrunners and drug dealers—but they were also more than the sum of their bad deeds, and I was in no position to start casting stones.

I'd like to think I'm more than just my mistakes. It's more complicated than that.

I wandered over to the bar and ordered a drink while I eyed the room, taking in the proverbial lay-of-the-land. Most of the tables were full, but there was a game near the back with only four players and an open chair, which looked like an invitation to me. I sauntered over to the edge of the shallow pool of light dipping over the table, keeping myself in the shadows, keeping quiet while I eyed the game with serious intent. I watched the players for a time, nursing my drink, sizing up the competition. After a few hands, I knew I could play and win.

"Mind if I buy in?" I asked to no one in particular. The loud and rowdy banter at the table ebbed to a standstill; four pairs of eyes held me in hard scrutiny.

"Never seen you 'round here before," a grizzled man, with arms the size of small tree trunks, said after a few moments. "How'd you hear about this place?" The question seemed harmless, yet a wrong answer would likely bounce my ass right out the door—and that was the best case scenario.

"Just passing through." I shrugged. "Looking for a good poker game, heard from a friend that this place might offer a little action … so, you mind if I buy in or what?" There was a long tight pause, pregnant with possibility, as Tree-Trunk Arms decided my fate.

"Ah, why the hell not," he replied with a toothy grin, sporting a few gaps. "It's a free country, old-timer. I'll be glad to take your money. Name's Uncle Frank, and we're glad to have you, partner. Buy-in's five hundred, the game is straight up Hold 'Em. You still in?"

"Call me Lucky," I said, "and you better believe it, though I was hoping for something a little more expensive." Tree-Trunk Arms laughed with a great belly rumble which shook his frame and the whole card table. One of his neatly piled chip stacks toppled lazily with a few soft clicks.

"Well partner, let's see how you do out here with us small timers—trust me, we'll be more than pleased to take all you got."

I nodded, cracking a wide grin of my own, while I pulled out a chair and he dealt me a hand.

And then I played.

I played and played late into the night, hand after hand, tune after tune, letting nicotine and music wash over me. Cool beer in one hand and slightly worn and bent playing cards in the other. I let the game take me, knowing I needed to win, and win big, if I was going to get a shot at Morse. I played for fun, drinking a little too much and enjoying it, because I knew in my bones that I'd already won. I was having a lucky night, and not the way normal people have a lucky night. With me, and people like me, luck is a quantifiable thing.

I would win because I *always* win when it comes to games of chance. No one knows why, but major practitioners fundamentally alter certain aspects of reality. Drawing in the Vis creates a sorta weak spot, which, in turn, creates a field of improbability, making things that wouldn't normally happen much more likely. What it boils down to is this: most world class practitioners are lucky as shit, at least in the small things.

This improbability field does have its limits—it's kind of like a small magnet, its field of influence will only affect things of a relatively proportionate size. A small magnet isn't gonna move a two-ton steel pipe, but it will pick up iron filings. Likewise, my improbability field isn't going to let me win the lottery (that's a *very* big field of influence), but it can alter small things like a throw of the dice, or a hand of cards.

I absolutely wreak havoc on games of chance like craps, roulette, and, to a lesser extent, card games. I don't get flushes, straights, or full houses every hand, but that's not too far off the mark. And let me tell you, being able to rig games by means of extraordinary luck sure does pay the bills. I can take a grand down to Atlantic City or Vegas and in a weekend walk away with enough cash to get by for a year. In fact, that's my business strategy: win big twice a year at different casinos, and whittle away the cash into several different banks accounts filed under my various aliases.

And yes, having extraordinary luck also means my toast never lands butter side down, which is about as cool as sliced bread.

It was ten to midnight and I was up by about five-grand when a man, who looked like the leather-clad offspring of a small rhinoceros and an Amazonian princess, approached me from the back.

"Been awfully lucky tonight." He crossed his heavily tattooed arms for effect. I shrugged my shoulders and sipped at my beer, feigning a total lack of care or interest.

"Boss says that if you want to play for some real high stakes, you can join the game in back."

"Buy in?" I asked.

"Just 'bout what you got on the table …" I gave a nod, a small smile flicked across my lips. Finally snagged a ticket to the Big Show, a chance to see Gavin Morse—Gang Lord, thug, and employer to his own Rakshasa. I really do lead a blessed life. I always get to meet the most interesting people—people who are usually trying to kill me.

Lucky indeed.

EIGHT:

The Big Show

I found myself sitting across a premium, felt-covered table, staring down the man I'd come searching for. Gavin Morse was not what I had expected. I figured the Saints of Chaos would have been led by someone ... well, more intimidating, more massive, more impressive somehow. Morse was a small, wiry guy—maybe 5'2" in boots, and 135 pounds soaking wet—though he boasted quite a collection of tattoos and scars across his arms, neck, and face. Lank, greasy, blond hair hung down to his shoulders, while a great beard, peppered with tinges of red, filled his face. I guess he looked pretty scary for being a card-carrying member of the Lollipop Guild.

He and I were the only players, though three men—including rhino-man, who'd fetched me from the public bar—encircled the large wood-paneled room. I didn't feel comfortable with so many armed men around me, particularly the two in my blind spot, but I couldn't reasonably expect anything else. Gavin Morse may have been a small-timer in the grand scheme of things, but he was still plenty big enough to require some substantial protection.

He was also apparently a smart bad guy. He may have been physically small, but he knew where he was weakest and had hired help appropriately. That's the mark of a good leader: not someone who can do everything, but rather someone who knows what they can and cannot do, and surrounds themselves with competent professionals to fill in the gaps. In my estimation, Gavin Morse was such a man.

So, there were lots of armed, professional looking bad guys which wasn't great. On the plus side, the scotch was fantastic. Springbank, single malt, 100 proof.

He dealt out the first hand, the *whisk-whisk-whisk* of laminated cards filled the air, and I let my tension and worry fade. What would be, would be.

The play went back and forth, hand after hand, chips passing to and fro with some regularity, though they mostly ended up in my pile. We made inconsequential small talk as we played, insulated from the sound of the main bar. My guess was that the walls were soundproofed, making this exactly the kind of place for both private card games and friendly interrogations. You know, the kind of friendly interrogations involving handcuffs, baseball bats, and sharp objects. Overall, very encouraging.

"So you're Mr. Lazarus," Morse said casually after half-an-hour of steady play. "You play like a fuckin' pro and you're lucky—good combo for guys like us."

Well, that sure as shit got my attention. Here I was under the assumption that I'd successfully infiltrated Morse's criminal enterprise and he'd been wise to me the whole time. I don't do Bond well, I tell you. I'm more the Captain Kirk trope—go in with my colors flying, punch the bad guy right in the kisser and never mind the consequences.

"You've known this whole time?"

"Hmm." He smiled smugly and nodded. "My boys have been watching for that car of yours. It's as flashy and over the top as a pimped out ice-cream truck. Easy to find. They picked you up hours before you ever got here—you can't drive around in my territory and think it'll slip my notice. Stupid ... your disguise is good—got that going for you at least."

I let go of the weaves of my conjured mask, cutting off the energy supply, and letting the image dissipate. No point in wasting the effort. As the illusion disappeared, I heard the uneasy scuffle of nervous feet all around the room. These guys were probably new to the supernatural game, so seeing an entirely different person suddenly appear in the room would be an unpleasant shock. They didn't immediately shoot me though, which meant they were a disciplined bunch. Morse's eyes widen for a fraction of a second, but then reverted to a business-as-usual glare. Damn, he was a cool character—I give credit where credit's due.

"Why not take a shot when you had the chance?" I asked, as I shuffled and reshuffled my stack of chips.

"I still have a chance. I haven't lost a thing. I got three straight-up killers in the room ... I wanted to see your move, watch you play your hand. If you were tryin' to kill me," he shrugged, "this charade seems like a lot of work to go through." He took a long slug of scotch. "I figured we could talk. Wager a little. If that doesn't work out, I can still kill you here. Dissolve your body in the back room, and wash you right down the drain—I have a barrel full of industrial grade sulfuric acid and an extra-large Rubbermaid container. Won't be much trouble."

"Isn't that ... inventive of you. Must be a real MacGyver fan." I smirked even though I actually felt like vomiting. You don't show fear to someone like Morse. Seriously though, how in the world did I end up sitting across a card table from a guy like this? What've I done to be on speaking terms with a guy who was sincerely considering washing me down the drain? Jeez, my life.

"Joking won't fix things." Rage lurked under the surface of his words. "I suggest you start taking this shit serious before I decide to add a layer of red paint to the walls." He pulled out a compact Ruger 9mm and set it nonchalantly on the table, safety off, barrel pointed in my direction. Guy was way too comfortable with a weapon.

"Listen," I said, letting a hard edge into my voice, "I didn't perform those hits—I don't care who your source is, they're wrong."

He took another swig of his scotch, fingers beating out some unheard rhythm upon the tabletop. "I find that hard to swallow," he said. "I got an insider on the force—"

Of course he did, and I had a damn good guess who that insider was. "Wait, let me take a stab here," I interrupted, "is it Detective Alan Harley with CGHD?" That gave him pause, though not much. Damn good poker face.

"Yeah," he said after a pause. "He's informed for us before. Was working the case and came to me a couple of days ago—said this whole thing was a supernatural hit. Said he'd seen shit like this before. Gave me his word that there was reliable evidence implicating you—nothing to go to court with. Not with something like this—not that I'm the kind of guy who takes things to court anyways."

"That's bullshit," I said. "What evidence did he give you? What overwhelming proof? Wait, wait, let me guess, *nothing*. Probably fed you some line about shadowy 'supernatural' sources, right?"

Morse sat motionless, the whirling buzz of on an overhead fan the only sound in the otherwise deathly quiet room.

"What else did he tell you?" I asked. "Did he give you Yraeta's name too? Did he say Yraeta was the one pulling all the strings?"

"Son of a bitch." His tone was flat, mirthless, thoughtful. He pressed his lips together making a thin cut in his bearded face.

"Who put you in touch with the Rakshasa?" I prodded.

"The fucks' a Rakshasa?" he asked.

"The thing you hired to murder me in New Mexico—the crazy, hyena-faced baddy who pumped my hotel room full of machine gun rounds."

"I didn't hire anything to kill you. I don't contract out—not on something like this. I'm gonna be the one to put a bullet in the person responsible."

"Why was your number in the Rakshasa's throw-away cell phone?" I asked, a little fire in my voice.

"Got me. But I didn't hire nothin' to kill you." I could tell he was on the level—he had no reason to lie. Son of a bitch, I'd been played. The Rakshasa must've been working for whoever was behind this whole clusterfuck. The crafty son of a bitch must've planted the disposable phone on purpose, knowing I'd go straight for Morse and either kill him or wind up dead myself. The Conjurer had done a bang-up frame job on me and had pulled the same trick with Morse. And I'd fallen for it hook-line-sinker like a giant moron.

"I'm new to all this freaky supernatural shit, ya' know?" Morse said, breaking my thought. "Two months ago I didn't know your name. Didn't know about demons—or whatever the fuck's been ripping up my people. Two months ago, I was worried about the ATF intercepting a gun shipment or the Aryan Legion moving into my territory. Fuckin' monsters skinning people? Families dead? No, this is all new ground … I didn't know what to think. When Harley came to me I didn't have any reason to doubt him."

The *tat-tat-tat* of Morse's fingers was a little too loud.

"Let's say I believe you," he continued. "Most of my guys know you came in here—if I let you walk, it'll make me look weak, soft. My position's not secure right now, not with the loss of so many of the crew. I look like I can't protect what's mine. If I let you go, it'll send the wrong message."

"I can help you, Morse—I'm going to end this shit." I looked him in the eyes. He glanced down at the table, unable to meet my gaze. I'm average in most ways, but not my eyes: faded and dusky blue-gray, sharp, searching, and too old for my complexion. Most folks unconsciously avoided my stare on instinct, the strangeness lurking there makes most folks uncomfortable.

"Look," I continued, "someone's obviously gone to a whole lot of trouble to put us at each other's throats. We can work together here."

"We're both gamblers," he said, arching an eyebrow, "why don't we play for it? You win, you live. Help me out. You lose, my boys shoot you dead."

Not exactly what I was hoping for. But better than nothing. I'd take that action, with my luck.

"Deal the cards," I said, gathering in energy, constructing a concussive wave of force for when things went bad, which I was sure they would.

He dealt, quick, methodical, face up.

He ended up with a pair of pocket aces. I got a 7 – 2 suited, almost the worst hand in poker. It's endearingly called *The Hammer*, because getting this hand is the poker equivalent of getting slammed in the groin with a hammer. It sucks. A lot. The 7 – 2 split are the two lowest cards you can have which won't make a straight—there's four cards needed between 2 and 7. Even though my cards were suited spades, the chance of getting a flush was low, and even if I did, it would be the lowest possible flush.

He, by contrast, had a pair of bullets looking at him, which is the best starting hand in hold 'em. Statistically, pocket aces will win more than any other starting hand.

Awesome. Good thing there wasn't a lot riding on this.

The grin on Morse's face was about a mile wide. I wanted to punch him right in his overly confident and heavily bearded face. I restrained myself, if only barely.

Stupid beard face.

I was fairly sure I wasn't walking out of here regardless of how the cards played out, but still. Morse was a good card player and a good liar, but I could read this play like a book. Even if I won, the outcome would be the same: me dead. Period. I kept playing though, building up the power for my working, using the time to run through possible exit scenarios in my mind.

The Flop—the first three cards dealt face up—sure didn't boost my confidence a whole helluva lot: A♥, 10♠, K♣. The extra ace gave him three of a kind, which is a tough hand to beat under ideal circumstances. Technically, I could still get a flush—the 10♠ was the only thing keeping me in the game and my brains inside my skull—but it was unlikely. If this were a regular hand, I would've folded before ever seeing the Flop and I sure wouldn't have stayed in for the Turn. I needed the next two cards to come up spades or I was dead, and if another Ace or King put in an appearance I'd be up a River—poker pun intended.

Morse flipped the Turn card.

Deep breath …

J♠

His smile faltered a bit, pulling back in at the edges.

"Any last words before we see the River," he asked, appearing to savor the flavor of his impending victory.

"Flip the card, Tiny. Games not over yet—chickens before they hatch and all that jazz."

His smile vanished, turning into an ugly grimace, as the River card landed face up:

9♠

How about that. A flush on the River, and with a 7 – 2.

Ha, take that universe! I won.

Something sharp stabbed into the side of my neck. Damn ... and here I'd been accusing Morse of counting his chickens before they're hatched.

NINE

Run

The first thing I noticed after being shot was that my head was still attached to my torso. The sharp pain in my neck, though uncomfortable, was not crippling. When I put a hand up to check the wound, I felt a set of tranquilizer darts sprouting from my carotid artery, like some kind of macabre jungle flower.

Still, tranquilizer darts were a good alternative to .45 or 9 mil rounds. Tranquilizer darts meant they wanted me alive. Maybe they intended to torture me. Probably intended to kill me ... eventually. Still, that meant I had a little while longer to breathe and a little while longer to try and finagle a way out of this shit-storm.

I slumped forward in my chair, letting my eyes drift close, feigning unconsciousness, as two of the gunmen approached with zip-tie hand restraints. They'd probably shot me full of enough tranquilizers to subdue a small elephant. They should've used more. The Vis grants me a far greater resilience to debilitating and intoxicating substances—unfortunately, including alcohol—so it takes a whole lot more to put me down. These tranqs would undoubtedly affect my system in a big way, but instead of knocking me out cold in thirty seconds it might take as long as ten minutes. Ten minutes to get the hell away and find a place to pass out safely.

Sounded like a frat rush challenge.

Though I might have been able to handle Morse and his boys outright, it would've been a risky endeavor: close quarters, surrounded and outgunned, and they'd shot me with friggin' tranquilizers for Pete's sake. Heck, even if I took out Morse and his boys, I couldn't possibly leave through the front—must've been thirty bikers in the main bar and most of them would be packing. I know bad odds when I see them and I wasn't feeling real lucky at the moment.

I wasn't completely up a creek, however. I still had the concussive wave of force which I'd channeled and constructed while Morse and I had played our last hand. Could only use that once though, so I had to make it count. With the front door out, I'd have to go out the back—even if it meant I had to *make* a back door. I pumped more energy into the construct, supercharging the working until all that accumulated energy made my head want to explode like an over-pressured boiler. More and more until I couldn't hold the power in anymore.

A barrage of raw force jolted out as the first gunmen placed his hands on me.

The construct rolled out of me with an accompanying flash of angry green light. Chairs flew end over end and guards tumbled through the air like scattered bowling pins. They'd be okay in a few minutes. The far wall—connecting to the parking lot—couldn't say the same thing.

Pieces of brick, concrete, and cheap red wood paneling flew outward in a confetti blast of rubble. The resultant sound wave was like the blast of a small-scale building detonation. What was left of the thick concrete looked like someone had taken an industrial wrecking ball to it. Precisely what my construct had been: a giant wrecking ball of channeled Vis.

I jerked the darts from my neck, stumbled to my feet, and shambled through the opening I'd punched into the rear of building, crouching down to hide my head and neck from any possible suppressive gunfire.

The sound of smashing wood followed me through the new emergency exit—the regulars in the main bar must've broken through the reinforced door to the back. Gunshots erupted from behind me, the roar of muzzle blasts shockingly loud in the night, while the whine of incoming bullets sent a wave of goose flesh running up and over my spine. I felt an impact under my right shoulder blade—my coat prevented the bullet from penetrating, but the impact hurt like a bitch and threw me off balance.

I managed to keep upright and moving in something that vaguely resembled a run. After about fifty feet, however, I found myself settling into a shuffling gait as my legs started to go numb.

I tried to draw up a reflective shield, but I might as well have been trying to fly away for all the good it did. I was already losing touch with my well of power—I tried to reach out and embrace the Vis. It was like a thick layer of molasses sat between me and my life sustaining force. I didn't have long then, and I didn't have access to much by way of defensive or offensive constructs. What I needed was a place to hide.

Once I broke clear of the infernal open parking lot, I hobbled into a narrow alleyway nestled between two large, run-down brick buildings—abandoned office spaces.

Everything felt so heavy, my legs and arms weighed about a thousand pounds each. Surely someone must have dropped a pickup truck onto my chest—no matter how hard my lungs labored, there wasn't enough air. I ducked down behind a metal dumpster, drawing my gun as I waited for my pursuers to close the distance. The alley was as good a defensive position as any. Decent concealment and a narrow opening, coupled with the trash bin, meant I'd have a nice shot at any approaching targets, while they'd have a terrible shot at me.

Can't ask for more than that.

Men hollering: someone—probably Morse—bellowing out orders. The orders were a bunch of incoherent jumbled gibberish to my drug rattled brain, but the general gist of the language was clear: get him without prejudice. Several bikers approached the alley mouth, mere silhouettes backed by the rough lighting of the parking lot. They had guns drawn and would start firing as soon as they got a bead on me.

I lifted my revolver with herculean effort and popped off a few rounds toward my assailants. Sometimes the best defense is a good offense—that's especially true if you've been shot with tranquilizers and only have about four minutes of consciousness remaining to your name. Defense is for people with time and I didn't have any. My first shot went wildly high—my colossal gun raising of its own accord—while the second careened into the building, sending a sizable shower of brick chips at the gunmen.

Damn, I couldn't even hit three goons, from thirty feet, in a narrow alleyway. They must have dosed me with a friggin' dump-truck load of tranqs—way more than I'd originally thought. It hadn't been more than three minutes and already I was losing significant motor dexterity; my hands felt like I had on a pair of oversized, stuffed mittens.

Running probably hadn't helped either. All that physical effort only served to move the toxin throughout my body more quickly. Nothing I could do about that. What would be, would be, I reminded myself. My shooting may have been terrible and far from lethal, but apparently it was enough to cause my burly, leather-clad pursuers to halt and seek shelter. I was up and moving again, even if more slowly and with a greater degree of instability—a drunk after far too many drinks. Several times I found myself supported only by the alley walls.

I soldiered on and eventually cleared the alley, lumbering down the sidewalk for all of five feet before a hammer blow of searing force ripped into my left cheek—and I'm not talking about my smiling face. Someone had shot me right in the ass.

Out maneuvered, flanked by another group of bikers. The attack hadn't come from behind me, but from the sidewalk running perpendicular to the alley, in front of the office buildings.

I fell. Hard. The rough concrete of the sidewalk rushed up to greet me like an old acquaintance who'd been long out of touch. When that sidewalk and I embraced, it felt like I'd been sucker-punched by every woman I'd ever done wrong. Another flash of angry pain seared across my chin as it bit into the pavement below, though that pain paled significantly in comparison to the bullet wound in my posterior. The wind rushed out of me, which might have been a result of either the fall or the gunshot. I couldn't tell since everything hurt so damn much.

I was bleeding, face down on the sidewalk, and about to pass out from tranquilizers, yet still I pointed my gun in the general direction of my assailants. I pulled the trigger twice, blasting a few more rounds, which brought about a satisfying cry of pain and an enthusiastic chorus of swearing. Sounded like I might've gotten a lucky shot in, which didn't mean much since I didn't have the energy to get up or pull the trigger again. My gun clattered to the sidewalk beside me.

I lay there for what felt like a long and painful ice age, horrible tension building as I waited for Morse's boys to finish the job. What a crap way to go out—plugged by a couple of low-level biker goons. Damn. I always thought it would be some dark godling, or maybe a Fairy queen, or, hell, even a ninja Rakshasa. I've even envisioned being trampled to death by a rampaging elephant, while playing the blues.

But capped by some Rube thugs while I was stuck drooling on a sidewalk with a bullet hole in my ass? No sir, never envisioned that. Undignified I tell you. Naturally, I should have expected something like this. I get no respect, no respect at all.

After a full minute, I got impatient—what in the world was taking these clowns so long? They could at least try and be professionals about this.

I craned my neck around, trying to get eyes on the goons. Instead, I saw the slick black Land Rover on black-rimmed 22s tearing down the block, automatic weapons sticking out from every window.

TEN:

Lucky Break

The shooting started about ten feet from me. The night air resounded with the *crack-hiss* of AKs, followed by the angry hum of rapid fire Uzi's. Bullets of various calibers chewed into the asphalt and concrete, glass shattered in sheets, car alarms sent up a cry. The crazy thing was that most of the bullets appeared to be aimed *behind* me, aimed at the bikers who'd been pursuing me. That's not to say a few strays didn't come my way, but it was clear that I wasn't the target.

Whoever these guys were, they probably thought I was already dead. I couldn't blame them for their faulty assumption. I certainly felt dead and from a certain perspective I probably looked the part. I heard a lot of shouting, followed by a substantial quantity of return gunfire, but the sounds were all starting to blend together, to blur and soften, taking on a certain fuzzy white-noise quality.

I read the license plate on the Land Rover as it zoomed by: 16KINGS1. Ha. How about that—instead of trying to kill me, Cesar Yraeta's crew was laying down suppressive automatic weapons fire, pinning my assailants in place, affording me the opportunity to escape. They were saving me, even if the act was unintentional. If Morse had been tracking my car, it stood to reason that the 16th Street Kings would've been doing the same thing.

They'd probably tailed me to The Full House, figured I was going to bring some retribution toward the Kings, and decided a little preemptive action was the best course. Yraeta's boys must've thought a good defense is a good offense too. Oh the irony of ironies—the Kings' bad intel had actually saved me, had given me a chance to escape. Finally, something that resembled a providential break, something as rare and glorious as a rainbow-farting-unicorn.

Except I couldn't move.

God must have one heck of a sense of humor. Just wish I wasn't always the butt of the joke. I needed to act, needed to move, otherwise Morse and his thugs would find me. It wouldn't be difficult since I was lying in plain view on a sidewalk three minutes from their front door. Dammit, this was not how I was going out!

Mustering my flagging will, I pushed through the thick layer of sludgy syrup separating me from the Vis, from the power I needed to save myself. The resistance was tremendous, both repelling my attempts to work through to the power beneath and exhausting me further from the effort. This wasn't molasses, it was a friggin' prehistoric tar pit, and it was about to swallow me like some ancient and unfortunate T-Rex. If I gave up now it would be the end for me, someone would roll by—whether Saints or Kings—and put a bullet in my noggin, just to be on the safe side. So I pushed, focusing my will into a drill, boring deeper and deeper into myself. Drawing on strength of conviction, resolution, hope, and anger.

A *lot* of anger.

"This is not the way I die!" I shouted through numb lips. Spittle darkened the sidewalk beneath me like the splatter of fat raindrops.

A trickle of power, a flow no greater than a leaky faucet, the merest pinprick of energy.

By God, I'd gotten through—manhandled my way passed the drug-induced haze clouding my mind. I didn't have access to much power, but I did have access to *enough* power. Drawing upon the earth, calling up the strength and resilience of ancient rock and man-made stone, I insulated myself in the stubbornness of dirt and bedrock. I wrapped that power about my mind like a cloak, blocking away the screaming pain in my body.

This was a dangerous thing to do, but not nearly as dangerous as staying where I was. Utilizing raw elemental strength and force to block pain is not the same thing as healing an injury—healing takes a crazy amount of power and time, not to mention some serious grade-A talent. This particular Vis application is a quick and dirty bit of business that allows me to push my body well beyond its natural capabilities and tolerances.

Though that may sound great, it's important to remember that pain, though not pleasant, serves a highly beneficial purpose. Pain is a warning sign that things are not okay in your body, a flashing signal which says: *STOP, decease, go no further, turn back idiot.* You ignore the warning signal of serious pain at your own peril, risking permanent damage if you push too far passed your limits.

The way I figured it, a fatal head wound counted as long-term permanent damage, so the risk was appropriate.

With that bedrock strength in me, I gained my feet—if only barely—and stumbled into a slow, lurching stride. My numb limbs carried me across the two-lane street running in front of the abandoned office buildings and onto an intersecting road, which would take me away from The Full House. By the time I limped across the intersection, my vision had become decidedly narrow— black crept in steadily around the edges until all I could see was a thin swatch of sidewalk in front of me.

I took plodding, methodical steps forward, each one carrying me a little further from Morse and his gang.

Left. Right. Left. Right. I let the words flow into me, the steady singsong cadence of a Marine Corps drill instructor.

I'm not sure how far I made it when my legs finally gave out and I crumpled to the ground. I'd crossed at least one more intersecting side street, so my guess would be about two blocks, maybe three—though that seemed like a stretch in my mind. It wasn't far enough away, not really, but it'd have to do. My body was finished, it flatly refused to cooperate in any meaningful way. Though the pain was still a distant thing, I didn't have a leg to stand on.

There was a dilapidated station wagon, which looked like it hadn't moved in a good long while, parked near me. I tried to push myself toward it with my legs, but everything below my waist had staged a mutiny. My arms were still hanging in there though, serviceable, if only just.

I pulled myself, inch by terrible inch, under the vehicle—a beaten up junker, in shades of green and rust—my body a dead weight fighting against my progress, my survival. Through a dirty puddle of water pooling at the curb—it smelled disturbingly of dog pee—but I didn't care. Well, maybe I cared a little, but I'd get over it.

A sense of peace filled me ... no, not peace, resignation. Yeah, that was it, resignation. I rolled onto my side, letting go of the Vis, letting my body surrender to the tranquilizer agent pulsing through my blood. I'd finally gotten to cover, finally found a haven of sorts, a place where I could pass out with at least a small hope of waking up. All that was left now was to wait. Soon drug-induced darkness would take me and I'd sleep. Wouldn't be so bad.

I couldn't feel my body anymore, my mind was a floating orb in a sea of nothing. Even that was fleeting as my thoughts took on the woozy quality of near-dreams ... my eyes filled with the vaguely lucid images that sometimes arrive on the front edge of genuine sleep.

I saw my boys. All grown up now, with children of their own—I couldn't remember much of their childhood. I'd left, missed so much: parent teacher conferences, holidays, music recitals, birthdays, football games ...

My youngest son was sitting cross-legged in front of the Christmas tree, his hair a mussed pile of burnt red, a large smile splitting his smooth and lightly freckled face from ear to ear. A little puppy—a shaggy thing with black and tan fur and a long lolling tongue—romped around in my boy's lap. Little tyke would send up delighted squalls whenever the puppy jumped onto his chest to plant puppy kisses on his face. It was one of the few good memories I had with my youngest.

Why had I missed so much?

I hadn't wanted that, had I? Why had I left them, left my wife? Lauren with her strawberry-blond hair, clear blue eyes, and small happy smile, the one that never left her face. God, she was lovely. I could see her on the day I proposed: she was hugging me, tears running down her cheeks in tiny rivulets, a new engagement ring cuddling her finger. She was smiling so big. Except the smile *had* left. Left with me—I'd taken it. What a bastard.

Shit. I hadn't wanted the road—the decision had been forced. I couldn't have given them anything good. I stole her smile though, made a pariah of myself, alienated myself from the boys. From leading a normal life. No nine-to-five. No retirement plan or health benefits. No cozy, white-picket home. No peace.

When's the last time I had peace, when I didn't have to look over my shoulder? What the fuck was wrong with me? Who in the hell would want that? I'm alone now. A homeless man who lives by himself out of a car.

I'm not a loser! Not a dead-beat Dad or a run out husband ...

What a bastard. I'm not ... the decision had been forced—I couldn't have given them anything good, not after ... not after I'd come into my power. I'd needed to give them a fucking chance! Shit.

You understand that, Lauren, don't you understand?

Where was I? Everything felt so fuzzy, my head all full of cotton balls, my thoughts jumbled ... where was my body? Was that dog pee?

Vietnam, that was it, I'd been shot. I was tired and dying.

ELEVEN:

The Bush

"**S**on of a bitch!" I hollered, my voice lost amidst the chaos and panic filling the jungle around me. I heard the *clak, clak, clak* of weapon fire, the wet *thunk* of thick vegetation exploding, the strident shouts of NCO's issuing commands, and the cries of injured Marines. Lots and lots of injured Marines.

I held the pistol grip of my M-16 in one tightly clenched fist. Training demanded I start firing at the VC who had to be out in the jungle somewhere. That's what I was supposed to do, what I'd been trained to do in this situation. But Martin was dead ... everything was different now.

"Son of a bitch! Someone help me!" I screamed again instead of firing, knowing I wouldn't be heard—not over the clamor of battle. I didn't know what else to do, so I kept calling out, hoping someone would hear.

Corporal Martin was dead.

My hip and thigh were full of heat, pinpoints of fiery light like hot coals—some the size of dimes, a few the size of quarters—covered my flesh. A part of my brain insisted I'd been shot, insisted I was dying and should give up. The rational part of my brain argued otherwise and was trying to slap the shit out of the gibbering madness in my head. I hadn't been shot, it wasn't that bad. Shrapnel was all, and shrapnel wouldn't kill me. Probably. It wasn't as bad as a bullet wound. Couldn't be.

I'll be alright, I'll be alright, I'll be alright.

Martin was dead though, so maybe I wouldn't be alright.

Shit, but it had happened so fast. The blast of light surrounding Corporal Martin, the dull pulse of sound, the *whomp* of air throwing me into the thick tangle of trees and foliage.

This was Greg's fault, that asshole.

Here I was bleeding with a leg full of shrapnel, eight-thousand miles away from a good bar or a decent set of tunes, and for what? I didn't want to trek through some jungle hunting for VC, weary of punji-pits, lobbing grenades and sending lead down range—I didn't even like camping. He'd convinced me to come here. I wasn't cut out to be a Marine, I wasn't fit for this shit. Greg had persuaded me—he was so gung-ho, decked out in his ROTC uniform, talking the Corps up.

I hoped he was okay. He'd been closer to the blast than me. He could be dead. He better not be dead, that asshole.

"You'll probably get drafted anyway, Yancy," he'd told me matter-of-factly after we walked at high school graduation. "It's not like you have other prospects anyway—don't kid yourself, you're not college bound."

"Doesn't necessarily mean I'll get drafted," I'd told him, "there are lots of other guys that haven't gotten snatched up and they didn't go to college."

He snorted. "You're not those guys, Yancy. You're the most unlucky sonuvabitch I've ever met," which was true. Everything bad happened to me. Bad things so improbable and absurd they could only be the stuff of high school nightmares, but weren't. During freshman year, my locker had exploded, littering the hall with pages from my personal journal—the whole friggin' football team got a real good laugh at all my innermost thoughts. Getting a date after that debacle? Forget about it. Took me three years to finally land a girl. Then, at senior prom, my pants had somehow spontaneously caught fire in front of the entire gymnasium. Had to rip them off to stomp out the flames.

Me at prom, in my whitey-tighties, doing a jig on my burning pants. Mortifying. Unlucky didn't begin to cover it.

"Chances are," he continued, "you'll get drafted into some shitty Army infantry unit—probably get three weeks of basic and end up over in Nam by month's end. No training, no friends, and unlucky as a rabbit about to lose its foot."

"I'm not a fighter, Greg. I don't like the ROTC bullshit—I'd never make it in the Marines. Officers yelling. Sergeants yelling. Shit, the cooks probably yell. No thanks."

"That's why we go in together, man." He threw an arm around my shoulder. "I've already talked to a recruiter—we can go in on the buddy program. We'll do basic together, go to SOI, hit the fleet in the same unit. I'll get your back. Help you make it through the training."

He was probably right, with my luck I *would* get drafted to some shitty Army unit; probably fall into a bamboo-filled punji pit four days in-country. Greg was a good friend, we'd been buds for a long time, and I knew he'd have my back—he'd always had my back. Since freshman year, he'd been there: locker explosion, epic bullying, flaming pants, all of it. Damn good friend.

And he was scared. Going to Nam was in his cards, and he was scared to face that game alone. He wouldn't ever say it, he was too proud for that, but I could feel it in him. He wanted me to go in for him, as much as for me. It was a little selfish, but I didn't hold it against him—he couldn't ask me like a regular person. Not Greg. This was his way of reaching out. No one wants to go through something like a friggin' war all by their lonesome.

I didn't have plans anyways, not really. I wasn't going to go to college and I didn't have a single job prospect lined up. Hell, I didn't even know what I wanted to do for work. I liked music and cards, but those weren't job possibilities, they were hobbies … truth be told, I was kind of a loser—exactly the type of guy that gets drafted and blown to pieces. Better to be in the Corps with Greg, than in the Army by myself.

He convinced me, sold me the dream. And I'd bought it.

But now I was bleeding in the Vietnam bush. If he was alive I was going to beat the tar out of him. I hoped he was alive. The thought of picking up his splintered limbs and ripped-up guts sent a few tears streaking down my face. I didn't want him police calling pieces of my body either.

"Son of a bitch! Someone help me! Help me!" I yelled. I didn't want to die here, I was so young—*too* young—I didn't want to end up like Martin.

I could see the explosion all over again, replaying in my mind's eye.

Corporal Martin and Benson had been playing some grab-ass game off to the right, killing some time while Sergeant Thomas and the Com guy, Schneider, put in a radio call to HQ. They were laughing hard about whatever the hell they were doing, really chucking it up. The platoon was supposed to be practicing sound discipline, but no one minded—not even the Sergeant. We'd been in-country for what felt like a lifetime, about a month in actuality, and we hadn't seen piss from the VC.

Everyday our butter-bar lieu swore up and down that Charlie was out there—"*don't get complacent Marines, complacency kills.*" Every day and every brief, the same shtick and the same sermon. Practice sound discipline, practice light discipline. Stay sharp, stay alert, stay alive. Complacency kills, complacency kills, complacency kills. Twenty-one patrols—some during the hot of the day, others by the light of the moon—and not a bullet fired, not a single VC spotted. We'd patrolled in thick jungle, swampy bright-green rice patties, and dusty little villages with straw and tin roofs.

A whole lot of nothing, save sore muscles and bug bites.

God, Nam had some friggin' bugs—Collins had woken up one night screaming, a fat black leech stuck on his tongue.

So it was fine that Martin and Benson were screwing around a little, having a few yacks during the break. It made things easier to bear if you could laugh a little. Even without VC incoming, Nam was still a shithole: the long humps and the driving rain, the crap food, biting insects, and sleepless nights. Watch every friggin' night. It was enough to make us all fray around the edges, and when everyone is armed with M-16s and grenades, frayed edges is bad-to-go.

Plus, we'd been humping for three feet-numbing hours, pushing passed vines and marching through knee-high grass. It was hot as balls and we were sweating oceans in the humid haze of the day. A little laughter was okay. And Sergeant Thomas was making a radio call, so we had time to kill and we deserved the break.

Greg and I were picking at our C-rats, just a little bite to eat—he'd been leaning up against a tree and I'd been standing in the open. Shit, but everything had been hunky-dory in that moment, the platoon could've been on a nature walk. It wasn't much different from the training exercises we'd done in Okinawa.

"What do you miss most?" I'd asked Greg.

He stared morosely at the beanie-weenies on his metal spoon. "Pizza," he said. Yeah, I missed pizza too. We all missed regular food. Nasty-ass C-rations. Even the good ones were awful, and the whole lot of them either plugged you up or sent your running for the shit-can. At least they came with cigarettes and toilet paper.

I picked through my 'spaghetti.' As if. "When I get back I'm gonna eat a fat ol' cheeseburger and fries." My mouth salivated at the thought. It was torturous to think about food when you were chowing down on C-rations—masochistic even—but it also made things more bearable. It helped remind us that someday we would go home, that cheeseburgers and pizza were waiting, and that Nam wasn't forever.

"You?" he asked. "What do you miss most?"

"I miss Lauren and my boys," I said without much thought. Lauren and I had been a serious item in senior year, but I hadn't thought it would work—long-distance wasn't my thing or hers. I'd accidentally knocked her up during boot leave, though, and everything changed. A son: little tow-headed, slobber-machine— he was a good kid. I missed him. My second son had been born right before Greg and I hit country. I'd had a week with him before deployment.

"Don't worry princess," Greg said, noting the look on my face, "I've got your back, you'll see 'em—"

He didn't finish the sentence. Everything had been hunky-dory.

One-step changed that.

I could see it all again, like a movie reel playing in slow motion:

Corporal Martin and Benson were playing some silly grab-ass game.

Dio, Collins, and Schmidt were getting down on an impromptu game of Hold 'Em.

Dickens, Sottack, and Litchfield chain-smoked a round of cigarettes in the shade of a young tualang tree.

Greg was telling me things were going to be okay.

Then: Corporal Martin tripped a little, staggering from a patch of sunlight into the gloomy shade of a squat palm tree.

Everything turned real slow, surreal, shrouded in haze and fog. Martin stumbled a little ... a terrible light enveloped him, made his face and arms shine for a moment with radiant light. For an honest to God moment, it looked like an angel had come and scooped him up—like the rapture had happened, maybe. It scooped him up and was kind of beautiful in its way. Then the light was *in* him, in his arms and legs, hands and feet, face and guts—they pulled apart.

The heat hit me like a wave and I was all caught up in the tangled undergrowth of the jungle floor. I'd never seen anything like it before, never seen death—not for real, not close up like that. The light had plucked Martin's ass right up and tore him to pieces; it scattered chunks of him into the tualang tree that Dickens, Sottack, and Litchfield had been smoking under. Great ropy strings of gray guts hung from the overhead branches like crepe paper at a party.

The light hadn't killed him, I knew. It wasn't an angel or the friggin' rapture, it was a rigged 105 round. The VC had killed him. Then, the shooting began. I didn't even know whether we were being fired at ... shit, I wasn't even sure there were VC up ahead. The blast had gone off and then the firing had started, but it could've been our side or theirs, I didn't know. All I knew for sure was that Martin was dead and that I didn't want to die.

"Shit. Someone help!—" I let the scream fall away. There was something rustling in the bushes behind me, I couldn't see, but I knew a person approached. *A VC ambush,* my brain shrieked. Some pajama-wearing Charlie was about to slit my friggin' throat! *Turn around,* my maddened brain demanded, *turn around and shoot that asshole into the next world!* I fumbled for my M-16 but it was useless, my hands didn't want to work and I couldn't turn anyways, the pain was too much. I steeled myself for the end ... *Please God forgive me, please take care of my family, please let that asshole Greg live through this. Oh God, Oh God, Oh God, please-please-please-please ...*

A hand fell on my shoulder and I almost let go of my bladder.

"I got ya', bud," Greg said. He moved into view. Raw red and black flesh—speckled throughout with pieces of melted cammie—wrapped around his left bicep. But he was moving okay, despite the wound. Probably riding high as a kite on all the endorphins and adrenaline running through him.

"I'm gonna get your ass out of here," he said. "Told you I'd have your back."

He bent low and scooped me up with a grunt, settling my bulk around his shoulders in a classic fireman carry. My leg wanted nothing to do with it, the hot coals in my skin rekindled anew, my eyes drifted shut from pain. He started running—running—through the jungle away from the VC and back toward our last forward outpost. A little chunk of cadence drifted into my brain: *Running through the jungle with my M-16, I'm a mean motherfucker I'm a U.S. Marine. Sight alignment, sight picture, right between the eyes—slow, steady squeeze and another VC dies. But if I should die in the combat zone, well box me up and ship me home.*

I saw a piece of Martin's face, charred black, lying in a sparse dirt patch, staring at me with one glazed eye. *Box me up and ship me home.*

TWELVE:

Game Plan

I woke up a lifetime later, flashes of Vietnam—like the brief burst of a rigged 105 round—fading into the dim, dusty vaults of memory. Martin's charred face stared at me for a moment, but I pushed it away. Some memories were better left forgotten and buried.

I didn't know where I was, but I was alive. Score one for me. I knew I was alive because of the pain: the hurt was an inferno in my bones and flesh, almost alive itself. The agony lashed upward from my wounded posterior, danced around my bruised ribs, and finally did a mean-spirited jig on my busted-up chin. Pain like this is only for the living.

But I actually felt better than I expected to. Someone—either Morse and the bikers or the Kings—had taken the time to patch me up and they'd actually done a competent job. I could feel the stiff edge of stitches running over the surface of my ass and there were squares of gauze affixed to my skin with paper tape in a variety of places, including my aching chin. My captors had even hooked me up to a portable IV (admittedly, it was hanging from a worn-down coat rack), which appeared to be pumping saline fluid and antibiotics into my veins. Nice, though I bet my co-pay was going to be hell. Gang health care is notoriously expensive in the end. Way worse than your typical HMO, though maybe not by much.

The next thing I noticed was that I couldn't move, like at all. I was still feeling groggy from the lingering effects of the tranquilizing agent, but my immobility was total—way more than some left over tranq juice could account for. I'd been Saran-

71

wrapped to a plastic, folding, banquet table, like the kind a church might use at an outdoor luncheon. I still had pants on, but my captors had stripped away every other article of clothing. The suffocating, squeaky tight plastic looped around my arms and torso in thick swathes, pulling at my body hair. My jeans masked the feeling of the wrap, but a constricting pressure—both above and below my knees—told me they too had been fastened securely in place.

Damn, Saran-wrap was a smart move. I couldn't risk cutting the stuff with an air construct, or I'd likely filet myself in the process. Likewise, if I tried to burn through the stuff, the whole mess would go up in flames and leave me one very crispy-critter—it'd be like getting blasted with friggin' napalm.

Well, at least I could move my head, even if it felt like trying to pick up a mountain. I sure hoped the fading aftereffects of the drugs would pass in time. I wasn't too optimistic though, the damn headache throbbing behind my temples felt like it was probably going to be sticking with me for a while yet. None of that mattered though—I couldn't afford to lay around waiting to fully recover. I could be dead by then. So, I made an effort to lift my thousand-pound noggin and take a little looksee, even though it caused a renewed wave of hurt to skip through my skull.

If I had any hope of getting out of here, I needed to first figure out where *here* was. I also needed to figure out what kind of defenses I'd be going up against.

The room wasn't anything special—certainly not the freaky old-brick dungeon I'd envisioned in my mind: a moderate sized living room, which wouldn't be out of place in any middle-class home. An oversized, wrap-around sofa hugged the wall to my left and disappeared behind my head. Directly in front of me sat a big flat screen, framed by a set of thick brown drapes, covering a large den window, with a reinforced front door to the left. A sparsely filled bookcase and a small table, holding car keys and assorted junk mail, off to my right.

The smell of red-sauce and grilled meat drifted from the kitchen, while the faint aroma of cigarettes and stale pot filled the room. I could hear a handful of muffled voices, mixed with the clink and scrape of silverware. The soft blare of a television, from elsewhere, carried the nasally laugh of Sponge Bob, followed shortly by the high-pitched shrieks of delighted children. Maybe my mind had been fried by the tranquilizers, because I couldn't figure this out.

I went through the last few things I could remember:

I'd been pumped full of tranquilizers, busted a hole in the back wall of The Full House, got shot in the ass, and had, eventually, passed out in dog pee under a car. Right?

So how'd I ended up Saran-wrapped to a table in white-picket suburbia? This was too small-time to be the Kings, which meant Morse had found me. But why bring me here, of all places?

It didn't make a damn lick of sense. Morse and the Saints must have had buildings better suited to holding captives, like that bar of theirs—or maybe a clubhouse or even an auto body shop—but not a place where there would be children present. Generally, bad guys don't torture people in front of their kids. That's taboo even for the worst of the worst.

A safehouse maybe? No, I doubted it. This living room felt … too lived in. Yeah, that was it. The piled junk mail on the table, the worn and picked through novels on the bookcase, the overall care of the abode. It all spoke of a loving, if busy, hand.

There was also a faint energy lingering in the air, kind of like the hot, muggy atmosphere of a New Orleans night—a palpable, if unseen force. It was the slow, dull, power that builds up around a home with a domicilium seal. Wherever I was, it was a place where people lived; a place where dishes were done and meals cooked, where teeth were brushed, and good night kisses issued. This house carried the weight of reality, charged overtime by the mundane and commonplace—it was more than merely a house, it was a home. There was only one reason I could think of for bringing me to a place like this …

A glance at the antique wall-clock, hanging by the TV, confirmed my suspicion: Five PM. I'd been out for nearly fifteen hours. It also meant it was Saturday evening and that the nightmare, who'd been tearing up LA, was only a few hours away from putting in its weekly horror-show performance.

Here I was, strapped to a table among Morse and his crew—a tasty appetizer for whatever was going to rip its way through the front door when the sun fell.

Morse was planning to use the seal of this home to try and ward off whatever had been targeting their club members over the past month. Morse may not have looked like much of a threat, but he was smart—the home's natural seal would be more likely to stop a supernatural baddy than all the humdrum human security defenses folks usually employ: concrete, bricks, razor-wire, or guns. Admittedly, those things are awfully handy to have around, even when the enemy you're dealing with has claws, fangs, or gooey tentacle thingies.

Never underestimate the power of good ol' vanilla human ingenuity.

The scrape of a chair cut off my thoughts—someone was sitting not far behind me, just out of view.

"He's awake, boss," said the sentry, his voice filled with the sounds of slight panic. "He's moving around—what should I do?"

A door opened and the stifled sounds of eating spilled out with greater clarity for a brief moment, before the door swung shut.

Someone drew near, given away by the muffled sound of footfalls on carpet.

"You sure know how to show a guy a good time," I said. "Good scotch, gun fights, intravenous fluids, and even Saran-wrap—pretty kinky."

"Glad to see the tranquilizers didn't do any permanent brain damage," replied Morse, "would've been a real shame to lose such a sharp wit and keen mind."

"I'm glad you recognize my invaluable gift to humanity—I am the great philosopher of our age, you know."

"Obviously," he said.

His tone annoyed the piss outta me. It was the same tone a long-suffering adult might use with a particularly petulant and dense child. I had thirty years on this guy, easy—age has to count for something, right?—though I suppose I could've been a little more grown-up considering the seriousness of my circumstance. But hey, if you can't crack a few jokes when the chips are down, what's the point of living? Sure, you can tranquilize me, shoot me, strap me to a table, feed me to a demon, or bore me to death with bad villain monologues, but you can't make me something other than I am.

"Has your keen philosophical insight given you some clue why you're alive?" Morse asked, drawing into my periphery.

"Yeah," I said. "I've given it some thought, but it's generally not my policy to divulge valuable info to the guy who's holding me hostage."

"Okay, Yancy—maybe it's better you don't talk anymore. That big mouth of yours is tempting me to put a bullet in your head, on principle." He took a deep breath, pulled a padded folding chair into view, turned it around, and straddled it with a hunter's ease. "Let me lay a few things out for you, so that you know why you're alive and how things are going to go down tonight."

"Please do tell," I said.

He pulled out his Ruger and set it on the table, six-inches away, muzzle aimed at my head. "How 'bout you just try real hard to listen."

"Okey-dokey."

"I don't think you're the asshole behind this and I don't think you're the fucker responsible for calling up this demon, or whatever. So I'm gonna take a gamble on you—I've got the whole crew here. The twenty one members left, plus their girlfriends, wives, and kids. *Everyone*. Can't tell who the Conjurer's gonna pick, so if we're all here, the monster has to come here. Right?"

"That's a terrible idea. If your plan falls through it's going to be a massacre."

"Yeah," he said. "If this thing goes tits-up, it's gonna go tits-up for everyone." He pointed a finger at me, "You included. I figure we got a better shot of winning this way though. We'll fight when we're at our strongest instead of waiting to get picked off one family at a time. And, assuming you're on the level, we'll have you too. Best game plan I can think of."

Reckless, foolhardy, and borderline suicidal, but as plans go, it wasn't bad I guess—kinda courageous even. He was willing to do terrible things for power and money, but he was also willing

75

to die for his people. That didn't make him a good man, but it did make him more than a hoodlum and thug.

People like Morse were the reason mankind is at the top of the food chain, even though there are creatures from Outworld whom are smarter, bigger, stronger, and more powerful. Humanity as a whole is an evil bunch of bastards, but when push comes to shove, the villagers can put aside their inner devils and take up the pitchforks and torches against a common enemy.

Still though, talk about putting all your eggs in one basket.

"Now, I admit I could be wrong about you," he said after a time. "You might well be the fucker calling up the demon, so I've worked out a vetting process. I figure if the demon *does* show, you must be innocent—you couldn't be the asshole responsible for calling it since I've got you here, right under my eye. Now, in this scenario, the demon shows, you get to live, and you help save all our asses. Following?"

"So far," I said.

"But, if the demon *doesn't* show … I'm gonna think that maybe you are the Conjurer and I'm gonna blast you into little pieces just to be on the safe side."

I'll say it again, Morse is one smart crook. I mean, *I knew* I wasn't the bad guy, but Morse couldn't be sure of that. This was a pretty solid vetting process and gave him the best of both worlds: if I was "guilty" he'd smoke me well and good, and if not, then he'd have a Fix-It man mage backing his play.

"So, you gonna play nice, or should I just cap your ass now?" he asked.

"I get my stuff back right?" I asked. "I'm gonna need my gear—and also being cut loose would be pretty handy."

He nodded.

At a quarter to seven, I found myself standing in a room which hardly resembled the one I'd woken up in—a room made ready for war. Couches and tables had been up-ended with sandbag barriers erected in front of each, a maze of potential covered shooting positions. Thick boards secured over the windows, the back door reinforced with thick gauge steel, while the front door stood wide-open, save for the thin screen. An open challenge if I'd ever seen one. Morse and his crew didn't intend to merely fend off their territory, they meant to kill whatever walked into this home.

The bikers had likewise undergone a similar metamorphosis as they prepared for the fight. All had donned para-military gear over their leathers: thick, beige flak jackets—sporting SAPI plates, no less—drop pouches, and about a million magazines each. And there were guns. Lots of guns. SAW M249 light machine guns. A refurbished M240. Couple of AA12 machine shotties—shotguns featuring a 32-shell drum and a fire rate of 300 rounds per minute. And a whole slew of customized, military-grade M-4s.

The fifteen men arrayed themselves in a staggered semi-circle, laying out unrestricted lanes of fire, ensuring that the only thing in line for a bullet was whatever came through the door. Or me. I was the front line defense, positioned squarely in the middle of the room, with the door to my front and all of those heavy-duty armaments fanning out behind me.

If this friggin' demon stood us up, these guys would riddle me full of bullets like a target at a firing range, and I'd be hard pressed to stop them. The drugs had worn off, sure, so I had access to the Vis again and I even had all of my gear. But this room was a friggin' death trap. Deflecting handgun rounds from a few shooters is one thing. Stopping a hailstorm of high-caliber bullets, fired from multiple positions, is another thing entirely.

Dying light trickled in around the curtains. Only a few scant minutes till the lights went down and the curtain came up on the evening monster movie. I could feel the tension growing in the room, mounting ever higher as the sun traced its course for the horizon. I tried to ignore it, focusing instead on all the half-formed constructs I had waiting for the party guest. In the hour Morse had given me to prepare, I'd cooked up some real doozies: all big hitters that'd land like a super-charged punch from Mike Tyson.

I was tired of getting ambushed—pushed around, kicked in the teeth, and generally made to look like an imbecile. Yraeta's guys had caught me unaware in the Big Easy, the Rakshasa had ninja sneak-attacked me in Las Cruces, and Morse had caught me with my pants down at The Full House. It was my turn now, someone or something was about to have a helluva bad night, which made me smile a little bit, a feral grin.

All that was left to do now was wait—wait and hold all of my ungainly constructs in place—but it wouldn't be long. There was power in the night and I wasn't the only one who felt it either. A quick glance around the room showed me necks and arms tensing, fingers easing toward triggers.

The energy building and rippling through the ethereal plane signaled the ritual was under way, approaching like some kind of fast, yet unseen, tsunami. The Conjurer was close—maybe within a hundred mile radius of this location—an important piece of the puzzle, which I filed away for later examination. There was no time for thinking now though. No time for fear or anxiety, or room for speculation and self-doubt. I was *present*, a knife being drawn from the sheath, a trigger squeezed tight just before the point of firing.

A dark energy seeped through the ceiling, an invisible mass of vile power, composed of thin strands of fire, wrapped in thick cables of earth and air, tied and bound with pillars of will, and immersed throughout with the Vim that comes from a taken life. Something—maybe a small animal or even several—had been sacrificed to help power the summoning.

That energy latched on to one of Morse's men: Uncle Frank, the good-natured, tree-trunk-armed guy from the bar—he would act as the anchor and the homing beacon for the summoned fiend. He was the primary target.

"I'm running out of patience," Morse said, his voice echoing around the room.

Morse's impatience was misplaced though, the waiting was over. A gargantuan form, shrouded in darkness and obscured by the grainy texture of the screen, manifested not ten feet from the front door.

THIRTEEN:

Fight Night

I didn't wait for the creature to get close enough to start throwing punches. I was well prepared and ready to figuratively smack the thing right in the damned kisser. My first defensive trap had been inlaid into the front lawn and concrete walkway: a seething mass of razor-thin strands of earth and rock, all looped about and reinforced with weaves of water and held together by my overburdened will. The creature surged forward with the speed and power of a stampeding elephant, but it didn't matter, all I had to do was release the pent up Vis stored in the ground. It was the matter of a thought.

Before the beast had gone three steps, a small forest of scalpel-sharp spikes, three-feet high—some the width of my wrist, some only the size of my pinky finger—leapt from the ground. The yard turned into something that vaguely resembled a porcupine. The spikes were a real piece of work. Instead of fortifying the LA top soil, I'd reached deep into the earth, pulling from the igneous and metamorphic bedrock, rapidly heating and cooling the substance until only scalpel sharp obsidian remained.

The spikes tore through the thing's feet and legs, gouged into its groin, and left it pinned in a pool of oozing black sludge.

The attack should've been a deathblow and it surely would have been to any mortal unlucky enough to end up on that lawn.

The creature was no mortal.

A dreadful growl of frustration and pain rang through the night like a tornado siren, setting off car-alarms, while dogs of all sizes took up a howling chorus. A hurricane of force and will exploded from the pinned creature, turning my neatly manicured yard of death-spikes into a whirlwind of shrapnel—glittering obsidian blasted through the door and into the living room proper like a swarm of venomous bees.

"DOWN!" I roared, as I thrust out my left hand, bringing my second defensive construct to bear. A shimmering bank of reddish fog coalesced into the air before me, fanning outward across the room and upward toward the ceiling. This was a super-charged version of the friction shield I'd use in the alley against Yraeta's thugs—it would superheat the incoming projectile particles, breaking them down into smaller less harmful particulates, while simultaneously deflecting and dispersing forward inertia. In theory the plan was great—I've used this construct loads of times without ever having an issue.

But the incoming projectiles weren't bullets, they were thin pieces of sharp obsidian glass. My shield worked exactly as intended: it obliterated the large rough-cut pieces, resulting in a swirling cloud of glittering glass dust. The shit would temporarily—or perhaps even permanently—blind anyone who was unlucky enough to get a face full of the stuff. Smooth move Yancy … that's why you're the expert getting paid the big bucks.

I heard several men—the few who had been too short sighted to don ballistic goggles—let out shrieks of agony as the powdered glass contacted their eyes. I let two of my partially formed defensive workings unravel, refocusing that pent-up energy into a large column of air, which sucked inward with a thunderclap of sound, before propelling the obsidian particulate cloud out through the front door and squarely into the face of the incoming creature. It dazed the approaching horror momentarily, but then the creature shrugged the stuff off like an MMA fighter getting slugged by a four-year-old.

That's the awful reality of fighting things from Outworld—they almost always have the advantage in virtually every imaginable department. Attacks that would easily wipe out a small army of mortals were a mild inconvenience to many things from the darker regions of existence. The cards are stacked heavily against us, I'm afraid. In some ways, I guess, that kind of gives humanity an edge, even if only in an unconventional sense.

Things like this are always overconfident, always underestimating what we, the little people, can put together with a little foresight. Often this means they never see the cliff until it's too late. This King Kong shit-head was standing right on the edge and I was gonna push it over.

Long talon-tipped fingers—rubbery black, slick, and each the size of a banana—ripped at the screen door, tearing the fragile aluminum structure from the house and pitching it into the air, quickly swallowed by the dark of the night. That was okay, the screen door had been the foci for my mega defensive construct. By removing the screen from the home, the creature triggered my housewarming surprise.

A freight train of force walloped into the black-skinned hulk, driving the thing through the evening air like a golf ball sent sailing down the fairway. Perhaps the creature wouldn't have ripped the door off its frame had it seen all of the Vis embedded sticky notes I'd plastered to the backside—nearly a hundred of the little buggers. Individually, they wouldn't have done much to the monster, when bound together, however, their cumulative effect was spectacular.

As the thing glided through the night, spinning topsy-turvy with a degree of grace impossible for a creature so large, the second prong of my construct lashed out. The house itself discharged a shimmering red-gold mist, the nebulous haze of a small sun, which coalesced into a tightly woven net of super-heated, lightning-fast energy. The net intercepted the beast midflight, wrapping around it like a second skin. Thin razor wires of golden power bit into slick flesh, carving out squares of black skin that splattered to the street below. A patter of wet *thuds*.

Ha! Eat that, ass-hat! Power through superior planning.

The last phase of my three-pronged defense came into play before the creature smacked into the light pole across the street and three houses over. The energy net continued to burn with the power of a small personal sun, yet I'd designed it to undergo a metamorphosis as it neared the end of its short-lived life. Originally, I'd fueled the net by pumping a ton of raw Vis into it. Once it had consumed all of that pre-stored energy, it drew in energy, specifically heat, from its surroundings. The temperature at the center of the net dropped to a hundred or more below zero—a layer of frost flash-formed over the thing's pebbly hide.

So far so good, but now I had to close the deal. Now it was time to take the fight out onto the street—I had put some distance between the creature and the home.

Fighting from the house, and the defensive protection of its domicilium seal, was strategically advantageous for me. The same could not be said for Morse and his guys. If the demon forced its way indoors, there was a good chance lots of people would die, and not just Morse and his guys. There were also the wives, girlfriends, mothers, and children cowering in the basement to consider. A misplaced bullet or Vis construct could easily kill one of those innocents, and that was something I couldn't abide.

I may not be a good guy in the typical sense of the word, but I'm not a monster either. There are lines even I'm unwilling to cross.

There was also my own livelihood to consider: the house might've given me a measure of safety from the creature, but it wouldn't do me any good against a stray round, fired by some overzealous, Kevlar-clad biker. If that thing did get in the house, Morse and his crew would initiate a shoot-a-thon of epic proportions, and I didn't want to be downrange from all those muzzles when the fireworks started. It would take everything I had to beat this nightmare and I couldn't afford to spend any extra effort shielding myself from accidental friendly fire.

It was for those reasons that I charged out into the night like some crazed and slightly senile dog: an old, rabid, rat-terrier chasing off a Godzilla-sized-mastiff a hundred times its size.

The creature collided with an aluminum light pole across the street—the pole crumpled in the middle, yet remained standing, its flickering light fully revealing the thing for the first time. I hadn't realized just how damn big it was until that moment. Sprawled across the black asphalt, I could finally get some perspective on its sheer size. Must've been eight or nine feet tall, and probably half as wide at the shoulders. It'd been crouched over before, hunched in on itself—the only feasible way it could have mashed itself into the house.

Thick slabs of muscle covered the creature's form; its dark pebbled skin was already starting to heal over the substantial damage I'd inflicted thus far. I also noticed it had two too many arms protruding from its elongated midsection. This guy must have been super handy to have around when it was time to clean beneath the sofa—why, he could lift the sofa *and* vacuum all at once. The supernatural baddies always get the neatest powers. Shirt shopping would be a bitch though.

The thing that made me nervous, though, was its head. So wide it didn't possess a neck, and surrounded completely with a jade lionesque-mane. Wide set eyes—dark and somehow vacant—framed in by a pair of curving ram horns, sprouting from the creature's tangled hair like a couple of sickly tree trunks. It wore a towering spire crown of gold, adorned with rough-cut rubies and festooned with a string of human skulls: all yellowed with age and sporting the signs of brutal death.

I wasn't a hundred percent sure what I was looking at, but I had a real strong suspicion that the ugly mug belonged to a Daitya, which, if true, was bad-news-bears all around. Like someone was trying to wipe out a big part of humanity, bad news.

The Daityas are a subclass of demonic giants who terrorized the Indian-subcontinent four thousand years ago, real Dark Ages type stuff: rape, torture, live human consumption. These things made the Mongol Horde look like a bunch of fluffy kittens prancing through a pile of yarn.

At some point in the dusty pages of history, the Daityas had also gotten a wild hair up their collective asses to wage an unholy war against God—in cahoots with a badass demonic-serpent the Hindus call Vritra. The axis of evil had lost, of course, because let's face it, if you go up against the Creator of the Universe you're going to get burned. Period. The fact that they tried, though, should tell you a little something about their overall disposition. Completely monkeys-with-laser-guns-riding-dinosaurs insane. As far as I understood, the punishment for their little revolt had been exile—banishment to a special place in Hell and denied access to our realm of existence.

FYI, in case you didn't get the message, God takes pretenders to the Throne *very* seriously.

These things were not supposed to have access to earth. Like Cuban cigars, there was a strict embargo on these S.O.Bs. But, also like Cuban cigars, it seemed someone was smuggling one of these shitheads into our reality. Thankfully, since this thing was still being summoned through a ritual, it meant the creature hadn't acquired enough life force, Vim, to manifest in our world on a more permanent basis. Right now the Daitya was just visiting, but the Conjurer was likely wheeling and dealing to get this thing a green card.

The Daitya was getting to its feet, rough chunks of ice flaked away in sheets as it stretched its thick limbs.

Shucks, why can't the bad guys show a little good sportsmanship once in a while and just stay down?

Holes riddled the friggin' thing's body—courtesy of my obsidian lawn trick—and it had hundreds of neat, square-cut patches in its skin, revealing ropey pink muscle beneath. Still, it appeared unruffled. A disturbing notion, considering the amount of thought, force, and will I'd already pumped into putting this thing down for keeps. It looked worse for the wear I guess. Still, it was standing upright and moving toward me—an implacable force of nature about to descend.

Yay me.

I struck out with a bar of white-hot flame, which plowed into one of the Daitya's massive shoulders. A plume of thick, choking smoke rose into the dark as it caught fire. The creature hardly noticed. I zigzagged my bar of flame across its torso and into its groin and legs. They too caught flame, yet the creature only slowed for a heartbeat. It raised one massive claw-tipped-hand and slashed at the air, the movement sharp and precise—my lance of flame disappeared, unraveled, as though the Daitya had pulled free all of the threads of my construct. I didn't think what had happened was possible, but there it was. The Daitya had access to some kind of Anti-Vis.

The flames about its body died away, choked out, leaving only a faint glowing trace of orange embers behind.

I started backpedaling as the Daitya closed the distance between us. I didn't have much of a game plan at this point, but I knew sure-as-shit that I didn't want this thing to get within "SMASH puny human" distance.

Damn, it was fast.

I pumped energy into the street, creating a layer of sludgy, hot, road tar between me and Mr. Big-and-Nasty. Each bounding step the creature took sunk it ankle deep into the road way—a mud bog of blacktop—buying me a little more time to gather distance. That worked for all of about four steps and ten seconds before the Daitya took to the air, a superman leap bringing it well into my discomfort zone.

A massive two-handed hammer blow raced toward me with the speed and force of a fast-moving semi.

I dropped and rolled left.

A small impact crater bloomed in the spot I'd vacated.

A wave of flame—a tree trunk of dragon fire—washed over me as I came to my feet. I had only enough time to condense a small bubble of air and water around myself, a loose protective shell, absorbing the flare of massive heat and jettisoning a bank of steam in return. The steam was not pleasant: it left my lungs burning and my clothes moist. Still, a helluva lot better than being charbroiled like a marshmallow during a camping trip.

Before I had time to catch my breath, a foot broke through the hazy plane of sudden steam and caught me in the ribs, a mule kick that sent me spinning to the ground five feet away. Thank God the blow had only been a glancing one and my coat had diffused some of the impact. Even so, my ribs ached with a knife-spike of misery—a crack for sure, but maybe something more.

I couldn't afford to let the Daitya land another blow like that. A straight on strike would kill me. The steam bank superficially gave me a temporary advantage—it hid me from the Daitya—but it also masked its whereabouts from me, and in the end, that wouldn't turn out well for the home team. Human beings rely heavily on sense of sight. Not so for most supernatural beings; they often possess a far greater sense of both scent and hearing, giving them a huge advantage when operating in sight-restricted environments. I needed to be able to see or the Daitya would eventually blunder into me and crush some fragile and generally important part of my anatomy. Like my skull, maybe.

I gathered in a small construct of air and propelled it outward in a semi-circle, letting the mist dissipate and granting me the vision of a rapidly incoming blue-black fist. I rolled again—I could feel the gush of displaced air as the massive appendage whipped through the space I'd occupied a moment before. Shit. This fight was going to play out in close quarters—an unavoidable truth, regardless of how much that favored the Daitya. I needed a card to play and I had one last Ace up my sleeve. With a small effort of will and a whisper, I muttered the phrase, "*gladium potestatis.*"

A thin, single-edged, azure blade, about three feet in length, and looking as fragile as lace, appeared in my outstretched hand.

FOURTEEN

Daitya

Yeah, you heard right, I summoned my magic sword.
Now, I know what you're probably thinking: *why in the world does some blues hound have a magic samurai sword?* Fair question. Back in my Marine Corps days I had been something of a martial-arts fanatic—*Enter the Dragon* wouldn't come out for a couple of years, but I was crazy for *The Jade Bow* and the *Buddha's Palm* series. Those were some major formative years for me and I regret nothing. Nothing. Mock if you want, but Kung Fu is amazing and I'm too old to care what anyone thinks about my viewing preferences. At any rate, before deploying to Nam with 3rd Battalion 3rd Marines in '68, I'd been stationed for two years with the 3rd Mar Division out of Camp Butler in Okinawa, Japan.

Put two and two together: goofy, awkward, young Marine with a passion for cheesy Kung Fu, stuck in *Okinawa* for two-years … of course I studied martial arts. It's practically all I did for those two years. I have a somewhat shocking confession: I was not always the elegant and easy-going social butterfly I am today. I worked at a couple of different martial arts styles, even studied Kenjutsu—the Samurai art of the sword. And I practiced a lot. Like no-life, six-nights-a-week, die from starvation playing World of Warcraft, a lot.

So what about the sword? It's important to point out that the sword is not actually a real sword, but rather a Vis construct, like any of the other constructs I frequently use. I invented it in August of '77, about four months after the first Star Wars film came out. Listen, Star Wars defined an entire generation. Star

Wars irrevocably changed the film industry forever and shaped the way all future generations think about cinema. It was also really, really cool. Badass squared, for sure.

I've always identified more with Han than with Luke, but the Jedi Lightsaber is hands down the single most badass weapon ever imagined. I mean a friggin' sword made of light that can suddenly burst into life? Yes please. It's like, dare I say it, *magic*. Took me four months, and a few significant favors, to figure out how to make the construct work. But damn if the effort wasn't totally worth it—a functional katana made wholly of air that I could summon at will. Neato toledo doesn't even begin to cover it.

The Daitya closed the distance once more and rained a series of fast moving hammer blows and jabs down on me. I managed to intercept and deflect each with my blade, narrowly evading each attack. The key to using a katana well is understanding that you never want to stop a strike; for that kind of thing you need lots of muscles and a serious European broad-sword, which is all about brute force.

Most things from Outworld have the upper hand when it comes to contests of brute force, which is precisely why the katana is such a good weapon. Kenjutsu is about movement, about redirecting force—an umbrella shedding water, say, instead of a brick wall stopping an incoming car—which means someone who is substantially weaker still has a chance in the fray. In Kenjutsu, you can make an enemy's strength work for you.

Our fiery tango had begun, and it was all I could do to keep from getting my head pounded into something resembling an overripe pumpkin after Halloween.

I slid from one defensive position to another: an overhand deflection, *uke-nagashi,* followed by a feeble attempt at a wave counter—a sweeping feint from the right, followed by a diving roll left.

My body twisted with the weight of the strikes.

My back ached from rolling over pavement. My shoulders had already begun to burn from the exertion of blow and counter-blow.

I wasn't in the kind of shape to be going toe to toe with something this powerful—treadmills and calorie counting aren't my thing. You only get to live once, and I'll be damned if I make my way through life subsisting solely on salads and diet smoothies. But boy, were all those ribs and burgers coming home to roost.

The creature's strikes came faster and faster, a feral light had entered its nightshade eyes. It was the look of a pissed off bad-guy—I stole your lunch money, kicked your puppy, and insulted your mother, pissed off. Good. Angry bad guys don't think clearly, which means they don't act clearly, which means they'll be prone to making fatal mistakes. The attacks were more powerful and harder to defend against since they lacked the coordination of any kind of formal combat. *But* they were also sloppy as a muck-filled pigsty.

The Daitya was no longer a boxer working an opponent on the ropes, it was a tornado descending on an Oklahoma trailer park: left jab, *swoosh*. Right hammer blow—crunched into the side of a parked car, shredding metal. Mule kick, followed by a brutal stomp—pavement rippled as its foot crashed down. Uppercut, narrowly deflected by my blade.

All rage and no grace. Completely reckless.

There: a wild cross-body haymaker, which would've knocked my head from my body, propelled it passed the speed of light and right into the next century. *But*, I'd seen the strike coming from a friggin mile off—so telegraphed my deceased mother could have evaded with ease. And there it was, the textbook perfect target: a large patch of exposed, purple flesh, right between the creature's overextended double arms.

I pivoted at the hips, dropping the tip of my blade low, and slicing diagonally up and across the body—*hidari jo hogiri*—through the naked skin between the arms and squarely into the Daitya's chest cavity. I'd been aiming to drive my blade all the way to the demon's opposite shoulder—tried to split that son of a bitch in two. Sadly, I only sank the katana up to mid-sternum.

Inky black goo leaked and sputtered from the terrible wound in places, a viscous river meandering its way to the street below. The creature was stunned, I could see bewilderment painted across its broad face. Its eyes grew a few sizes too big; massive arms floundered stupidly for the protruding sword handle, while its legs swayed and wobbled. The Daitya was a felled tree about to topple, but it wasn't down yet.

I tried to pull my Vis sword free, but couldn't—it'd been thoroughly lodged in the demon's chest, and I didn't have the remaining stamina to wrestle the blade loose. Whatever. Wouldn't have been able to maintain the construct for much longer anyways. The thought of doing anything more than sleeping was physically nauseating, and the thought of drawing more deeply from the Vis made me want to shoot myself in the face.

Thankfully, I'm not that rash. Instead, I drew my pistol, leveled it at the Daitya's grimacing mug, and shot *it* in the face. Six quick trigger pulls filled the night with fire, though the sound was not much greater than the *pop-pop-pop* of a few Blackcats going off.

From such close proximity, my gun was highly effective. The first two rounds punched into the creature's nose and left cheek, leaving colossal craters in the landscape of its face. The next two rounds pulverized its shocked and staring eyeballs, leaving only a couple of gapping, cavernous holes in their wake. The last two impacted the bony ridge of skull beneath the towering crown, perched so neatly atop its thick head. The Daitya began to fold in on itself. Like someone had turned on a miniature black-hole right in the center of its abdomen—a vortex in our plane of reality, recalling this crippled, otherworldly denizen.

The form continued to twist and distort, drawing in ever more tightly.

With a thunder-crack of displaced air, the Daitya vanished, leaving behind only a small mountain of green goo which would further liquefy and wash away in time. I hadn't actually killed the demon—it was far too powerful for that. I'd just damaged its assumed form so badly that it no longer had the energy to maintain a physical presence here. It was the best I could do, given the circumstances, and it had nearly killed me.

My pistol dropped, clattering on the asphalt. Odd, since my hand seemed to be working okay. A second later, I was staring up at the stars overhead, a scattering of rough diamonds laid against velvet cloth, and had no idea how I'd gotten there. My eyes felt damn heavy, but I didn't mind. Tired, so, so tired … I deserved to indulge in some shuteye. Yeah, I was in the middle of the street in the dark of night—not typically the best place to nap, but that thought was far away. Sleep was close, a good friend waiting to embrace me.

I let it.

FIFTEEN:

Cry for Help

Someone slapped me gently on the face, the *smack-whack-smack* of their palm on my cheek sounded like a soft bongo drum in my ears. And I was sleeping so peacefully. It was a woman hitting me—something I'm not entirely unfamiliar with— the soft, smooth texture of her hand and the clean sent of lilac told me as much. She was talking to me. I couldn't understand the words themselves, they were all a jumbled assortment of mush, but her voice was soothing and kind. The voice a kindergarten teacher might use with a student who'd taken a bad fall.

I lay unmoving, not wanting to open my eyes, not wanting to remember where I was or how I'd gotten there.

I just wanted to be still, to let my weary body take its ease, to imagine I was safe and everything was okay. Maybe I was with a beautiful woman.

Maybe Rosie—the long-legged, funny-as-hell brunette from Kansas I'd hooked up with a couple months back. Yeah, maybe Rosie had once again welcomed me into her apartment and in between her bedsheets. It hadn't been serious. I don't do serious and she'd known it, but it had been good. I'd been safe there, warm in her queen-sized bed, cotton sheets entwined around my body. She bought me donuts and coffee from the Krispy-Kreme the next morning.

God, how I wanted that to be my reality.

It wasn't and I knew it.

I couldn't remember what'd happened, but I wasn't with Rosie. I wasn't in Kansas anymore, literally, and to hell with the cliché. Though I wanted to indulge my fiction, I was sure there were more pressing concerns to deal with. I blinked my eyes open.

The lighting in the room was harsh—felt like staring into the sun on a cloudless day.

"I think he's coming t ..." said the soothing female voice, "it looks ... starting to open ... eyes." I only caught snatches of her words, the syllables blurry and indistinct. So was her form, though it definitely wasn't Rosie. Rosie was brunette and this lady was blond, almost platinum.

"Good," said a gruff, recognizable voice followed by footsteps. A man came into view: Morse. That asshole.

Oh right. I was in LA. The Saints of Chaos. Yraeta and the Kings. The Daitya ...

I must've passed out after my fight with the demon. Drawing too deeply from the Vis can do some funky stuff to the mind and body. I had, in the way of the Vis, just finished running an Ironman Triathlon—you know, those insane things where people swim for a couple of miles, bike for like a hundred more, and then run a friggin' marathon, all without a break? Athletes who participate in such events routinely suffer from serious physical injuries and what I'd done while fighting the Daitya had been of a similar magnitude, even though our royal rumble had taken no more than ten minutes.

Morse stood over me smiling. I was on the same banquet table from earlier. This was an all too familiar tableau ... at least I wasn't Saran-wrapped down this time around.

"I've got to stop waking up like this." I propped myself into a sitting position, legs dangling down—the motion sent a wave of dizziness coursing through my head, threatening to lay me back out.

"My gamble paid off. Fuck, you're better than a room full of machine guns," Morse said, a large toothy grin cut his face in half. It was a genuinely happy smile, one that reached all the way to his eyes. He lifted a half-full glass of something amber and delicious looking, and offered a toast. "You smoked the shit out of that thing. Six shots right to the fuckin' head—fuckin' A, dead as dead. To Yancy Lazarus." In that moment any bitterness or animosity I harbored against Morse melted away, a snow bank too long exposed to the glow of the sun. He cared about his people, cared about their well-being, their families, their livelihood and lives.

Morse was a predator, a jackal who'd gladly rip your throat out, but he was also more. The people in this home were jackals of a similar nature, but they were his pack and his fierce love for them was obvious.

He thought I'd killed the Daitya—understandable from his perspective, like he said, I'd shot the thing six times in the head—and I hated to disappoint him. Nothing to be done about that though.

"Not dead," I said. The cheerful buzz of celebration, filling the room with its optimism, died into an uneasy whisper.

"What?" Morse asked, his smile gone as quickly as it had come.

"Not dead. Temporarily out of commission."

"Bullshit. I saw what happened, you blasted that fucker back into the Stone Age with that hand cannon." His shoulders were unconsciously raised, tension knotting his muscles.

He wanted to believe the Daitya was gone and this nightmare was over. It was obvious he couldn't bear the thought of facing this tribulation again. His eyes held the same wild look I'd seen a hundred times before. In Vietnam, lots of guys would get that same look after a firefight, especially if it was the first, and especially if they had to go back outside the wire: fear mingling with anxiety, resolve waltzing with cowardice, self-preservation arm wrestling with duty. It was the look of a gambler counting odds, *how long would the dice come up 7s?*

"No bullshit, Morse. All I did was buy us some time—a week, to get this situation straightened out, or we'll be facing round two. And next time, the demon is going to be expecting an ambush. We won't get so lucky again."

The glass, raised to me in salutation a moment ago, flew from Morse's hand. The *tinkle* of broken glass resounded in the room.

"Fuck!" He bellowed. "Fuck, fuck, fuck!" He stomped over to the living room wall and sunk his fist deep into the drywall with a *thunk*.

"Listen Morse, it's not too late to fix things. We can prevent this asshole demon from manifesting again." The room was utterly still. The fuming Morse withdrew his hand from the wall and stood stock still, a feisty wolverine waiting for something to maul—an animal backed into a corner. A few chunks of drywall crumbled to the carpet.

"Alright. Alright," he finally said, reigning in his temper. "You said it's temporarily out of commission. What the fuck does that mean?"

"Creatures like that are conjured here from a different plane, but they don't actually belong to our reality—they're just visiting. Think about it like this: you can't waltz out onto the highway without getting smashed into little pieces, you need a car. Well, a creature like that demon can't just walk around in our reality. It needs a particular construct, a vehicle, to operate. The Conjurer pumps a ton of energy into a construct—what you might think of as a magic spell—in order to provide the being with a body to move around in. All I did tonight was rob the demon of enough energy that it was no longer able to maintain its physical presence in our reality. Basically, I busted its car to shit."

"So what … next week the Conjurer dickhead that called this thing just repairs the car?" Morse asked.

"Yahtzee."

"Everybody out of the room … Now." Morse commanded, swiveling about to make sure all of his underlings got an equal piece of his glare. His voice was not loud, but it demanded obedience, and the fistful of men and women in the room were more than happy to oblige. Each, in turn, slinked away like a dog caught picking through the trash, until only Morse and I remained. Morse pulled out an I-phone, thumbed through its contents for a moment, and then showed me the screen.

A little boy, maybe nine, with red hair and a dusting of freckles, clung to a thirty-something-woman with striking red hair and a low cut blouse of burgundy. The mother had her arms entwined around the little boy. Both were smiling—maybe laughing—while they peered into the camera. It wasn't a professionally done photo, just a phone picture. The quality of the photo was poor, yet its authenticity made it more powerful. It reminded me of my youngest son when he had been that age.

With a flick of his thumb, Morse brought another picture onto the screen: a selfie of a gruff man in his fifties with a spattering of scars and small tattoos across his face and around his neck. The woman next to him was maybe forty, with too tan skin and too blond hair. They were at a bar, the fuzzy shape of a pool table and the glare of neon lights told the story. The pair would have blended in at the Sturgis rally without remark; both bikers and both, obviously, happy. The way their faces pressed together, the way her eyes looked up toward his—they were in love.

Morse showed me another three pictures: two couples—one old, one young—and a father cuddling a small girl.

"Why are you showing me these?" I asked.

"These are the people the demon's already killed—these are my brothers and sisters, and children. You met Uncle Frank right?"

I nodded.

"The older guy with the platinum blonde. That was our Sergeant at Arms, founding member of the Charter. Uncle Frank's older brother with his wife. Dead two weeks now, flayed alive … you've got to help me." His voice broke a little. "I can't see any more of my people hurt. And the kids … I don't want to see another kid fuckin' die."

His words hit a nerve somewhere deep inside of me, something hot burned in my guts and blood. I wanted to eviscerate the guy who'd conjured the fucking Daitya. Wanted to smash his face in with a rock, to bludgeon him until his head caved and his eyes didn't work anymore. I wanted to set him ablaze and watch his skin slough off for hurting those kids. The sensation was a nauseating visceral thing and it made me sick. I'm no stranger to violence but I've never *wanted* to hurt someone—not like this. Maybe in Nam, but Nam had been a long time ago.

"Please help me," Morse said again, his eyes downcast at the carpet.

"Okay."

He seemed to relax with my answer. "I'm gonna need to track down the Conjurer, and I'll need some help from you and your guys to kill this dickhead."

"Anything," he said, and I knew he meant it.

SIXTEEN:

Frank's

I was at a blues joint down in the city—a hole-in-the-wall called Frank's, featuring a rip-roarin' house band and a mean set of southern-style ribs. The house band was a bunch of gray-hairs like me—well, I would be a gray hair if I aged properly—and they were belting out a hard bop tune called 'Sack O' Woe,' by Cannonball Adderley. And they were making it sound good. The piano bobbed in the background, while the lead sax player—working a beautiful, brassy, vintage Martin Handcrafted alto—slipped and garbled his notes, in typical Cannonball fashion. All sassy-ass 1950s slurred pitches. Nice.

The music was exactly the pick me up I needed. Some blues men are real tormented types, their music is harsh and tawny. Not Cannonball Adderley. The set before could have been the meanest, dirtiest, down-and-out blues you ever heard—dead dog, tornados, and a rabid lion mauling—but Cannonball's stuff was always a ray of sunshine. Its energy was so upbeat it was contagious: you could've lost your job, your wife, and your home all in the same day, and a tune like Sack O' Woe would still leave you tapping your foot halfway through. Such was the power of the blues—it said, *so you've have a bad day, well that's life fella. Now pick up your damn feet and get back to walkin', shit, get back to dancin'.*

Considering the past few days I'd had, that was exactly the message I needed to hear. Just needed to pick myself up and get back to dancing.

If that wasn't enough to put a little bounce in my step, I also had a frosty Pilsner on the table, half a rack of ribs left on my plate, and a full side of cinnamon apples. Nothing in the world is better than a plate of ribs—it's my single greatest weakness. Well, I guess there's also, alcohol, gambling, women, and bullets, all weaknesses in their own right ... on second thought, maybe ribs aren't my greatest weakness so much as my greatest guilty pleasure.

I was born in Plentywood, Montana, but I grew up poor on the outskirts of Raleigh, North Carolina. My Dad had been a gambler like me—like his Pa before him—though not a successful one, a big part of the reason we were so poor.

When my Dad wasn't betting the ponies or playing poker over at the VFW hall, he and Mom—along with the family—ran a little barbeque joint, Pops. My Dad made ribs, the best in the county. We called them Last Meal Ribs, 'cause if you were about to hang or fry those were the last thing you'd want to taste. The night before, Dad would skin 'n' trim those puppies and throw on an overnight dry-rub marinade. Then, come five AM, he'd pull his ass out of bed so those bad-boys could simmer on low heat for six hours.

Best ribs in the county—maybe the state (I'm a little biased though)—the pork equivalent of an angelic choir singing in your mouth. But ribs were for the customers, folks who had the money to pay. They were a luxury. As a kid, I'd ferry those platter out, breathing in the meaty aroma of pork and sweet barbeque, but never getting a chance to indulge.

Except on my birthday. On my birthday, I got ribs too.

Now, every day could be my birthday if I wanted.

I had a big ol' mouthful of tangy baby-backs when Greg pulled out the barstool across from me.

"See you're still alive," he said.

"Ditto," I mumbled, mashing the sweetmeat into pulp.

"Wanna' tell me what happened?"

"In a minute Greg," I said, before washing down my food with a swig of Pilsner.

"You're a piece of work Yancy—get me out of bed at eleven thirty, make me drive across town on a Saturday night, then expect me to sit here and wait on you. A real piece of work."

"Am I inconveniencing you Greg? Let me tell you about inconvenience. Inconvenient is getting a call from an old friend which results in driving halfway across the country. Inconvenient is getting sucker-punched by a supernatural assassin, being pumped full of horse tranquilizers, Saran-wrapped to a table by an insane gang of bikers, and then fighting a friggin' demon. Oh, and inconvenient is getting shot in the ass. I got shot in the ass, Greg. Bullet. Ass. So I am so sorry if I'm 'inconveniencing' you."

"Apology accepted." His voice as dry and dusty as the Mojave. "Make sure it doesn't happen again—this isn't R and R y'know. We've got work to do and I don't have time for your drama-queen-cry-fest. So," he made a curt *get moving* gesture with his hand, "fill me in already." I knew he was joking. I still wanted to give him a thousand paper cuts and throw him into a piranha tank.

But I would be the bigger man—I refused to let his childish taunting get under my skin. With a grunt and a sigh I clued him in to my highly eventful night. The Full House, Morse, the Daitya. I gave him the full skinny and never even pointed out what a colossal jerk he was. A colossal and *petty* jerk.

"Well, while you've been lollygagging around, drinking beer and eating ribs," he said, "I've done some real footwork and found out some good stuff from my end."

Scratch that, I didn't want to throw him in any ol' piranha tank, I wanted to throw him into a tank filled with genetically modified super-piranhas carrying tasers and bullwhips. Asshole.

"First off, I got some traction with Yraeta and the Kings. Talked with a little bald guy with glasses—looks like he should be working as a CPA, really dislikes you. No surprise there."

"*Huh,*" I grunted noncommittally, thinking back to the bureaucratic little man with the Benz. "Yeah, Mr. H & R Block. We've meet."

"So I guessed. Despite Mr. CPA's extreme dislike for you, we were able to deal. Tight-lipped little fella, didn't want to give me much. From what I gathered though, Yraeta isn't behind the Conjurer—doesn't even make sense, from a business perspective."

"I don't understand—business perspective?"

"Course you don't understand yet, I haven't told you. I'm gettin' there if you'd stop bummin' you gums for a minute or two."

Genetically modified super-piranhas carrying tasers and bullwhips, galloping on man-eating tigers.

"Mr. CPA says that the Kings have a loose business arrangement with Morse and the Saints—the bikers have muled coke a couple of times, done a little gun-runnin' too. It's not a firm contract or anything—nothing on paper—but they're friendly. Certainly no outright animosity."

"Okay, so why does that prevent the Kings from targeting the Saints? Gangs do dirty shit all the time—most gangs aren't exactly beacons of ethical integrity."

"This is different, this is business. Morse and his crew act as a buffer between the Kings and some goose-stepping, skin-head group—The Aryan Legion, I think they're called—who won't deal with Yraeta because he's color. The Kings could squish the Legion in a month, but it'd take some effort, maybe mean some losses. Easier to let the Saints stay in place."

"*Huh.*" I glanced away, taking another bite of ribs. I chewed in relative contentment. I wasn't in immediate danger, there was good music thumping in the background, and I had southern-style ribs. Life wasn't all bad. Okay, so Yraeta wasn't our guy—even if we didn't know who the culprit was, at least we'd eliminated a suspect. Not all bad, though not all good either.

"So we know it's not Yraeta." I washed down the meat with another swish of Pilsner. "Other than eliminating a single suspect, did you manage to turn up anything useful—so far you've got no good leads. Only dead ends." It made me feel a little better to drag Greg down a notch or two, even if I was feeling good already.

"Wipe that smug look off your face. I've got another lead. The PI called me a few hours ago—"

"Whoa there braggadouche, hold your horses. You mean *my* PI called?" I asked. "'Cause if it's *my* PI than it's not your lead, its mine."

"Now you're just being petty, Yancy. We've got serious business to be about. Don't have time for your quibbling."

That's it. I was going to swing by *Thurak-Tir* and sell him to the wicked Fae—maybe some particularly malicious Sprite would curse him into a giant toadstool or something.

"Apparently," he continued without even a smirk, "my detective pal isn't as clean as I thought. Remember I told you that IA had taken a look at him?"

"Yeah."

"Well, it turns out that IA suspected he was an informant for, guess who—"

"I already know he gave me up to Morse," I said.

"Yeah," he replied, "but not only Morse. He's also informed for Yraeta and the Kings."

The dots were a little clearer.

"Okay," I said, "so Al gives me up as a scape goat to Morse and also drops my name into Yraeta's lap after you told him I was getting involved?"

"Your guess is as good as mine." He shrugged, "but that's my guess too. He's the only one with connection to both Yraeta and me, and he had access to the info. I don't know what he stands to gain by letting this horror show play out, but I'd say it's worth payin' him a little visit."

"Okay, okay—that's good. Another lead to run down. I also had some thoughts on the Conjurer. Drum roll please ..." I picked the last chunk of meat from the bone, letting him stew in silence.

"Well get on with it already—can't stop flappin' your damn lips, until you actually have something to say, then you clam up like a Puritan on a first date."

"Fine. You've suffered long enough." I took another deep gulp of Pilsner, finishing my drink, before waving down the waitress and pointing to my empty bottle. Greg could stand to suffer a little more. Arrogant, good-for-nothing, ass-face—stealing my thunder and my leads.

"You done with your tantrum?" he asked.

I didn't justify his dig with a response. "I'm thinking it's gotta be someone from a serious Hindu background—Indian subcontinent for sure."

"That's a stretch, Yancy—lots of big hitters contract out Rakshasa."

101

"Yeah, but a Rakshasa and a Daitya? Both are from the subcontinent, and it strikes me as a little strange that they should both be batting for the same team. Whole thing stinks like a hot porta-john after an all-day chili convention. Plus, Daitya are big time—you're not gonna hook one of those on the end of your line with any run of the mill conjuration. I'm thinking the ritual has to be old as hell, probably before the Daitya war and the exile. Means the ritual would have to be done in Sanskrit, or maybe Pali or Magadhi. Not a lot of world class mage-folk running around speaking those languages these days."

A long-legged waitress of maybe twenty-one, deep red hair, obviously dyed, brought me my third Pilsner of the evening.

"Excuse me ma'am," Greg said, as respectful as a ten-year-old boy to a catholic nun—the guy is chivalrous, if nothing else. "Can you please bring me and my friend here a pitcher of Coors, and two glasses, frosted." She smiled and nodded, blushing slightly, before wandering off toward the bar. Greg might be old and crusty as the bottom of a battleship, but women love him. Beats the absolute hell out of me. Not that Greg would ever do anything about it; maybe once upon a time and way, way back when. Not now. Cancer had taken his wife ten years ago, and he'd never moved on.

"Maybe," he continued, "let's say you're right. Sai Hari could have done it, but last I heard, he was a senior member with The Guild, hobnobbing with the Arch-Mage even, so he seems like an unlikely candidate."

"Yeah," I said, "Maybe, Vihaan Vohra? Doesn't he have a reputation for freaky juju like this?"

"Yeah, he did Yancy—but *did* is the operative word. Past tense. Guild hunted him down four years ago. Dead. Maybe if you kept up to date with The Guild you'd know that too."

I looked away. I didn't want to have this conversation again—I was done with The Guild. Bunch of tightwad, hypocritical, self-righteous, self-serving, bathrobe-wearing geezers. There were a few members I still kept in contact with, but by and large, if their super-secret headquarters were on fire, I wouldn't take the trouble to call the fire department. Shit-parrots, the whole lot. Okay, mostly the whole lot.

Let's just say we had a catastrophic falling out and leave it there, buried like all good skeletons ought to be.

"We're not talking about that." Now it was his turn to avert his gaze. He knew it was a sore subject, one I wouldn't appreciate him pushing at—he's never been good with personal boundaries, so it was tough to be mad at him.

"Alright, alright. Sorry for prying … hey, Arjun Dhaliwal could be our guy. He's been on the lam from The Guild for years and he's got the supernatural muscle for it."

"Yeah," I said, "and he's bat-shit crazy, too … I remember him. He's got deep connections to India—was always jawing about a unified India. *Hindutva*. Bat-shit crazy and fits the bill."

The waitress showed up with our pitcher: deep amber in the low light, with the perfect amount of head on top. Greg slid her a twenty and told her to keep the change, which earned him a big smile and another blush.

"So what's our game plan, Yancy?" He picked up my mug and poured, nice and slow, before filling his own glass.

"Well, I say we kill this pitcher—and maybe another one, since you're paying—I'll play a set with the house band. Then we'll catch a few winks at your place and track down detective Al in the A.M. See if we can't get him to talk."

"And if it is Arjun? Guy like that is dangerous. Will you get in touch with Ailia? She could tell us for sure, maybe even give us a location." Ailia. Jeez. Talk about uncomfortable discussion points. She, like The Guild, was a conversational no-man's-land, chock-full of razor wire and anti-personal mines. We'd been together for a while, one of my few serious relationships, and it had ended … well, *badly* is maybe a bit too mild. It would be more accurate to say it ended like a thermo-nuclear blast: complete devastation and long-term health risks. She was still around, but we weren't exactly on speaking terms. On pain-of-death, actually.

"Let's see what Detective Al gives us before we decide to go swim with the sharks," I said.

Greg smiled, but it was the grimace-grin of a man about to go into a combat-zone. "But before that, let's drink—maybe more than we should."

He smiled again and this time it was sincere, crow's feet spread from the corner of his eyes.

You've got to enjoy life as it comes. The reality is that no man is promised tomorrow and God knows two days is a helluva stretch to expect. You never know when some demonic baddy is going to pulverize your face, or when a city bus will plaster you all over the road.

Tomorrow would be a tough day, maybe my last tough day, and it would have plenty of worries all its own. So Greg and I would leave tomorrow's worries for tomorrow; those were problems for Future Me. Tonight we would enjoy life. We would eat, drink, flirt with good-looking women, play a little music, and smoke a few cigarettes—while we still could. Gotta enjoy the little things, because they're what make life worth living.

SEVENTEEN:

Detective Al

Greg and I idled out front of a little ranch style in Burbank. The home was cute: yellow siding, red brick edge work, neatly trimmed green lawn sporting a few manicured hedges, and a smattering of miniature pink hollyhocks. A realtor would have called it a "starter home," though in this part of Burbank, this house probably ran for a small fortune. The cute home, which showed all the obvious signs of loving attention and a meticulous hand, belonged to Detective Al and his wife Judy. My PI from out east had given Greg the scoop on Al, who wasn't as squeaky clean as his neat and picturesque house.

I rubbed at the bridge of my nose and took another slug of my, now, cold coffee. Tired, so friggin' tired. We'd been sitting on this house since 6:30—it was already a quarter of ten and we hadn't seen notta from inside. No Al. No Judy. No walking horrors. Nothing. The only thing I'd seen so far was the bottom of a couple of cups of coffee. We'd gotten up early for no good reason, which made me want to blow something up on general principle.

Greg had insisted on an early start—*to cover our bases*, he insisted—but I think he was just being a sadist. He knew I wasn't a morning person. It took fifteen minutes to brush my teeth and toss on some cloth, another ten to grab a cup of gas-station-joe, and forty-five more on the 101 to get here, which put wake up time at twenty-after-five. Let me tell you something, twenty-after-five is a time that shouldn't appear on an alarm clock. Its criminal and a blatant violation of the sixth amendment: freedom from cruel and unusual punishment. Anything that has me up before eight comes with a one-way ticket to Grumpsville.

It was even worse this morning, though, because Greg and I had stayed up well passed one at Frank's, enjoying the music and the beer, drinking in the atmosphere and patently ignoring all the catastrophic problems looming over the horizon. Past Me had really screwed Present Me over and I was regretting his poor decision-making—lousy, no good, drink-too-much bum. Partying it up and then footing me with the bill.

It also didn't help that Greg looked as bright-eyed and bushy-tailed as ever. The man was sixty-six for crying out loud, yet somehow he was as spry as a college kid, up early for class after a long night out. He had always been a morning person though, probably why he managed so well in the Marine Corps: an organization that runs off little sleep and lots and lots of early mornings.

I'm not a morning person, never have been and never will be. I like staying up late and sleeping in late.

Apparently, Detective Al and his wife also subscribed to my sleeping philosophy. Most folks would've been up and off to church, or at least poking around the living room a little—watching some pregame football show or maybe a bad Sunday movie.

Not Detective Al. This house was dead: no flicker from the television, no lights on, no telephone rings. Dead. There was even a week's worth of newspapers congregating on the front walkway, a sickly looking bunch, expecting welcome, but left out to fend for themselves. Sure, there was a car in the driveway—one of those new Chargers, that looked just a little too slick for my taste—but that didn't mean anything.

The whole scene had an uneasy feel about it. I've never been good when it comes to numbers, but simple arithmetic isn't beyond my grasp, and this scene wasn't adding up. Game is afoot, Watson! My guess was that Detective Al and his missus had checked out—either they'd skipped town when things got too hot, or someone had taken them out permanently. Either way, I'd have to take a closer look to know one way or the other.

"That's it Greg, I'm going in." I set my coffee in the cup holder and grabbed the door handle of his Ford Focus, not waiting for a response. There was too much going on to kill another hour or two waiting at this obviously vacant house.

"Give it another fifteen." He took a sip from his foam cup, no further explanation offered.

"You kidding me right now? We've been here for more than three hours. Another fifteen minutes isn't going to change anything. Shit, fifteen minutes of snooping around and I'll know everything I need to know ... we can blow this popsicle stand and stop wasting our time on this stupid-ass, waste-of-time, stake out."

"So why the rush? It's just another fifteen minutes, right? You said so yourself. Listen, I have a hunch here, let's play it out. Make an old man feel better."

Smarmy, know-it-all jerk, turning my words against me. I wasn't going to sit here all morning, hunch or no hunch. I popped the handle and pushed the door open, sliding out of the seat and into the empty Sunday morning street.

"You're only a year older than me, Greg," I called over my shoulder as I closed the door with a *thunk*. I could practically feel his eyes boring into my back and though I didn't possess ESP, I could almost hear his thoughts. *You sure look like a young man to me—and I think your damn brain has the same malady, too much youth, too much impatience.*

I pulled open the screen door and found the front door locked up nice and neat. Now, you might be thinking, a little ol' locked door, well that shouldn't be a problem for a world-class mage, right? Wrongo. Remember, this house, like all real houses, was protected by the presence of a domicilium seal. Using any type of construct to force my way in would be rough going. Could I hypothetically blow the door off the hinges with a mega blast of fiery force? Well, yeah, I probably could. But it wouldn't be easy, it would take an elephant-sized amount of force and willpower, and it wouldn't be inconspicuous.

There is, hands down, no better way to get the cops to show up then to explode the door off a house at 10 AM on a Sunday morning—especially in a nice part of Burbank like this.

And, what if Al and Judy were home and just late sleepers? It would be inconsiderate to bust up their stuff for no good reason.

Instead, I fished out a black leather case containing my lock picking gear. Why yes, I am a fan of the age-old art of lock picking. It's a little old-fashioned and more of a hassle than blowing the door off its frame, but it's a sure fire way of gaining unlawful and unwelcome entry into any home. That whole pesky supernatural barrier thing has no effect whatsoever on the efficient, yet utterly vanilla, ability to pick a lock. Plus, no unnecessary property damage. A win, win all around.

Lock picking isn't necessarily difficult, but it's also not as easy as they make it look on television—you can stick a bobby pin in the lock and wiggle it around for a bit, but if the lock opens it will be more luck than skill. Realistically, you need to have a decent set of picks and torques and some serious practice if you hope to confidently gain entry passed those bothersome locks designed specifically to keep you out. Admittedly, having a bit of supernatural luck on your side also helps. With my luck, I might be able to stick a bobby pin into the dead bolt and see that puppy pop right open.

But hey, it's always better to have the skill and not need it, than to need it and not have it.

I slipped my torque into the lock and applied a little pressure, all the while working my pick until all the stacked-pins were in place—the dead bolt released with a satisfying *clunk*. The whole thing took maybe fifteen seconds, but bear in mind I've had years to practice this unsavory art.

I turned the brass-plated door handle and pushed the door inward on silent hinges.

The lights were out and the air felt stale, the way things get in a too hot room that's been vacant for a while. Inland California can heat up year-round and today already felt like it had the makings of a scorcher, but no AC pumped into the house and the overhead ceiling fan sat still. A motley assortment of dust bunnies—in the Marine Corps we called them ghost-turds, charming I know—decorated the fan blades. Unfortunately, in the circles I run in, ghost-turd means something entirely different, something involving actual ghosts and residual ectoplasmic residue. I'll spare you the details. You're welcome.

Everything looked nice and neat: clean brown carpet, big flat screen on the far wall, brown leather sofa sitting opposite the

TV, a dark wood coffee table, and a plush recliner. Above the TV hung a family portrait—Detective Al and the missus. In my mind, I could practically see the guy leaning back in his Lazy Boy sipping a frosty beer while watching a Pirates game, all while the overhead fan whirled lazily away. There was no sign of a struggle or home invasion—no broken down doors, busted locks or shattered windows—the home was just empty. Like maybe Al and Judy *had* packed up and left town for a while. Maybe they were off in Malibu sunbathing and sipping strawberry margaritas.

But the car was parked out front. Maybe they had another one?

I moved through the living room and into an adjoining dining room: a cheap white-topped table and a set of matching chairs, but nothing of a more sinister nature. The kitchen, main bathroom, and master bedroom had obviously colluded because they all told the same tale: *yes, the occupants were currently away, but no need to worry, everything was fine and dandy in this neck of the woods.* Everything was clean—though not too clean, which would have been suspicious in its own right. All of the furniture appeared to be in its proper place and there were no giant, man-sized bloodstains or dead bodies in evidence.

Still, this felt all wrong. This whole situation was the equivalent of a Rube glamour—a coat of paint to hide the grime laying beneath. There was no basement, normal for this part of California, but I spied an unattached multi-car garage through the dining room window. The only place left to check. By process of elimination, if there was anything fishy going on that was where said fishy thing would be swimming.

I exited out through the kitchen, via a sliding glass patio door, which let out into a tiny backyard. The grass, though a little long, was thick and green—except near the garage door ... there the grass had wilted and yellowed. A cockroach, chitinous and brown, scuttled across the lawn and disappeared beneath the garage door. Believe it or not, that little roach was a clear sign that I was on the right trail and not running down some dead end lead.

Rakshasa are nasty creatures—even other nasty creatures think Rakshasa are grimy. They literally live in filth. The grimier the better for a nest of Rakshasa. They like dark, rotten places, full of death and decay, old garbage and insects: cockroaches and bedbugs mostly. Like I said, *Nasty*, with a capital N. Like humans, Rakshasa usually adjust their new living accommodations to suit their particular tastes. And it starts to show quick. If a Rakshasa is around, the paint will start peeling, the plants will start to wither, the floor boards will begin to creak, and every cockroach and bedbug for about five miles will come over for the party.

It'll also stink—the sour sweet smell of compost and rot. The closer I got to the garage the more obvious the odor became. Looked like pay dirt.

I tested the garage door and found it locked. Unlike the house proper, however, the unattached garage was far enough away from the main property structure that I wouldn't have trouble popping the door with a Vis construct—no seal in place to stop me. I didn't want to blow the door off the hinges though, because if anything was home, that would surely cost me the element of surprise—all I had going for me, at this point. I drew my revolver in preparation and inhaled a trickle of Vis, only enough to perform the simple working I had in mind.

I forced a thin stream of air into the keyhole, which then expanded throughout the length of the plug, naturally pushing up the individual stacked pins until they all rested in their proper positions.

The lock twisted open with a faint, nearly inaudible click, the knob turned in a loose weave of air, and the door swung inward with a rusty creak—so much for the element of surprise. I drew in a little more Vis, pumping out raw energy into a small orb of light that floated an inch above my outstretched left palm.

Oh man, I didn't want to go in there.

From the stink wafting out of the opening I already knew I was going to find something—or even lots of somethings—dead. I took a deep breath and went in, despite my common sense screaming *STOP* in the back of my head.

First thing I noticed: there were no Rakshasa home—I could tell immediately by the fact that there weren't any flabby, gray-skinned, hyena-faced, monsters trying to rip my head from my torso. So far so good. The second thing I noticed was the incredible stench emanating from the hot little room, a nauseating mixture of raw sewage, burnt hair, and the putrid scent of decaying flesh. Not nearly so good. I doubled over, woozy from the stink and heat. That's when I noticed the cockroaches scuttling across the floor a few inches from my feet.

The room had been mostly dark, and with only a trickle of light from my glowing construct, it had been easy to overlook the thousands of little critters crawling over nearly every surface—floor, walls, windows. Their bodies moved back and forth in a living tapestry, the scuffle of their legs and wings created a soft background buzz, the sound of a Brillo pad running across sheet metal.

Oh God. Not only did I feel sick, but now I wanted to run back to Greg's Ford Focus, shrieking like a small girl. Yuck. Seriously. Cockroaches are gross, folks. Maybe this is my western, ethnocentric brain speaking here, but I have to imagine that cockroaches are hated universally by every people group on the planet.

Seeing one made me want to take a bath. Seeing ten thousand made me want to take a bath in a vat of acid. For a month.

So gross.

I was so distracted by roach-a-palooza that it took me a few seconds to notice the mutilated bodies—partially obscured by insect forms—lining the far wall. There were nine bodies, all told, stacked against the wall. Flesh distended and gray, stained with splashes of old, mud-brown blood. Many of the corpses were missing pieces: arms, legs, ears, chunks of abdomen. They were all, uniformly, missing their hearts. Rakshasa will eat anything—garbage, bloody-road kill, paint cans, you name it—they're living garbage disposals, and human beings are right at the top of the menu.

It was obvious, from all of the missing body parts, that the corpses had been kept around for afternoon snacking. But why were all the hearts MIA you may be wondering, and rightfully so. Aside from being man-eaters, Rakshasa also have the unique and utterly unfortunate ability to shift into the last person they consumed—provided, of course, that they ate the heart while it was still beating. Just one more trick which made Rakshasa very good assassins.

Near the bottom of the stack, I spotted Detective Al. He was dead and far along in his decomposition, which meant the Detective Al that Greg had been consorting with was a doppelganger Rakshasa. The rest of the bodies probably belonged to a bunch of Al's neighbors or friends, cover for the pack of Rakshasa that had moved into the area.

Finding Al's body in the stack answered a few questions, specifically how my name had gotten thrown into the mix in the first place. When Greg had gone to the phony Al and informed him of my imminent involvement in the case, the hyena-faced, turd-monkey must have scampered off to Morse and Yraeta—probably hoping one of the gangs would get me something nice to wear. Like a toe-tag.

So these attacks had nothing to do with me at all. I was just another innocent—well sort of innocent—bystander who'd gotten pulled into the mix by a misplaced word to the wrong set of ears. I'd have to punch Greg in the nose when I got back to the car, it was only fair.

As I looked around at the bodies—trying to commit each face to memory in case I ran across that face again—I realized I had bigger problems than I'd thought. Not only did I have some maniacal mage, a minor Indian godling, and a Rakshasa to contend with—I had a whole friggin' nest of Rakshasa on my hands. Craptastic. My life officially rules.

The smell finally got beneath my skin—I turned from the room, doubled over on the yellowing lawn, and let my breakfast fly: coffee and burrito chunks formed a small river, which splashed across the lawn.

I'd gotten vomit up my nose, which is about the worst thing in the world, *usually.* In this case it was actually a blessing. The vomited coffee and burrito bits smelled a helluva lot better than a stack of month old bodies.

As I sat there, trying to shake off my nausea, my blood started boiling. I was pissed. All those innocent people stacked up in there like a bunch of cordwood, waiting to feed the hungry fires of Rakshasa bellies. I didn't know those people, but I sure as shit knew they didn't deserve to have their hearts ripped out from their beating chests.

I knew it wasn't okay to have their final remains piled in the back of small garage, afternoon snacks for bugs and baddies. There was no dignity in what I'd seen, no fairness, no value. Whoever was behind this whole shebang had racked up a tremendous butcher's bill, and I was starting to cherish the idea of paying him back in kind.

"I do hope you are quite all right, Mr. Lazarus," a man said from somewhere within the garage. His voice was a deep baritone and coated in the off-British accent so common among well-educated Indians and Pakistanis. It was the voice of the demon-conjuring ass-hat who was running this carnival show, I was sure. I bounded to my feet, placing my back against the outside of the garage wall, before peeking around the corner, hoping to get eyes on the enemy while maintaining at least a little cover.

The garage was empty, save for the cockroaches and the corpses, and there wasn't any room to hide. The space, while rather large, was open and otherwise unadorned.

"Over here," the voice said, chuckling softly. There was a vague, man-shaped thing coalescing in the corner. Naturally— because my life absolutely cannot get any better or less weird—the man-shape was made of cockroaches, which continued to scuttle about in an ever-shifting blur of movement. "I suppose it is about time that we had a face to face Mr. Lazarus—"

"A face to face, really? I want to blast you in the 'face' with a can full of Raid, freak."

"Let's be adults about this."

"Obviously you don't know me very well," I said. "Also, you're made of cockroaches. Not something your typical adult does."

"Are you quite done now, Mr. Lazarus?"

"No. Because you've killed like twenty innocent people in the past month which makes you both a sociopath and an asshole. Not a reasonable adult."

"I am not the sociopath you have named me—though, perhaps, from your perspective it may appear so."

I could feel my shoulders knotting. Was this guy actually trying to justify his acts of cruelty and murder? I'm not a big one for God, but I figured this guy deserved a good smiting. I guess I would have to settle for setting him on fire myself, which I was sure would be cathartic even if it didn't bring justice.

"Let me save you the trouble of trying to explain why you aren't such a bad guy. You, Roachzilla, killed women and kids. *Ergo* sociopath. *Ergo* it's go time. End of story."

"A sociopath feels no remorse over his actions, yet I deeply regret these deaths. I wish these souls hadn't perished. Their deaths were not needless, however, they will serve a greater purpose and a greater good."

"I'm sure that'll be a tremendous comfort to the orphaned kids and the widowed spouses of all these people." I pointed my pistol toward the bodies stacked against the wall. "Can we cut out the whole evil-villain banter thing, and get to the part where I set you on fire?"

"You lack vision," he said.

"And you lack scruples and good hygiene, *Arjun*." A telling silence hung heavy in the air. I'd thrown a friggin' bull's-eye.

"So you've figured it out have you."

"It wasn't hard," I said. "There's a nest of Rakshasa running around and a minor Indian dark god. You're the only guy who fits the ticket, bub." The truth was, of course, that I hadn't actually figured it out—just an educated gamble, but sometimes a good bluff is your only play.

"Though it may not have been hard to piece together," he replied, "no one else has done so. You are, surprisingly, smarter than you look—precisely the reason I wanted to avoid your involvement in the first place."

"Oh, I'm smarter than I look huh? Ever heard the saying, 'don't cast stones in glass houses?'" I asked. "Maybe I should remind you that you're made out of dumpster bugs—plus, you're bat-shit, evil-villain, crazy. So, minus thirteen in the smarts department …"

"No vision, Yancy," he said again. "Greatness always comes at a price, to pay it is not madness, but courage. Did the Allies weep for the death of the women and children who perished during the Bombing of Berlin? Did not the Nazi's need to be stopped, even if the cost was terribly high?"

"Apples and oranges, bug-boy."

"Not so, as it has been said, 'kill one man and you are a murderer, kill millions you are a conqueror.' I mourn for those who have passed, but I will do my duty for the greater good of all men. You of all people should understand—you participated in war and you routinely do violence in the service of good."

"Shut up," my voice barely a whisper, "don't talk about what you don't know. We're nothing alike ..." I could see Corporal Martin horsing around with Benson, could see the light envelope him and hurl him into the tree—his arms and legs flying apart at the seams. I hadn't wanted to kill the VC, not until then. But they'd fucking killed Martin, he was the first. It was different.

"Like I said, no vision, Mr. Lazarus. But you do have a good heart. That much is plain—even if your smart mouth says otherwise." Though the cockroach man had a face devoid of human features, the place where its lips should've been twitched slightly in mirth. The motion made my skin crawl.

"It would grieve me to see you killed unnecessarily. You are, in a sense, a man of duty and morals like myself."

"Arjun, you better believe I won't feel even the slightest regret when I wipe your smarmy, psychotic, cockroach-wearing ass right off the planet. Scorched earth, dude. Scorched earth." He smiled again, which didn't improve my temper one iota.

"Even so, *I* would regret your loss, so be warned. My plan will go forward, despite any efforts on your part. If you interfere again I will have you killed, I will show no quarter. Give me your word, bound in an oath of power, not to interfere further and I will let you walk free from this place uncontested." What Arjun was asking for was no simple sworn oath, he was asking me to make a pact, one imbued by a powerful construct of pure spirit, which would literally compel me to cease my involvement. Making a power bound oath in my circles is a *big deal*, it's a nearly irrevocable contract.

And he could kiss my ass if he seriously thought I'd do such a thing.

"I think it's about time we started the barbeque." I conjured up a glowing orb of azure flame.

"As I suspected," he said, slouching over, perhaps in resignation or indifference. "It has been a pleasure, though sadly this will be our final parting. My Rakshasa were only a few minutes away when you broke into their nest—finishing a little morning task for me—they should be converging on you shortly." Arjun fell apart; the constituent bugs crawled away from the constructed form and back to their respective places along the walls, floor, and ceiling.

I heard the snappy *rat-tat-tat* of Greg's compact M-4—things were already headed south and in a hurry.

EIGHTEEN:

Shoot Out in Burbank

I sprinted around the outside of the house, dropping to a crouch as I neared the front side of the building. The heroic thing would have been to jump headlong into this snake pit full of trouble, but as a general rule I try not to be a hero. Ever. Heroes don't live long. Let's be real here, it wouldn't serve anyone for me to run out guns-a-blazin' only to find myself pumped full of holes because I hadn't taken the time to figure out the lay of the land. Remember, pragmatism before heroism is always the best policy in a gunfight.

I cautiously rounded the corner, keeping my back against the house. Greg was pinned down behind the far side of his vehicle, directly across the street from my position. He kept a low profile, rising just long enough to send a handful of well-placed shots toward the three assailants advancing on him from the neatly trimmed front lawn. The three looked mostly human, except for the fact that a multitude of bullet wounds littered their arms, torsos, and faces. No human could survive that. The 5.56 caliber, M-4, NATO rounds weren't going to put these guys down for keeps— that much was clear—but they were giving them pause and putting a little hitch in their giddyup.

Fortunately, Greg and I had come prepared, *Semper Paratus*. Greg also adheres to the policy that pragmatism beats heroism any day of the week. Vis constructs are virtually worthless against Rakshasa—like ducks and water, my friends—but there are still things that pack a major wallop for their kind. There are few things in this world, and that includes the preternatural world, which are truly invulnerable. In my experience, every Superman has their kryptonite.

Rakshasa have their own version: either lots and lots of large-caliber bullets, or industrial grade insecticide. There's not a pesticide I know of that will kill Rakshasa outright, but most serious pesticides will impair their cognitive functions, reaction time, and ability to heal rapidly—all the things that make them so irritatingly difficult to kill. Greg and I had coated our bullets in Fipronil, which is one of the active ingredients in most cockroach sprays and baits.

Firpronil is some foul stuff and is poisonous to just about everything under the sun, including people and, more importantly, Rakshasa. It disrupts their central nervous system, but it doesn't work instantaneously. It has a delayed toxicity which—in the amounts we'd used—would kick in after a few minutes. These poor sons a bitches probably didn't even realize anything was wrong yet. Maybe they were feeling an incy wincy bit slower than usual, but not anything to write home about. That would change in a hurry.

I brought up my revolver and lined up my shot on the baddy closest to Greg's car. Just an average looking guy—maybe 5'10" with a slight paunch and wearing a pair of glasses, khaki pants, and a neat button up which had been scattered with bullet holes. He looked like your typical dad, maybe a sales manager or a high school English teacher, *sans* the bullet holes. I remembered seeing his bloated face in the stack of bodies in Detective Al's garage.

The flesh-mask wearing Rakshasa was gaining ground on Greg's position, but the poison was obviously taking hold in a big way. The creature's steps were the disjointed, lurching movements of a boxer too long in the ring.

I squeezed off two rounds, letting the gun settle back into place for a second after each pull, making sure the shots fired true. The gun's report was so subtle it was nearly nonexistent—especially with the angry buzz from Greg's semi-automatic firing in the background. The effects, however, where immediate, devastating, and anything but subtle. Both of the creature's legs flew apart at the knees: great bloodied chunks of gray flesh somersaulted through the air with a lazy grace, as its calves flopped to the pavement. So much dead meat.

Mr. High School Teacher tumbled to the ground with a gasp and a wail, its human flesh-mask melting away, replaced by the flabby, gray-skinned thing beneath. Its head rolled about, its eyes reeled frantically, trying to make sense of this new world of hurt, trying to understand how such a thing could have happened. It lay on the pavement mewling—the feline sound of a dying lion—and for a split moment I felt kinda bad. I *almost* wanted to waste a perfectly good round and put the damn thing out of its misery, even though it was no longer a threat and each bullet was precious.

Nobody ever said I was smart.

I steeled myself, envisioning those bodies stacked up high in the garage. Human beings murdered mercilessly and nibbled at like finger food by this monster and its ilk. I could see the face of the man this creature had hid behind: eyes glazed over in death, body rigid and black with rigor. He probably had a family—a wife and kids, parents and in-laws, siblings, coworkers, friends—they would all miss him. His corpse would never be found, the Rakshasa would ensure that much, and those people would mourn him and remember him. But they would also wonder about him. There would always be those lingering questions.

There would be no closure.

Had he run off to escape bad credit? Maybe he'd taken on a mistress, abandoning his wife and kids ... no, not a good, upstanding guy like Mr. High School Teacher. But then who could really say, he had disappeared hadn't he? Maybe he'd driven off to the woods and offed himself—a little Saturday night special to the temple because he couldn't take it. Maybe he'd gotten sick. No one would ever know.

Death is a terrible thing. Not knowing is worse, in its way. My ex-wife and kids got asked those questions a lot after I fell off the face of the map.

Now, the family of the poor schlub in the garage—who'd done nothing except be in the wrong damn place—would have to undergo that same trauma. Would have to grapple with the uncertainty and all those uncomfortable questions. I let those thoughts feed me and sustain me whenever the cry of my bleeding heart bubbled to the surface. Screw this legless shithead. Let it suffer.

I shifted my stance and took aim at the second beast— disguised as a petite, mid-thirties, brunette in a black pencil skirt. It too was stumbling toward Greg and hadn't noticed its buddy had dropped out of the game. Clearly, its reaction speed was declining. She looked like a drunk sorority girl after a wicked bar crawl, which was all to the good for me. When I pulled the trigger a bright spray of black and gray filled the air—half of her midsection just disappeared. Incredulous eyes turned on me, but I didn't have time to gloat in my victory.

The last Rakshasa—disguised as Al himself—knew something was off and darted behind a tree on the adjacent lawn, no longer in my line of sight. Well, the element of surprise could only reasonably take me so far. And hey, two for three isn't *too* bad. I moved left, leaving behind the safety of my firing position, advancing on the California ash the Rakshasa had disappeared behind on the connecting lawn. Rakshasa are not small creatures and though the tree was good sized, it seemed unlikely that the creature could have disappeared so thoroughly, even in its human flesh-mask.

I crept forward, gaining ground. The hell? Something was wrong here … I felt the slight tingle of a Vis construct. My stomach sank, the Titanic had hit the iceberg and things were about to get messy. The construct was a rough thing—lacking the refined quality of a genuine mage's working—but it was a bona fide construct nonetheless. An *illusion*. I'd missed it because I hadn't even thought for a second to look for something like this. Rakshasa don't use the Vis—not to say it's impossible, mind you, but rather to say I've never heard of such a thing. Shit, it was even possible that the thing was some sort of charm, made up by Arjun and handed down to his flunkies. Yeah, that kind of fit.

Really though, the how didn't matter a whole helluva a lot. What did matter was this: the Rakshasa who'd thrown the illusion up was now somewhere else.

Probably behind me.

I felt something—the equivalent of a living monster truck—collide into my lower back, sending a thunder-crack of sensation along my spine and into my neck.

Yep, behind me.

Excellent, the crap-alanche had officially commenced. Wouldn't want things to get too easy—I like to stay sharp. I went down in a heap, tucking my head beneath my jacket while simultaneously drawing my arms and legs in toward my stomach. While the fetal position may not be the most heroic of fighting postures, it is an absolute lifesaver if you're about to be on the end of a serious pummeling.

Generally, the backside of the body is tough; it can take a substantial amount of punishment without suffering serious long-term effects. Ask the hedgehog or porcupine. But the same cannot be said for the soft underbelly, which houses all of your fragile, gooey, and highly critical organs, like your heart, spleen, liver, or kidneys. These things are essential for living—and also drinking (thank you, liver), which makes them even more crucial—and thus they should be protected at all costs.

And let's not forget that I'm not a hero, just a pragmatist. The fetal position is highly pragmatic.

The first series of blows landed in the vicinity of my shoulders—felt like a couple of enthusiastic construction workers were giving me the business with a pair of sledge hammers. It was actually an okay thing. Sure my shoulders felt like over tenderized beef-slabs, but at least the Rakshasa had missed my head. Small victories, right ... the next few blows impacted across my ribs, while a wild kick crashed into my belly and lifted me momentarily off the ground. I tried to stay curled up tight, but it was an arduous chore. The world blurred, and all of the oxygen I'd been enjoying suddenly left me without so much as a Dear John letter.

Noise filled my ears. Screaming maybe, but not mine since I had lost that ability, along with the air in my lungs.

More hammer falls crashed into my body. My jacket absorbed a portion of the tremendous violence, enough to keep my bones from exploding from the strikes. This thing was going ape-shit on me—it was going to beat me to death. There was no doubt in my mind. And I couldn't do a damn thing about it. I'd been too careless, too overconfident, and now I was out of options and paying the price. I couldn't think, couldn't focus, couldn't muster the necessary concentration to pull out a working.

That sound again. Not screaming, something else, and getting closer. Gunfire and ... sirens. Yeah, that was the sound. Honest to goodness police sirens.

The Rakshasa yowled—a hateful trumpet blast of sound—and then the heavy fist falls ceased. The sudden absence was startling, even overwhelming. I was going to survive? Bullshit. The idea was absurd. The sirens were so close now. A set of hands pried themselves into the space beneath my armpits. I fought this new invader, clenching my biceps ever tighter into my sides, wanting to survive.

"Yancy!" It was Greg. "Loosen up your damn arms son, we got to get to the car, the cops are gonna roll up here in about thirty seconds."

I let him help me to my feet. My body didn't want to function properly and my limbs seemed to be wrapped in wet blankets, but somehow I got my legs moving, though Greg was obviously carrying the majority of my bulk. My weight returned to me for a moment as Greg pulled open the passenger-side door and unceremoniously shoved me in like an oversized bag of dog food, which was exactly how I felt: pulverized and processed meat in a bag.

The sirens were too close—no friggin' way we'd get out of the neighborhood unhindered. We'd be stopped, questioned, and searched. Then? Then we'd be arrested. Greg and I were both packing some serious heat and there were bullet casings and a variety of fluids littering the street, not to mention a garage full of dead bodies.

I'd been saved from the Rakshasa, but the cops would cause a metric shit-ton of trouble all their own. I am a wanted man, after all.

"We need something here, Yancy," Greg hollered, trying to get his words to penetrate my addled brain. He was right, we couldn't get caught here like this, it would be far too difficult to sort out and we didn't have time for that shit. I could barely think, but I didn't need to think, because I could feel the Vis waiting for me just out of reach. I let go of my pain, drawing in sweet life, pushing the agony away, insulating my body so I could work, so I could pull our collective asses out of this sling.

On a better day, I would have tried to throw up an illusion to cover the scene. Today was not a good day. It was a terrible day. So instead, I went with a quick and dirty glamour. Now, in some circles the term glamour and illusion are used interchangeably, and understandably so because they achieve nearly the same effect: they deceive.

They are not, however, the same thing even if they bring about similar results. Illusions, or veils, fool people by actually creating a different image, which is projected over a person, object, or scene. Illusions exist, in a manner of speaking, in real time and space; they work by tricking the optical nerves in the eye.

Glamours, on the other hand, deceive not by tricking the eye, but by tricking the mind. A glamour doesn't create an image that the eye sees and sends back to the brain. Instead, a glamour suggests directly to the brain that something appears to be different than it is in actuality. Most low-level glamours—like my jacket, say—are basically amped up suggestions planted in the brain, *these are not the droids you're looking for*. You get the idea. But heavy duty glamours are not so much suggestions as they are commands.

Most magi avoid doing stuff like that. It's not exactly illegal, but compelling the freewill of thinking beings is taboo and there are lots of folks who don't look kindly on that sort of thing. If a glamour is too heavy duty, it can actually enthrall people—enslave them to your will—which is a serious no-no. Go around enthralling people and you're guar-an-teed to get your mug plastered on The Guild's most wanted list.

Like I said, today wasn't a good day, I wasn't in a good way, and I didn't have the time or energy to whip up a fancy illusion. So instead I pushed out a glamour with the force of a bomb blast:

EVERYTHING IS NORMAL HERE, MOVE ALONG. My command must have encompassed two or three blocks, though I formed a small bubble around Greg to prevent him from being unduly affected. It was a powerful working—maybe even powerful

123

enough to enthrall—but spread over such a broad area, no one person would be harmed. Still, tiptoeing along the edge of some serious gray area shit …

I opened my eyes in time to see a pair of black and whites pull by, theirs flashers winking off. Greg pulled the car out behind them.

"You survived," he said, cruising along without looking at me.

"*Humph*," I grunted—sure didn't *feel* like I'd survived.

"Congratulations. You should've waited out the fifteen minutes like I said. Pays to listen to your gut."

"Duly noted," I replied, as I closed my eyes and drifted off to a sleepy playland, devoid of pain, cockroaches, heart-eating monsters, or stupid know-it-all friends.

NINETEEN:

Brainstorm

"**A**rjun," Greg said.

"Yep," I confirmed from my place within the bathtub full of ice. My torso looked like something Van Gogh might've painted on a dark day: black and blues swirled and intermingled across my ribs, chest, and shoulders, blending with the faded yellowing bruises from my encounter with the Rakshasa in Las Cruces. Looked a little like Starry Night, which was both cool and aesthetically pleasing. Also asstastic, did I mention that?

"What's the end game?" Greg asked. "Long term, where is this thing going?"

"Like I've got a clue." I shrugged my shoulders and immediately regretted doing so. "Greg, I've been playing some hunches and following a few leads, but mostly I've been bluffing so far. You know that planning and forethought aren't my strong suits."

"You're right—better to give the dyslexic kid the road map than ask you for insight and direction."

"Why are we friends again?" I splashed some water at him, drawing minutely on the Vis to make sure he got a face full of freezing human-soup. "I have to admit, though," I said after a moment, "Arjun struck me as sincere—whatever the hell he's playin' at, he sure thinks he's doing good. He's crazy as a horse in a tuxedo, but he's got good intentions." The sound of slushing water filled the quiet of the room.

"We better kill him quick," Greg said, mopping the water from his face absentmindedly with a hand towel.

"Yeah" I agreed. "He's the most dangerous kind of bad guy—one with a good cause. The quicker the better."

"So how are we gonna get him into his pine box?" Greg asked.

"I don't know. But we're not going to be able to do it alone. I don't have a clue where he's holed up—he's somewhere in L.A. but L.A. is a big friggin place. Might as well be operating in some fallout shelter in Pakistan."

"And he's got a small army of monsters standing in our way," Greg added.

"Right. So even if we get to Arjun, there's no way we can handle nine Rakshasa popping out of the walls. Let's not forget that he also has some serious hoodoo to fling around and a pet Hindu demon in his pocket."

"You're a real well of hope and optimism," Greg said, unamused. "Now how's about you stop whining and start thinking about solutions, princess."

"How about you grow up a little, Greg. Name calling? We're senior citizens, it's … well frankly, it's beneath us. So, if you could please just give me a friggin' minute you crotchety, old, backed-up-well-of-septic-waste, I'll sort this all out. Okay?"

"Whatever," he grunted noncommittally, which I took as his assent. I closed my eyes and let the water sluice over my body, let my arms relax and float upwards, clearing my mind of the pain, worry and anxiety. Feeding all those unhelpful emotions into the fire of the Vis, letting energy and life fill me, while I floated in the coolness of the water. I always did my best thinking in the water, there's something primal and inherently creative about water. I also needed the liquid buffer for the small construct I was preparing.

In the black, empty space that my thoughts, hurts, and emotions had previously occupied, a picture coalesced. But to call it a *picture* is somewhat inadequate because this place is, at least to me, more real than anywhere that exists on earth. Plush carpet, dark wood-wall paneling, and mahogany furniture—all old, finely made, and smelling of lemon oil and leather. A padded leather chaise sat against one wall, a hulking desk framed in the back wall. An antique globe—which also served as a flip open liquor cabinet—sat in between a pair of burnt-leather club chairs. On the wall in front of the paired chairs sat a ginormous wall-mounted flat screen, which I used to review memories when the need arose.

I'd created this private space long ago as sort of a safe haven for my mind to go to in times of stress and trouble. A place I could go to be alone, to think, to work through my issues ... and boy do I have some sumo-sized issues to work through. Shit, I have a convention center full of sumo-sized problems, so you can probably imagine the amount of time I hang out here.

I took a seat in one of the club chairs—a scotch with water appeared in my hand. I didn't drink, but let it just sit while I waited for my guest to arrive.

"Don't let that scotch go to waste," said a voice from my left, "you look like a month-old-jock-strap: stretched, sweaty, and terribly abused. You could use the drink." The man who was insulting me so casually—and doing it well, might I add—occupied the second club chair. The newly arrived guest was ... *me*. Or maybe me as I'd looked ten years ago, with skin the color of seawater, and without all the bruises and lacerations.

He was my instinct, my subconscious, a living being, of sorts, permanently bound by the Vis with an Undine: a water-elemental from of the Endless Wood, just outside of *Glimmer-Tir*—the golden city of the High Fae of Summer. I'd saved the spirit as a young, naïve mage, and it had taken up residency in my head. It's kind of hard to explain actually. Our relationship is ... complicated, I guess. But that's a whole other story.

Now this is pretty out there, I confess, but most people talk to themselves right? Sure, usually it's a bit more of a monologue than a dialogue, but let's not sweat the details here folks. The important thing to take away is that my subconscious partner in crime is great for all kinds of things, and allows me the perfect springboard for a solid brainstorming session.

He's kind of like a DVR for my life—he helps me to remember things I've forgotten, points out details my waking mind might overlook, and helps me to find connections that the more rational part of my brain would never make. He also has a sharp tongue, which he feels free to unleash on me whenever I go against his advice and get us into trouble.

"This whole mess is a real shit-storm, you never should have gotten us into this business."

"Well we're involved, that ship has sailed," I said. "What I need now is advice not your general smart-assery, so stow it."

"Look, the best advice I can give you is to jump back into the Camino and drive for Vegas. We don't need this kind of trouble and we sure as hell don't need all this publicity. We've been doing a good job of staying under The Guild's radar—but this is going to remind them you exist and that you threatened to blow them all to the moon last time you were around."

"Not going to happen," I said. "We're committed. We're going to make things right here."

"We can't make things right here," he said. "We can't bring all those people back." He rubbed a hand through short hair, a look of pure exasperation on his face. "Look, this thing is a friggin' amputation operation—maybe we can stop the bleeding, but we're not gonna be able to save the leg."

"You're not going to convince me. Better start giving me something to work with or else we're both going to wind up in Al's garage as Rakshasa food."

A whiskey appeared in his hand, a double, neat. He drained the thing in one long pull and put his head back, eyes squeezed shut. "No talkin' you outta this?"

"Nope. We're staying on till the end."

"Stubborn." He shook his head. "Alright, let's review the tapes." The lights in the room dimmed and the wide-screen TV blinked to life. Two men appeared on the screen, Morse on the left and H & R Block, representing Yraeta, on the right.

"Let's start here," my instinct directed. "Morse has lost a lot of men and has a damn good reason to want to deal Arjun a little payback, right? But he's not your only ally. Yratea's also taken a helluva hit. At this point, it's safe to assume that doppelganger Detective Al fed Yratea the bad info on you, which cost him manpower, and this mess is likely going to cost him a profitable business alliance with the Saints. Yraeta's pissed and that's good for us. We can use that. He might be annoyed with you—who wouldn't be? *I'm* annoyed with you—but it's a safe wager that he'd rather settle the bill with Arjun."

All good points, though that didn't actually solve the problem for us—Morse and Yratea might be weapons, but I didn't have a target for them.

"Okay," I said, "let's say we can use Morse and Yratea. Then what? Still doesn't give us Arjun. We don't know where he is or have a way to get at him."

"No, but Greg was right. Ailia could find out for us ... "

"No," I said, the iron in my voice unyielding. "There's a reason I'm in the driver's seat and you're not—I make better decisions." He cast me a speculative glance that said *then why are you here asking for my help.* "Usually I make better decisions ... sometimes," I amended. "But I'm not setting up a meeting with Ailia. It's a bad idea, like Chernobyl bad." Though I'm occasionally prone to bouts of over-exaggeration, this was not one of those times. Setting up a meet with Ailia was about as smart as skinny-dipping with Great-Whites.

Ailia and I were a serious item, once upon a time. Really, she was the only serious relationship I'd had since my ex-wife. But that had been a lifetime ago and I knew things wouldn't end well if I called her up out of the blue. Ailia could help me, sure—or rather the Morrigan, Irish goddess and general badass, who currently had possession of her body could—but the cost would be might hefty. Too friggin' hefty. I just didn't think my heart could handle seeing her again, hearing her voice, smelling the sweet lilac scent of her skin. Even if I could use Ailia to find Arjun, the emotional trauma of being with her again wasn't worth it. Ailia was a closed door and I needed to remember that if I wanted to stay alive.

"No, there's got to be better options. What am I even keeping you around for if that's all the originality you've got?" I asked.

"First, I am a part of you—"

"Apparently the incompetent part," I muttered, though he kept right on going as if I hadn't said a thing.

"So you'd better watch where you cast your accusations. Second, it's not like you've got a load of options—you burn bridges faster than a chain-smoking arsonist—and lastly, I am the one that comes up with ninety percent of the plans that keep us breathing."

"All I'm hearing is a bunch of whining. When are you going to get to the part where you come up with something useful or insightful or whatever?" I asked.

His shoulders slumped, the cast of his face told me he was about a second away from throwing something at me before disappearing like a wraith, abandoning me to my fate. But I knew he wouldn't. This was *our* fate, he'd stick it out as an act of self-preservation.

Everything was still and quiet in my mind as both my instinct and I weighed and considered options, looking for any avenue which might deliver us Arjun.

"What about Harold the Mange?" my instinct asked after a minute. "We still have a working relationship with him, sort of. He could probably do what we need."

"I dunno … things didn't end so well last time we were together," I said. Last time Harold and I parted ways, it was after he'd tried to cocoon me in his lair with the intent of devouring my innards. Take note all you members of geekdom, trying to cocoon someone in your lair is not a good way to create long-lasting relationships.

"Yeah, but it was nothing personal," my instinct continued. "He just lost control of his hunger. I'm sure he won't hold that fiasco against you. He's reliable, at least so far as Hub Dwellers go."

"Still …"

"Listen asshole, it's either Harold or Ailia—I'll let you make the call."

Well if those were my options. "Fine, I guess Harold might work. But it'll mean a trip into the Hub and I don't have anything to sell him, so I'll owe him one." Owing someone a favor might not sound like a whole lot, but in the preternatural community a favor can be a big deal. In the regular world of Rube mortals, owing someone a favor means you'll help them take an old couch to the dump. Heck, if it's a big favor you *might* even help them move.

In my circles, however, it meant I would be indebted to Harold in a big and official capacity. But that was a worry for

Future Me. Plus, I could always try to barter with him, if I played things right I might even be able to set some decent terms to the favor. A little mercy for Future Me wouldn't be a terrible thing if I could manage it.

I didn't want to go into the Hub, I didn't want to deal with Harold, but I *did* want Arjun. And since the only other option was Ailia, Harold and the Hub seem like a regular bouquet of sunflowers and daisies.

"I can see those wheels a turning," said my instinct.

I drank my scotch in reply. "Alright, we'll try Harold."

I opened my eyes, letting the padded leather room vanish back into my mind. Greg was staring off into space, apparently as absent as I'd been. I splashed around in the water, stretching cramped arms and legs, which had been still for too long.

"So what's the plan?" he asked as I settled back into place.

"We need to go make friends."

TWENTY

The Hub

I filled Greg in on the plan: his job was to connect with Morse directly and Yraeta, through H & R from New Orleans, and see if both organizations would be willing to play ball. If Greg could play the diplomat well enough—and I was confident he could—I'd have some significant firepower at my disposal. With the combined criminal forces of Morse and Yraeta, it'd be easy to get rid of the Rakshasa army for long enough to give me a clear shot at Arjun. All that left me to do was bounce on over to the Hub, track down Harold the Mange, see if he had the goods on Arjun, and then strike a potentially life threatening bargain.

No problem.

I left Greg to his work. He'd have his hands full, but then so would I. I got into the Camino and headed out to the 101, which eventually dumped me onto the 126. I cruised north and west for maybe twenty minutes, before stopping in Santa Paula.

In Santa Paula, there's this old-timey, glass-fronted butcher shop: Sam's Meats. The store had been there for ages; a yellow brick building, sporting big glass windows with prices and sales stenciled on by hand in big green, orange, and white script: *Sale, Top Sirloin $6.99 per pound*, read one glass panel. There aren't too many places like Sam's anymore. Most little family run butcher shops have gone the way of the dinosaur, driven to extinction by the giant asteroid that is big market business.

I could feel for Sam. He was a relic and a curiosity from a different age, hanging on against the march of progress. Most days, I'd say that describes my life too.

I've bought ribs from Sam on a number of different occasions—let me just say that the man knows his shit—but that wasn't the reason I'd come today. A shame all around. Instead, I'd come to Sam's because there also happens to be an entranceway to the Hub nestled right behind his rollaway dumpster.

Every major city—and even most minor ones—have one or more doorways to the Hub: portals that cross over from the material plane and into an in-between place, which I like to think of as Earth's waiting room. LA, and its surrounding areas, has fourteen entrances to the Hub that I know of for sure, though in a city as big as LA there could be lots more.

What exactly is the Hub, you're probably wondering? It's a real shithole, is what it is—and this is coming from a guy who's seen about every filth-covered dive bar or motel in America. The Hub is the plane of existence which directly connects to our material realm, and it's the place where most beings from the far-flung reaches of Outworld cross over. If you're a troll or hobgoblin visiting from The Endless Wood, you have to cross over via the Hub. If you're a Valkyrie on leave for a long holiday weekend of skiing in the Alps, you're still going to have to pass through the Hub.

Think about the Hub as the material plane's version of a Greyhound Bus station: the Hub doesn't connect to every plane—Heaven and Hell for instance—but it's where a guy can enter or exit from our plane of existence into another. There are, of course, exceptions to this rule: Angelic messengers, for instance, have free-reign to go wherever the hell they want, whenever the hell they want. Human magi can also summon a being directly into our plane by acting as an anchor into our realm and then tearing a hole in reality.

Generally though, for most things—leprechauns, Low Fae, or other dark denizens—the Hub is the revolving door in and out. One big bus station. Like any normal bus station, you might well get rolled if you fall asleep there and it smells a little like urine.

Harold the Mange was a Hub Dweller and Harold was my best chance at getting to Arjun, which meant I had to suck it up, put my feet to the pavement, and trek through the Hub. I opened myself to the Vis, letting energy flood in, filling each cell. Opening a doorway to the Hub, even a pre-established one, takes a lot of energy. At least it does for me.

Creatures from Outworld can more or less come and go as they please with relative ease—they're just less materially real than human beings, so crossing over is no big thing. Most of them can just kinda phase through the weak places.

For humans, crossing over is a bit trickier and takes some power—though, admittedly, I've seen magi who can open a door to the Hub with a trickle of power so low, it wouldn't be able to snuff out a candle's flame. I can't, for the life of me, figure out how they do it. There's some trick to the thing which I've never mastered. Fact is, not everyone is good at everything: portals, conjurations, and dimensional crossovers are not my bag, too much finesse. For me, opening a way to the Hub never feels like turning a doorknob, it feels like prying the door off a safe with a crowbar. But, the end result is the same and that's what matters, right?

Doorknob, crowbar, potato, potahto. Whatever.

To me, results speak their own language.

I focused my will, spinning hundreds of razor-thin strands of radiant heat into a rough lattice square, overlaid and woven through with streams of air, and knots of earthen power. The immense structure—though invisible to the naked eye—vaguely resembled a medieval castle gate, which is kind of what it was, I suppose.

I forced the working into position, overlapping the weak spot in our plane, which hid the entranceway to Hub. My body strained to hold all of the separate strands of construct in place; keeping all of the pieces of this weave together was like juggling a half-dozen chainsaws, while mowing the lawn, and cleaning a sink full of dirty dishes. I was hurting.

When I'd finally finagled the construct into place, I let it unravel while simultaneously whipping up a force shield to protect myself from the blow back.

A quick lesson on Vis constructions: all constructs are composed of a variety of elemental pieces. Each woven together in an endless number of patterns and forms. For all you knitting buffs out there—there's got to be a few, right?—it's a little bit like knitting, (it's the best analogy I have to work with so cut me a little slack). In knitting, there are a whole slew of different yarns to work with, a ton of different patterns to choose from, and about a million different shapes a piece can take—socks, washcloths, ridiculous sweaters you'll never wear. You get the idea.

But if you don't tie off the piece correctly, those socks will fall apart on you every single time.

Working with the Vis is no different. If you pump a whole bunch of energy into a massive construct and don't shape it through an effort of will, the damn thing will unravel and literally explode in your face. So when I said opening a way to the Hub is kind of like prying open a door with a crowbar, what I really meant is that it's like blowing a door off the wall with a shape charge. The construct I'd made was basically a big, shape-specific bomb—amped up with a whole bunch of juice, and then left to blow up as the underlying lattice unraveled.

FYI, this is not a safe thing to do, and is generally frowned upon by the magi community. Irresponsible and wildly dangerous, they say. Meh.

Like I said, results speak their own language.

A thunderclap ripped through the night as my incomplete construct denoted with a flash of silver light, sending out a rush of hurricane force air and a whirlwind of particulates, mostly dust and trash from the alley way. The blast was big. My force shield deflected the majority of the debris, though the strength of the explosion did rock me back on my heels for a second. I blinked my vision clear from the light of the explosion. Before me hung a black hole falling in on itself where my working had been moments before.

Believe it or not, the black hole of doom was actually part of the plan. The first detonation was the initial result of the working coming undone, but the implosion would actually create the door. Once there was sufficient gravitational pressure, the weak spot in our plane would cave, granting temporary access into the Hub. The black hole condensed—the gravity of its vortex immense, falling ever inward. Eventually, the doorway opened with another thunder crack. A jagged rip, eight by ten feet, hung suspended in the air, the Hub's hazy, mud-colored sky filling the view.

I dropped my shield and let the Vis go, yielding to the gentle pull from the now open portal. I didn't want to venture into the Hub, but it was better to be done with the thing. The rift let me out into the back alley of a notoriously ill-reputed bar called The Lonely Mountain, which boasts a list of clientele that reads like the horror shelf at the local bookstore. It was also one of the frequent haunts of Harold the Mange, my target and possible ally. Even if Harold wasn't in residence this evening, there would probably be someone who could give me a clue as to his whereabouts.

I made my way around to the front of the bar. The building was a hulking thing made of craggy, gray stone, which might well have been transported out of the Arthurian era—part mountain, part castle. High windows, fixed with black metal bars, shed both orange-red flame light and the muffled—though barely—sound of other worldly orgasmic moans. The Lonely Mountain is mostly a bar, but it also doubles as a high-class brothel. Brothels in general are a no-go in my book—real men shouldn't pay for women—but this place carried an extra dimension of grossness ... I've seen some of the ladies *and* gentlemen working this place—it's not a pretty sight.

A man in his late fifties attended the door: black hair, flecked with gray, ashen skin, tattered clothes, and a blank, vacant look etched across his face. He was a zombie. There are a great multitude of zombie species—everything from sentient, nearly human zombies, to the mindless brain-eating kind which fill the majority of movies these days. This guy fell somewhere in between. He was dead, and recently, by the look of him. Someone with access to the Vis (and a dark inclination) was animating the body through a construct and feeding the creature a basic set of instructions to follow. *Throw out troublemakers*, maybe.

I marched passed the zombie bouncer, who never even noticed my presence, and pushed through a pair of frosted double doors that read: The Lonely Mountain, followed by a stern warning, *No Fighting, No Trouble, Violators will be Incinerated.*

The Lonely Mountain was such a popular and happening joint due, in large part, to the fact that the proprietor was a fierce and unforgiving man named Firroth the Red. Firroth wasn't actually a man at all, but a Red Dragon—hence *the Red* part. Like most Dragons, Firroth was ferociously jealous of his treasure, which happened to be his bar and brothel, and would, literally, incinerate anyone who threatened its safety. The Zombie bouncer out front was only a formality since everyone this side of the Hub knew that Firroth was the bar's real enforcer. It made The Lonely Mountain a great place for business meets, though, since no one wanted to put a toe on the wrong side of the line where Firroth was concerned.

Harsh, thumping music poured from the room. Muted red, orange, and amber lighting filled the space with pockets of illumination, though overall the bar remained a dark and foreboding place, a cave dimly seen—it actually kind of reminded me of The Full House. Maybe Morse and Firroth had the same interior designer, stranger things have happened.

Smoke—both the tangy aroma of tobacco and the musky, sulfurous stink always hanging around dragons—loitered in the air. The ground level was cavernous, chock-full of jagged hanging stalactites, glowing in various hues, and deep recessed booths housing the bar's assorted patrons. In the Hub, buildings are often much larger on the inside than they appear outwardly, which was certainly the case with The Lonely Mountain. I didn't look too closely into those shadowed booths, I didn't what to see what nightmares were walking tonight.

I also didn't want to be seen. Magi are not well loved in the Hub. To most preternatural beings, human are prey animals—snack food—and to them, magi were a perversion of the natural order.

A cursory glance didn't immediately reveal Harold, but that didn't mean much, he might well have been lurking around somewhere. Aside from having a massive ground level, The Lonely Mountain was also several stories high.

I'd have to ask around, something that could prove to be a bit trickier than it sounded.

TWENTY-ONE:

The Lonely Mountain

I pulled up a stool at the bar. Though most of The Lonely Mountain's patrons were tucked away in the recessed and secluded booths lining the bar's interior, a few forlorn souls lingered at the bar proper: eight men—or what I presumed were men—and one woman, all of whom looked more or less human, though that didn't mean much, not here. Lots of things can look human with a little effort. There was even a chance some of them might be. People of all stripes, classes, and nationalities have found their way into the Hub from time to time: thralls, slaves, or tourists who've made terrible deals with varying supernatural factions. Shit, in the New York Underground, there's even a portal that any Rube can come through—no Vis required.

On the stool to my right sat an overweight and slovenly man with thinning hair, nursing a dark brown stout. He looked like the Horsemen of Death was stalking his trail. Off to my left, with one stool between us, was the female customer. She was a plain Jane: dark slacks, a silky-white button down blouse, dark shoulder-length brown hair pulled into a ponytail, and a pair of thin black glasses. Her face was thin and angular, a little too harsh to be beautiful, though she could pass for handsome.

She looked entirely out of place here, which immediately set my instincts a ringin.'

Firroth the Red stalked up to me from the far end of the bar. Though he was a dragon's dragon, he wore the guise of a man—a huge and dragon-ish looking man. He must have stood at eight feet and had a swath of fiery-red hair, which shimmered gold and orange in the light. The guy was also built like a straight-up brick house—his muscle's had muscles large enough to lift weights at Venice Beach. Scrolling tribal tattoos of blues and blacks snaked up his arms and around his neck, so delicate and finely worked they looked like artful scales, which they may well have been. A cigar—fat, black, and reeking of dragon stink—jaunted from the corner of his mouth at a rakish angle, always burning but never diminishing.

His eyes were the color of molten-gold, slit by a thin razor cut of black—they were the cold and cunning eyes of a reptile. Lots of things in the Hub might be mistaken for human, Firroth was not one of those things. He may have elected to sport a human suit, but it was an unconvincing costume.

"What's your order, mage?" he growled, and I was immediately reminded that Firroth is not the kind of bartender you come crying to after a rough day. He's friggin' terrifying.

"What've you got?" I asked, lowering my shoulders, trying to appear casual and unimpressed.

"Everything," he said flatly. "I've got anything and everything for the right price. So what's your drink?"

"I'll take a Jack, neat, and any information you've got on Harold the Mange."

"Don't know what business you've got with the Mange," he said—picking up a filthy glass, wiping it gingerly with an even filthier rag, before pouring my drink and setting it in front of me—"but this place is strictly neutral. You saw the sign, right." It wasn't a question.

"Listen, Red." His eyes flashed in response, and I knew I'd made a misstep by not keeping things wholly professional, but I soldiered on. Best to never show a predator that you're weak or nervous. "I'm not out to break tables, throw chairs, spill blood, or otherwise bring trouble to your fine establishment. I just need some info."

A wave of smoke, hot and heavy, billowed out from Firroth's cigar. The thing looked like a friggin' jet engine. As the smoke cleared, Firroth shot me a wink and pointed toward the woman on my left.

"The drinks on me, but drink quick," he said, before stalking down the length of the bar and disappearing behind a set of swinging doors into the back.

I swiveled on my chair, my drink forgotten and untouched—I'd probably catch the plague from the glass—and turned my gaze on the less-than-lovely-bar goer.

"So I imagine you were following that exchange right?"

"Quite." She dipped her head in agreement. "It's always valuable to keep your ears open—as they say, knowledge is power. And you, Yancy Lazarus, are looking for information on the Mange."

"My reputation must proceed me," I said.

"Hardly. You flatter yourself, I'm afraid," she said. "One of my many gifts is *knowing* things, including a limited knowledge of my own future. I saw you coming ages ago."

"Well, this is awkward" I said. "Best we move on. If you know me, then it's likely you know what I want. Where is Harold holed up tonight?"

"Indeed, I do know what you want—our meeting is quite fortunate for you—but there is, of course, a price."

Yeah, of course there was a price, how could there not be? People in the Hub—hell, people in general—are a selfish lot, always trying to find out what's in it for them. No free meals.

"What're you asking?"

"Nothing much. Just consideration, should I ever need help from you. Not a favor, nothing so binding, just goodwill between you and I. I have always believed that if you help others in their time of need, they may well help you in yours."

"And who are you?" I asked, wanting to know whom exactly I was giving consideration too.

"If you want Harold the Mange, it's better that you do not pursue that line of inquiry."

I probably should have walked away from the table—it's always wise to know who you're making deals with—but I needed Harold and this wasn't a formal favor.

"Fine." I rolled my eyes, annoyed. "Should such a time arise in the future when you—whoever the hell you are—need help, I will *consider* it." Her lips pulled back at the corners in a tight smile, which left me uncomfortable and twisting in my seat.

"Excellent," she practically cooed, which made me more uncomfortable still. "Harold has moved shop. He is currently taking inventory." She pulled out a slip of thick, expensive, cream-colored paper and scrolled an address on it with her finger—no pen required. Not human, check.

The address was for a dump over in Remington corridor, a slum even by Hub standards, and a known haunt for the Little Brothers of the Blade. I curled my lips in a chilly smile of my own, before excusing myself from the bar and heading out of The Lonely Mountain to hail a cab.

Once outside, I waved down a passing 67' Austin FX3—the classic black taxi of London—all sleek black and chrome, with the bright amber *Taxi* bobble on top, shining out into the night. The car pulled over with a squeal of brakes, followed by a chorus of honking horns and bristly curses from passing motorists. I slid into the back without much thought. The interior was black velvet instead of the slippery, cheap vinyl stuff you would expect, while the doors were framed with sleek hardwood and more chrome.

The Hub, though disgusting in many ways, was also a place of excess and luxury.

I shut the door behind me, the black, bulletproof glass—a safety mechanism against would be carjackers—rolled open to reveal a bulbous creature with glimmering blue-skin and an old-fashion cabbie cap. A Kobo. Kobocks mostly lived down in the Deeps, sheltered in their closed off communes while they worshiped forgotten Dominions and dusty Powers of old. A few commuted to the surface for work though. The Kobo cabbie turned down his screeching music: Hub hip-hop. No thanks.

"Where to?" His voice was sludgy and uninterested.

I gave him the address in Remington corridor.

"Looking to get a kidney or a heart from the Little Brothers?" he asked. "I might know a guy."

"Not interested," I replied curtly.

"Whatever." He shrugged his lopsided shoulders and shut the partition between us. Thank God, I had no desire to listen to the awful music I'd heard squawking from his radio. It also saved me from any painful or awkward conversations about Hub politics—a subject that could bring considerable trouble if you weren't careful with your tongue.

I put him out of mind, knowing he'd get me to my destination. He was certified, after all, which meant he could be trusted not to murder me horribly and steal my wallet. Probably. Instead, I focused on the passing sights.

The buildings were a varied lot, crafted out of every imaginable material—red brick the color of blood here, reinforced steel-plate there, plaster and stucco further on, and lots and lots of concrete. Gaudy neon signs were plastered to every available surface; glamorous and garish things in a hundred different shades of color, all of them unnatural, and each vying for attention. An alley snaked away between the buildings: a row of shanty homes made from plywood, warehouse pallets, and car tires. A little further up lurked a towering, off-kilter building made of electric-blue granite and studded with skulls—the Temple of Suicides.

Off on the left, a fire-engine-red woman, sculpted of neon tubing, winked on-and-off, a promise of illicit pleasure to come. On the right, a pair of bouncing green and blue dice caught my eye—a sure spot to find a little action and maybe make a little money. Who was I kidding? Everyone and their brother would know I wasn't playing a straight game. Magi aren't welcome to games of chance, and trying to disguise yourself as something other than a mage is a sure way to get disemboweled.

Personally, I've always thought it's a bullshit double standard, in the Hub *no* one plays fair—there's always some hustle going on. And usually, you're the mark.

I pushed it all out of mind, better that way. The Hub can be an alluring place in its way—everything is so much brighter, so much more vivid, and the stakes are always higher here. But the place is like a cancer, it'll eat you up if you let it. And that was just up here on the surface where the denizens at least pretended to play nice; down in the sprawling Deeps, it's even worse. The Hub is sort of like New Orleans, Bangkok, and Vegas all rolled into one—except that even Vegas would blush crimson if it took a ride down the Hub's central boulevard.

Shit, the Hub would probably slip Vegas a roofie, take it to a sleazy motel, and carve out a lung for the black market.

After fifteen minutes the taxi pulled onto a narrow street, devoid of sidewalks, and littered with trash and filth of every assortment and description: slowly smoldering tires, mounds of plastic bags and rotting foodstuffs, open sewage trickling along building fronts. Even worse, were the pieces of flesh and bone—often whole limbs—dotting the pavement and protruding from the sour-smelling refuse piles. Evidence that the Little Brothers of the Blade had been out and busy, taking fingers, hands, and feet as payment from the unwary. Hacking and cutting with their gleaming sling-blades and sharpened shrub-sheers. Much of the blood sprinkled about was still fresh, which explained why the street was so empty.

Creepy as hell—no amount of flash and glitz could make me want to cool my heels here for too long. Give me the Big Easy's gator problem over the snake-faced Little Brothers any day of the week, thank you.

The shops and homes lining the way were oddly leaning things of concrete and cinder blocks, sporting tin roofs and broken windows covered by reinforced black rebar. Rats scampered about in the gutters—big furry things that had grown bold—while an accompaniment of otherworldly, pale-blue, corpse toads, chortled their subtle song.

Not all of these buildings were as they seemed, I knew, many of these homes were probably no more than mere facades: a mask to cover what lay beneath. If you have a nice car in a bad city, there's a good chance someone will eventually try to jack your wheels, chop your ride, and leave you standing high and dry. But if you're driving around a multicolored Ford Gremlin, circa 1986, with two-hundred K on the odometer, and no stereo, it's an even bet that your car will always be waiting for you.

Well, operating on the same principal, many Hub dwellers went to great lengths to make it appear as though their homes looked—at least superficially—like the run-down equivalent of the Ford Gremlin.

Harold the Mange was a no-shit master of disguise when it came to camouflaging his lair. And he needed all the protection he could get because he had his grubby, fat-little, paws into just about everything. He was not a power player by any stretch of the imagination, but he had a great number of resources. Mostly, Harold was a middleman, a broker who dealt in information, favors, and the occasional rare artifact. He was also a shady bastard, not to be trusted further than he could be thrown, which wasn't far since he was prodigiously fat. Being such a crafty little shit had made the guy a lot of enemies, hence the camouflage.

But if anyone could get me the info I needed on Arjun, Harold could, even if the price would be through the roof.

I strutted up to a townhome: a little, two-story building, painted a splotchy matte white, with thick worn boards covering the windows. It was a rundown hovel, surrounded by a host of other rundown hovels, and if I didn't know better, I would've walked right on by. Which was, of course, exactly the point. But I did know better.

I exhaled the air in my lungs and breathed in fresh air filled with Vis. I dipped into the well and carefully drew out the power I needed. I sent out a fine weave of spirit, a gently probing web which lay lightly over the house. This construct was a delicate thing, finer than a spider's wispy webbing—it gave me a read on any constructs, veils, or barriers without setting them off. Hopefully.

I could feel an illusion, expertly crafted—though made piece meal—concealing the home's true nature and urging the casual passerby onwards. There was also a set of defensive wards placed around the doors and windows—pesky things that would turn any would-be thief into a pile of dust if he tried to force the locks. The wards were well made but lacked the power to keep a big leaguer from getting in. If a High Sidhe noble wanted in, Harold's wards weren't going to do the trick (though the solid steel door would help).

It also wouldn't keep a supremely talented mage out.

I'd probably be able to get in too.

Whatever Harold was, he wasn't human, and the Hub was a place of partial spirit, so I didn't have to sweat dealing with a domicilium seal. Places here don't have 'em. I pulled in air and earth, drawing from the ground beneath my feet, feeling the strange soil and rock composing the Hub. With a heave of will I ripped out a hunk of pavement the size of a motorcycle, and with the aid of heat, air, and water, shaped the material into something resembling a medieval battering ram.

My siege weapon hung suspended in the air, fifteen feet from the front door. I created a super dense pocket of compressed air behind it: the Vis equivalent of a high-powered potato launcher. Except instead of potatoes, I was firing off a two-ton piece of sculpted rock. Tension built and grew behind the rock, the air filling the enclosed space I'd created to contain it. I pumped more Vis into the enclosed space, knowing physics would eventually take over and do all the work once I'd accumulated enough pent up kinetic energy.

My constructed barrier ruptured with a great *woofing* sound, which hit me like one massive pillow. The hovering rock, however, received the lion's share of the stored energy and hurtled through the space between me and the reinforced door like a friggin' freight train. The door never stood a chance. The rock collided with a *crash*, twisting and bending the door inward, amidst a flare of angry blue flame. The home's wards released on impact, but I was far enough away to feel nothing more than a faint trickle of warm air.

A pleasant summer breeze.

I stepped around the crumpled metal door and clamored over the rock, all while trying to avoid the sharp wooden splinters sticking out from the now ruined door frame. There's nothing worse than a splinter, and considering the overall hygienic quality of the Hub, it was best to assume a splinter would give me dysentery. Or something worse. In general, being in the Hub for any extended length of time made me want to bathe in hand-sanitizer, on principle.

The interior of the house was a mess. The walls sported tattered and peeling wallpaper and a variety of stains, which didn't bear thinking too deeply on. The dark, hardwood floors were pitted, chipped, and scraped, though free of the layer of dust which I'd have expected in a place like this—a sure sign someone had been here recently. Four doors lined the hallway, one off to the left stood open, revealing a gutted bathroom. Both the doors on the right were closed, but I knew the rooms behind them were as barren and broken as the rest of the house—my gentle probe of spirit, told me as much.

The door I wanted lay at end of the hall: the last door on the left. It looked no different from its fellows, yet I could feel a thrum of power—concealed to most, but obvious to me—emanating from the space.

I'll take what's behind door number four, Monty.

I tried the handle and found the door locked, but it was just an average old door lock. Nothing fancy and no wards I could discern. Harold wasn't big time and wards are not a cheap thing to come by if you have to outsource. Harold's definitely not a mage, a member of the High Fae, or a godling, so it stood to reason that he'd contracted out. He'd chosen, and wisely, to prevent people from getting this far by putting his muscle right up front. And, if that failed, Harold had created the illusion of abandonment to deter any highly motivated thieves (not that there would be many down in this part of town in the first place).

A gentle effort of will and a thin weave of earth helped me to kick open the door without a hitch—one well-placed boot ripped the lock right from its home. The door swung inward, revealing a short rock hallway trailing down into a low ceilinged cave, lit by a mixture of torchlights and electric miners' lamps.

Harold the Mange looked up at me from the center of the claustrophobic chamber—maybe thirty feet away—the corners of his mouth turning down into a grimace.

TWENTY-TWO:

Harold the Mange

Harold the Mange was a sight to behold, but not in an awe-inspiring Grand Canyon, Mount Rushmore, or even that sorta awesome, but also kinda terrible, *Killer Klowns from Outer Space* way. I'm talking a sight to behold like the world's largest landfill or Jabba the Hut: a sight that leaves you cringing a little and feeling kind of dirty inside. He was a pasty thing, inordinately fat, with rolls and rolls of maggot-white skin, straining around his neck, arms and midsection.

Mostly bald, though a few wispy strands of graying hair stood out around his ears, while mud colored liver spots adorned his scalp. He had no legs—or if he did, they'd been buried by his bulk and died long ago. Instead, he perched atop a set of spindly, dusty, metal legs: eight of the electrical limbs fanned out beneath him like some strange spider. In the Hub, techno-organisms are a common enough sight. Harold had gotten the upgrade long ago, presumably to allow him to eat ever greater amounts of cheeseburgers. The guy was a freak show.

No one—at least no one I was aware of—actually knew what in the hell Harold the Mange was, due to the fact that he is a deceptive, manipulative, compulsively scheming SOB, who probably clubs baby seals for fun in his free time. The guy is a world class ... well, pick any pejorative and it would stick.

If you believed Harold—which isn't generally a prudent or wise move—he was among the last of a nearly dead race of ancient Dwarves, called the *Cragwier*. Once upon a time, and long, long ago—as legend holds—the Cragwier played a pivotal role in creating the pocket dimension, which, overtime, gave birth to the

Hub itself. Now, Harold was a liar, thief, sometime charlatan, and not somebody you'd want to turn your back on. Not for a minute. But about the whole Cragwier thing … well, I sort of believed him. Harold doesn't have a lot of talent, but he is good at three things: getting information, finding rare treasures (a Dwarven impulse, if you ask me), and manipulating the Ether and the Ways.

His whole cavernous home, filled with shelves, cases, and metal file cabinets full of shit, was a personal pocket dimension Harold had created. The damn place was a vault and a nearly impenetrable fortress, existing within the Ether—the spiritual realm containing all known dimensions—but outside of the Hub. This place didn't exist in the world and it only had the single access point which Harold created to allow customers to come and go. Harold can manipulate the Ways, not an easy thing to do. It takes either access to god-like amounts of energy or a special talent.

Harold sure as shit didn't have the former—I wouldn't dare bust down his front door if that were the case—but he had scary good talent when it came to the Ways.

If I could get Harold to play ball, I could kill a couple of birds with one large stone. Harold could not only give me the goods about Arjun, he could also create a custom made, pimped-out portal. One which would dump me right into Arjun's super-secret, highly villainous, Legion of Doom headquarters. I didn't have a ton of options and I needed Harold, but he didn't know that. Exactly the way I intended to keep things.

Basic economics was at work here, the law of supply and demand in full swing: he had something I needed and if he knew how bad I needed him, he would charge me through the nose. The way to undercut the market was to make it seem like I had loads of options.

So, I pulled out my behemoth, widow-maker pistol—not that Harold was married, let's be real here, the dude has weird metal spider legs—and leveled the cannon right at Harold's flabby chest. Tip: sometimes gun-barrel diplomacy is the best way to proceed, though resorting to such overt thuggery should never be your normal tactic.

"Yancy," he croaked, spreading a wide, nervous grin. "It feels like ages—how have you been?" His voice was a low gurgling thing, the sound of a great bullfrog speaking through human lips. I responded by stepping forward, closing the distance between us, keeping my iron trained and unwavering on his torso.

He took a few anxious scuttles back, folding in his shoulders as though he hoped to implode and disappear from the sights of my piece. His heart was beating fast, I could hear it, and his labored breathing filled the cavern. His eyes darted about, searching for an exit or maybe a weapon.

"Listen, I know things ended poorly last time …" he said apologetically. "It's the legs, partly made from a real spider, you know." He scuttled a few more paces back into his lair. "Technomancy has some dangerous and often unpredictable side-effects—you know that—I can't be blamed for my actions."

I strode forward, ever nearer.

"L-l-loook," he stammered, "we can make a deal. Things needn't get messy. You must need something since you haven't pulled the trigger."

I squeezed the trigger ever so slightly, not enough to fire—there was quite a bit of tension in the trigger mechanism—but enough for him to know things could get real bad, real quick.

The fine art of negotiation for you. I am something of a diplomat.

"You tried to eat me," I said, raising my hand canon level with his prodigiously pudgy head as I drew closer.

"And you knocked down my door, but it's best not to point fingers." He dry washed his hands, as if to say *what's done is done.* His words actually gave me pause for a moment, *I'd knocked down his door?* Seriously?

"Harold, those are not comparable situations—I mean we're talking apples and oranges here. On the one hand, permanent bodily damage, irreparable maiming, and possible death— gruesome death. One the other hand, a door. Get your priorities straight."

"I do have them straight," he muttered darkly, and a part of me wanted to pull back the hammer, just to see him squirm, but I resisted. I needed Harold. "But it's all water under the bridge, Yancy. We can both be reasonable men. Let's talk about this."

I waited, letting the tension build between us. It was a calculating move, meant to make him think I was the one doing him a favor by, you know, not killing him. The tension was clawing at him—great blobs of sweat beaded on his head and rolled down his face.

"Alright," I said, "let's talk." I released the slight tension in the spring and dropped the weapon to my side, glad I didn't have to hold the damn gun up any longer. Heavy son of a bitch—I was already feeling it in my shoulder. I relaxed, just a little.

Which was when Harold flew at me like a pudgy, white wrecking ball. He may have been inordinately fat, but his mechanical appendages let him move like a friggin' hawk with a jetpack. His weight slammed into me, knocking me back a step or two, while his arms sought to enfold me. I wrestled feebly, caught unaware and unprepared for this encounter. Harold isn't known for his bravery, courage, or physical prowess, and I'd expected him to cower and give over with only a little intimidation. But that's the thing about playing the thug card: if you play it too well, sell it too much, there's a good chance you'll put your target's back against a wall.

When things—human or otherwise—are backed against a wall, with few options and death looming over them, they're liable to respond in all sorts of unexpected, out-of-character, and often violent ways. I know this from a lot of personal experience, though usually I'm the one against the wall. It was like fat, plodding Harold the Mange had morphed into a crazy, nasty-ass, Honey Badger.

I flailed my arms weakly, but with no luck. His upper body was surprisingly strong, and he had little trouble wrapping me up and tossing me deeper into his cavernous lair. I extended my arms and tucked my body into a wheel, rolling over the uneven floor, and back upright.

I came to my feet and pivoted, holstering my gun in the process. Harold had his blood up now and I couldn't risk accidentally shooting him in a tussle—as much as it pained me, I needed him if I was going to nab Arjun. I'd played a bluff and lost.

By the time I turned around, Harold was on me, filling my vision with his bulk. I lashed out with a solid punch, but he reared back with a metallic hiss and my fist sunk uselessly into his heavily padded mid-section.

I danced away, not wanting to stay still long enough to give him a chance to land a blow.

He lashed out with a metal leg, its wicked point aimed toward my knee but I weaved out of the way, darting first out and then in for another quick strike to the torso. The blows didn't faze him in the least, there was too much mass between his vital organs and me. My strikes would never do any real, fight-ending, damage.

I'd need to tag him with a couple of solid hits to the head to end this scuffle, but those metal legs of his made that increasingly unlikely. Every time I moved in for a strike, he shifted out of reach with ease, and I simply didn't have the height I needed to mess with his grill. Throwing down with a good ol' fashion bout of fisticuffs obviously wasn't going to get 'er done.

He lashed out again with another metal appendage. I dodged without too much trouble, but another of his legs caught me smack in the stomach like a hammer. The blow was a serious one, momentarily picking me up off my feet while simultaneously emptying my lungs of air, like a couple of popped balloons. I stumble-walked, tripped over something, and fell into one of the bookshelves lining the wall. My head took a brutal bump, but I hardly noticed it as I wheezed, trying desperately to find some oxygen.

Harold the Mange was kicking my ass. The hell was happening here?

I could never, ever let anyone find out about this. Never. It felt like getting beat up by the supernatural version of Steve Urkel. In my defense, however, it'd been a rough couple of days. The way I figured it, there was a big asterisk next to this throw-down.

After a moment, I shook off the hit and reoriented on Harold. He hadn't closed the distance, but instead was looking at me with a mixture of uncertainty and gloating pride. The conflict on his face was clear: should he play things safe and flee while he had the chance or press his advantage and kick my mage-ass right out the front door? Stupid move. He should have done one or the other, but waiting around was gonna cost him. Sometimes no decision is the worst decision you can make. Now that I had a little breathing room and time, victory was a sure thing.

I drew in Vis, creating a quick and dirty little construct. Force, raw and unseen, whipped out at knee level, a single strand of power as thick as my wrist. Harold couldn't see the blow coming and thus stood staring on as my working crashed into his metal frame like a tractor-trailer. His legs rushed out from beneath him with a screech and his enormous torso toppled forward liked a demolished building.

Fear and panic raced across his face in turns, his eyes bulging as he hurtled toward the ground. He slammed into the rough and dusty stone floor with a dull thud that rattled the earth beneath me; the tremendous momentum from the fall rolled him onto his back.

I wasn't about to waste my advantage like he had, so I gained my feet, darted right—deeper into the cave—and conjured a set of stone shackles which clamped down over his wrists and neck, securing him to the floor.

I rubbed gingerly at the back of my noggin, a small goose egg forming where my head had so kindly been introduced to the bookcase. It hurt and I wanted to punch Harold a couple of times.

"Ouch! Uncalled for Harold—not okay." I prodded the bump gently. "That's not the way you treat a guest, turd-bag."

"You're not a guest," he said from the floor, his breathing coming in great labored pulls. "You're a former enemy and a house invader pointing a giant, highly menacing weapon at me."

"Yeah but … but you …" Well shit. He was right. Damn an ass whupping and an ethics lesson from Harold. Man was I off my game. "Fine … I guess you're right. Stupid, asshole … tried to eat me …" I let the earthen bonds dissipate. "Sorry, I broke into your house and menaced you, Harold," I said, tracing my foot through the sand like a five-year-old who'd broken a window after being told not to throw the ball inside. "That was kind of a dick move I guess."

He ponderously made his way upright, breathing hard the whole while. The guy needed to see a doctor, he was scary-out-of-shape with all that huffing and puffing.

"Well, I did try to eat you last time, so maybe your response was not wholly unwarranted. I accept your apology—we can call it even." He said, grumpy but mollified. He carefully brushed rock dust from his chest and arms, the movement dainty, considering his girth.

"Yeah okay, even" I responded.

"So what drags you all the way into my neck of the woods," he said eventually, "so far as I remember, you've never been a fan of the Hub."

"You can say that again—every time I come here something terrible happens. Every. Single. Time. I just got my ass handed to me by Harold the friggin' Mange."

He shed a wicked grin. "You know I have surveillance equipment recording around the clock. I think our little tussle will definitely go into the archives."

I moved my hand toward the butt of my revolver, and frowned. "Don't push your luck ass-bag."

"Of course, no need to be hasty. We can be friends—I assume you're here after some information, or maybe a specialty item?"

"Got it in one. I need to find out about Arjun Dhaliwal. You know him?"

Harold snorted and shuffled over to a series of large silver file cabinets built into the cavern wall. "Do I know Arjun? Of course I know Arjun—I keep rough tabs on every mover and shaker in the game." He fished a large metal key out from between several rolls of fat and unceremoniously opened one of the cabinets, rifling quickly through a set of folders within. "I've had my eye on him lately. Word around here is that he's brewing up some serious trouble—there's even talk that Vritra is stirring."

Well crap. Vritra was an ancient, demonic, hard case. A Hindu deity, responsible for drought, famine, death, and a whole slew of other craptastic things. Vritra had been in the clink for a long, long time and for very good reasons.

"Yeah," I said, "well I can't speak to that, but Arjun and I have a dispute that needs settling—what's your price for the info?"

"The info I'll give you for free … let's call it a peace offering. Plus, Arjun's a real prick—one of those holier-than-thou types. Always going on about karma and moksha. We'll call this one a freebie, an act of good karma ..." He smiled, the grin downright devilish, "but that's not all you need." He pulled out a brown folder, faded around the edges, wrapped about the middle with a piece of twine. He scuttled toward me with the folder extended. "You don't just need the info, you need a Way." He thumbed his nose and blinked at me conspiratorially. "The info is free, but the Way will cost you."

"Hold on now." I snatched the folder before he could consider taking it back. "Thought we were on good working terms again—you're going to gouge me here?"

"Its business, nothing personal." He began dry washing his hands again, a shiesty used car salesman coming in for the kill. He knew I was going to bite, and I knew I was going to get a lemon on this deal.

"First," he continued, "I want my door fixed. I want new defensive wards—and good ones—installed, both on my exterior and interior door. And I want one unlimited redeemable favor, good at any time, for any situation."

I laughed, a raspy, wheezy thing I knew would grind his gears. Harold hates being laughed at. Who doesn't? *But* he had asked me for the equivalent of a blank check, which was a ludicrous, laugh-out-loud funny demand.

"Now the door isn't a problem," I said, pretending to wipe a tear from the corner of my eye, "it'll take some time, but I can get it done. A blank check favor, though? Not gonna happen, amigo. I'll give you one reasonable favor and I get to decide which job it'll be."

"Define reasonable."

"I'm not going to go kill someone and I won't play your thug," I said. "Everything else ... " I shrugged. "You make a request and we'll talk." I could see the wheels spinning in his head, his eyes had the light of speculation and cunning contemplation, which made me more than a little uncomfortable. Harold isn't tough in the traditional sense of the word, but he's crafty as a fox-in-chicken-drag, which is often more dangerous than brute strength alone. This deal would come back to get me sooner or later.

"Redeemable at any time?" he asked again.

"Yeah—but I get to decide whether the job is reasonable."

"Fine." He licked his lips, savoring the word. "You need only give me the specifications for the Way and I will build it to order—from one location to another, mind, and I will need a few hours notice. These things do take a little time. I will, of course, make it to specification, but I would like to cash in my favor now."

"Funny Harold," I said, "But I've got shit to do, so stop joking."

"Not a joke," he said again, dry washing his hands some more and giving a slightly apologetic shrug of his shoulders. "You said I could redeem the favor at any time and if you want me to build your Way, you're going to have to abide by the terms of the deal."

Ugh. My life. I knew this bargain was going to get me, but I hadn't thought it would be *this* soon.

"Really Yancy, I literally cannot do what you want if you don't help me—it's in your best interest."

"What's the favor?" I grumbled.

"Please follow me. I'll give you a brief on the way down to The Pit."

"The Pit? Seriously?" I asked. "Not exactly filling me with overwhelming confidence here."

He smiled and scuttled toward the back of his cavernous stony cave.

TWENTY-THREE:

Down the Rabbit Hole

The back of the cave tapered into a narrow tunnel, which hardly seemed big enough to accommodate Harold's bulk. The guy was surprisingly agile, however, and he moved through the darkened passage without thought, a spider patrolling his web with easy, familiar, movements. The surface of the rock walls were smooth, almost polished, bored out as though by the passing of a river. I knew better though—Harold can secrete a caustic saliva that'll eat away rock or flesh with equal ease. He'd nearly slathered me with the damn stuff during our last encounter, the one where he had tried to cocoon and eat me.

"Making me nervous, Harold. This feels suspiciously like a trap—my trigger finger's getting a little itchy. I'd hate to break our fresh new partnership so early on."

"No worries, good chap," he said, which did absolutely zero to ease my worries. "Trust me, I have no intention of seeing you harmed. At least not at my hands." He chuckled as though making a grand joke. "Your break-in was fortuitous for me. Just a little further, now—I'll show you."

The path wandered for another five minutes, ambling left and right in a series of gradual and unpredictable switchbacks.

"You made this place right?" I asked, trying to fill up the unbearable quiet, broken only with the clicking metal of his spidery appendages.

"Yes, yes," he said absently. "It is my home, my creation, my love."

That wasn't creepy or anything. After a moment: "Why in the hell didn't you make it go in a straight line? What've you got against an economical floor plan?"

"This place is built in the Ether …"

"Yeah, I know. That's my point—the Ether's just like a bunch of empty black space—perfect for straight lines."

"No, no. The Ether may seem to be empty, but it is not, as you shall soon see. No, the Ether is home to a myriad of things and there are all the other worlds to consider, each one unique, with its own atmospheric imprint upon the Ether."

"Fascinating, Professor Science," I said. "How about you get to the part where you answer my question?"

"Right, right," he sputtered. "Well, you cannot simply traverse through the Ether linearly—there are unseen currents which must be accommodated for: fluctuations, quantum-foam, drifting dark-matter clouds ... also, this twisting hallway's loaded to the gills with traps of all shapes and sizes. A whole mile worth of them, each pulled from the deadliest regions of Outworld—no one will get to my hoard." He cackled, more than just a little bit mad.

Yikes, a mile worth of booby-traps. I guess Harold might also be a teensy bit more dangerous than I gave him credit for. Check, don't try to raid Harold's booty. *Ewww.* Harold's booty—there was an unfortunate word pairing sure to haunt my dreams for decades.

"So if you're all bunkered down for eventual Armageddon, what could you need from me?" I asked.

"Here we are," he said as we turned a final corner which let out into a cavern, about the size of a large warehouse, housing rows and rows of metal shelving. The shelving units, in turn, housed clear plastic Rubbermaid tubs of artifacts. Strange and ancient stone carvings next to turn of the century brass antiques. There were also weapons of every shape and size—maces and swords, AT-4 rocket launchers and apace-age looking laser guns and doodads. Damn, his collection was more expansive than I ever would've wagered. I didn't know what it all did, but a bunch of the stuff was probably dangerous as hell.

Cool. Harold went up a notch in my book.

We walked down the central walk for a moment or two, me staring around like a slack-jawed country-bumpkin. I have to admit, I've seen a lot in my days, so it's hard to offer me

157

something completely new, but Harold's massive treasury—or maybe armory—had done the trick.

In the center of the room sat what could only be The Pit: a giant hole, thirty-feet across, recessed into the floor a good five feet, and covered with a massive steel door which looked like it belonged on a friggin' space shuttle. A guardrail encircled the thing, interrupted only by a single set of wide metal stairs, leading down to the gargantuan, space-age, manhole cover.

I had no idea what it was or what it did, but I was immediately certain I was going to hate it when I found out.

"This," Harold said as he gestured grandly at The Pit with both flabby arms, "is The Pit."

"Gee," I said, "and here I was thinking it was your indoor swimming pool."

"Barbarian," he said. "This is the machine which allows me to manufacture Ways—it is a permanent and malleable rift, which someone with the right ability can manipulate to create ripples in the Ether. Ways."

"Amazing," I said, voice as flat as the Nebraska plans. "Can we get to the part where you ask me to do something wildly reckless and insanely dangerous? I've got shit to do."

"Dammit, man! I so rarely have visitors down this way—can't you indulge me in a bit of the theatric? I mean really, is it so much to ask for you to play your part here?"

"*Jeez.*" I rolled my eyes. "Fine ... wow, Harold," I said in mock wonderment, "The Pit you say? Amazinggggggg. Please tell me more ... I'm *soooo* interested—oh, oh, when are we going to get to the part where you ask me to do something wildly reckless and insanely dangerous? Can we get to that part? Please, please?"

"Fine. If you're going to be such a poor sport about it. I have inadvertently attracted the attention of a Dara-Naric—it's lurking on the other side of the door. After I pop the safety hatch, I'm going to need you to go into the rift and scare it off."

"Dara-what-ic?" I asked. "And hey, I already told you I wasn't going to play hit man for you."

He laughed at me, a great long heaving thing which did nothing to improve my general mood. Getting laughed at really does hurt. Stupid karma.

"Good God!" He said in between gales of mirth. "You can't kill a Dara-Naric! They're eldritch beings that dwell in the depths of the Ether. They're a terrible rarity, really. I, who travel the Ways daily, have seen their ilk only a handful of times. Each is completely unique and, to my expansive knowledge, indestructible … honestly, I was rather unfortunate in attracting this one on my last outing."

"And I can't kill it?"

More laughter.

"No, no you can't kill it. Perish the thought! You'll be lucky to survive it."

"Come again?"

"You'll be lucky to survive it," he said, speaking slowly, enunciating each word carefully—a grown up speaking down to a child.

"Well then why would I go in there? This seems like a terrible idea."

"Oh, it is a terrible idea," he agreed, bobbing his enormous head energetically. "But if you want me to make you a Way to Arjun, I need access to my Pit."

Well shit.

"So how do I get rid of it—err, scare it off I guess."

"*Well …*" he said, drawing out the word in a way that told me he didn't have a clue. "There's not a lot to go off, mind—Dara-Narics are rare and few people who encounter them live to tell the tale. But I have gleaned that they detest fire or maybe light—being creatures of the darkest depths—and that they also hate music."

"Music." I said, feeling completely ridiculous. "Like AC/DC or B.B. King? Just music?"

"Quite right. The Dara-Naric are beings of quiet and chaos. According to old, old sources the sound of even the simplest melody can drive them mad."

"So what? I'm gonna hop into your Pit of Doom, shoot off some fireworks and play a few tunes—maybe throw in a little dancing or juggling for good measure?"

"Yes." He smiled with a shark's grin. "Something like that." I considered turning and walking away, this idea sounded way worse than trying Ailia for help. I mean she'd probably kill me, but at least with the Morrigan I knew what I was dealing with. Some giant, unkillable, creature of chaos, dwelling in the blackness between worlds—a creature I'd never in my life heard of? That sounded like a really dumb plan.

Sure, Harold and I had made a deal, but he hadn't come through with his side of things yet, and I had specified that I could choose the job, so backing out now wouldn't be a big deal ... but I was so close. Harold could get me what I needed before anyone else had to get hurt or killed by Arjun and his demon carnival.

"Do you have anything for me to play?" I asked, resigned.

"Look around my friend. I have anything you could ask for."

I couldn't go in with a piano—it's a damn tricky business to fight a giant monster while hauling around an eight-hundred pound Steinway. Playing guitar also wasn't an option: I needed at least one hand to sling some fire.

There was one thing that might do the trick. I asked Harold if he had what I needed and, after a few minutes of impatient waiting, he scuttled back from his endless shelves handing me the requested items.

With a long sigh, I made my way down the metal steps and right up to the edge of the metal-shielded Pit. Ready to jump into the darkness of the Ether and do battle with an eldritch monster armed with, drum roll please ...

A Hohner Special harmonica and a cushy neck-holder, like Bob Dylan used to wear. Some days, I swear.

TWENTY-FOUR:

Into The Pit

Harold moved over to a complex and boxy computer terminal on the far side of The Pit, typing away in a flurry of key strokes and button clicks.

"You won't have long," he said, not looking up from the screen. "I'm going to prop the gate open for five minutes—it will be on a time delay—but no longer. If you haven't gotten the job done in five minutes then I will assume you are dead and the door will lock. The gateway is also motion sensitive—if you pass back through within the designated time it will close automatically, so no worries about the Dara-Naric following you through."

I had the harmonica secured in place around my neck, my pistol drawn in my right hand, and the weaves for a fire construct in my left. Fat wet drops of sweat littered my brow, my stomach seemed to be doing Olympic floor dancing: turning and flipping in a horribly queasy way. It was the kind of feeling you get when you're about to go down the big rollercoaster drop, or maybe skydive. Without the parachute.

Shit, this was a bad idea. I was breathing too hard, close to the edge of panic. Being confronted by something nightmarish is one thing—you don't have the time to think about being scared—but willingly venturing into the dark lair of a creature so terrible it can't be killed is altogether different.

"Are you ready?" Harold called from the ledge, still punching buttons with master speed.

"No," I said, "but open the door anyway"

"Disengaging locks in *Three ... Two ... One.*"

The door let out a hiss and a puff of steam as a series of overlapping plates slid and rotated open, revealing a hole as black as darkest space. With a gulp, I jumped down into the chasm, expecting to fall into some great, unending abyss. Instead, I found my feet instantaneously connecting with some sort of walkway. The hell? There wasn't anything beneath my feet, just more unending blackness, but I could feel the presence of something solid under my boot-soles.

A glance back showed me the thirty-foot Pit, except, impossibly, it was standing upright—no longer a hole in the ground, but an upright doorway. I'd jumped down, but now found myself standing on a wall, a wall that felt like the floor. It was like one of those trippy MC Esher paintings—the ones that tinker with perspective so bad you can't tell which way is up and which way is down. I shrugged my shoulders ... whatever. I'd seen stranger things.

And speaking of seeing this, I could see. The blackness before me was unending and unbroken, yet paradoxically, my vision wasn't restricted in the least—my hands, feet, and body were as clear to me as they would've been on a perfectly sunny day.

I took a few tentative steps forward, trying to slow down my breathing, fighting to get my panicked heartbeat under control. I don't know what I'd been expecting—I'd never heard of a Dara-Naric, so I had no frame of reference to work from—but there wasn't a damn thing in here. Just emptiness and more emptiness. Everything was okay, I'd gotten all worked up over nothing. *Everything is okay*, I told myself again urgently wanting to believe it.

"Nothing's here, Harold!" I called back through the portal, the sound of my voice as loud as a gong, but hollow and distorted.

"Oh, it's still there," he called, his voice faded and far, far away. "I can feel its presence, lurking, waiting. It's part of my gift. Trust me, keep standing around, it'll find you ..."

"Well, I don't know what to tell you," I hollered again. "I can't fight what's not—"

Something, roughly the thickness of a tree trunk, swatted me into the air like a fly. I tumbled freely, twisting and turning as though in some gravity-free vacuum or maybe some crazy-ass traveling-carnival ride. I braced myself for impact, expecting a head-on collision into something with the grace of a car accident.

Instead, I landed softly on my feet, which came as a helluva shock. Now, I was upside down, well sort of. I felt right side up, but the Pit's opening was directly above me by about thirty-feet, hanging unsupported in the air like some otherworldly flying saucer—

And that's when I saw the Dara-Naric, its bulk hiding behind the portal opening, lying in-wait directly above me. It was the biggest living thing I've ever seen, and I've seen a school of blue whales. Its head was the size of a large house: black, inky-skin stretched tight over vast muscle and thick bone. A massive ridged plate ran horizontally across its great face, making me think instantly of a hammerhead shark, and beneath that sat a cruel hooked-beak the size of a car, filled with ragged tearing teeth. It didn't have any sort of eyes—at least none I could find.

A damn shame—its eyes would've been the first place I shot. Eyes can be a tremendous vulnerability for a creature so large; they make perfect targets, and let's face it, no one likes getting poked in the eye.

Its similarity to anything even remotely earth-bound ended at its head. Its body, stretching out behind it, was a craggily, rounded mass, more like an asteroid than a living thing. It had no arms or legs—nothing that might resemble feet or hands or claws—but it did have a shit-load of tentacles. When I say shit-load, I'm talking a crazy, incalculable, cloud of lazily swinging and swaying appendages—some bigger than skyscraper support columns and others merely the size of your average lawn tree. It was one of the latter that had taken a swing at me.

The slimy son of a bitch was a real piece of work, something straight out of a Lovecraft tale.

"Huh, that's definitely a new one," I said just to hear the sound of my voice in the void. This thing was out of my league—hell, I was sure this thing was out of *everyone's* league. Maybe an angel (or a battalion of angels) could smite it, but human folk were never meant to tangle with something like this.

I stood still, my heart hammering in my chest like a blacksmith working the forge, trying to decide what to do. The Dara-Naric wasn't particularly aggressive, it didn't seem angry or vicious. Just giant and menacing—and maybe a little curious. I think if it was hungry or angry there wouldn't have been enough of me left to fill a mop bucket at this point. I was sure this creature could dispatch me without a second thought or bother if it wanted too.

I didn't think it wanted to. No, the sense I got was ... loneliness and playful interest. A giant child left to frolic in the emptiness of the Ether. A giant, lonely, child who had suddenly happened upon a shiny, new toy: me.

That first tentacle snaked toward me again, shortly joined by three or four more cautiously probing limbs. So, maybe this thing didn't want to kill me, eat me, or do any of the other, generally horrific things most supernatural things like to do. Still, it was really, really big, and I thought it might accidentally pop my puny head off by playing a little too rough. I was not interested in ending up like that Barbie doll with no head—the one every little kid has in the bottom of their closet.

I fired three shots into the nearest tentacle, my normally quiet gun roaring like thunder in the silent space. My bullets plowed into the Dara-Naric's rubbery flesh, instantly absorbed without leaving anything even remotely resembling damage. The limb withdrew though, drawing back toward the creature's moon-sized body. It had flinched when the gun fired, not when the bullets impacted. Harold was right, it wasn't a fan of the light. That was probably why it was hiding behind the portal—so that when it opened, the earthly light wouldn't disturb its sensitive nature.

Ha, sensitive nature ... maybe the Dara-Naric wasn't a kid, but a moody goth teen, brooding in its room behind closed curtains.

One of its other limbs struck out like a cobra, so fast I almost didn't catch it. I narrowly sidestepped the strike and fired the remaining three rounds into that tentacle—at this range, I could hear the meaty, wet thuds. Again the creature withdrew the limb, unperturbed by the rounds themselves, but clearly uncomfortable with the muzzle-flashes. The other approaching appendages moved with greater purpose now, no longer lazily seeking out some new oddity, but instead searching for a potential threat. Maybe prey.

I needed to end this quick before the creature became outright hostile and I ended up a smear of bloody tomato paste.

I brought up my left hand and unleashed a stream of fire so bright it hurt my eyes. The flames washed over the creature's beaked-maw—it lurched back in shock, a deep rumble of anger so massive it literally shook me where I stood. The fire poured into the creature's flesh, but the Dara-Naric refused to ignite—there was no smoke, no embers, no flame, save what I dished out.

It wasn't burning, but boy was it was pissed, *mondo* pissed. Godzilla battling Mothra pissed. Hundreds of its limbs flailed about in a downpour of dark meat; a score of bobbing tentacles struck blindly at me while others crashed down hundreds of feet away in mindless rage. But each incoming limb avoided the touch of my lance of flame at all costs, as if each tentacle were semi-sentient.

Okay, my flame beam didn't do jack to actually hurt the Dara-Naric, but it wanted no part of the terrible light. Time to change tactics.

I cut the fire lance off abruptly, and ran right, away from the bulk of the incoming tentacles. Seconds later a sputtering cyclone of flame, about five-and-a-half feet tall, sheathed me in its soft yellow furnace light. I know what you're thinking: *awesomesauce*, tornado of fire ... but simma down now—it's only a flashy gimmick, designed for show, but with little practical value. At least until now. I can't actually surround myself in burning flame—that shit would flash-fry me like a like a gooey, deep-fried Oreo. This little baby only looks like fire. It won't burn a sheet of notebook paper, but it doesn't take much juice and it's bright and flashy as noonday in summer.

If the Dara-Naric had been pissed before, now it went positively mental. Its shriek of rage sounded like the billow of a T-Rex using a megaphone, and it started aiming its blows right at me. I dashed forward, zigzagging and dancing among falling tentacles, rolling here and jumping there to avoid being crushed beneath the weight of the creature's fury. A pesky mosquito avoiding incoming hand slaps.

So far so good. Kind of, I guess. I mean, I'd taken a peaceful, curious creature the size of a small planet and turned it into a raging death machine ... sounds kind of stupid and reckless when I put it like that.

Harold had been right about the light, so now it was time to sooth the savage beast with some funky harmonica blues and I knew the perfect tune—let's face it, I always know the right tune. I pressed the mouth harp to my lips and belted out a fast, punchy, upbeat version of Robert Johnson's "Cross Road Blues."

Lots of people think that the harmonica is some kinda ignoble pocket toy—the kind of thing you might give a kid as a stocking stuffer. It's not some hoity-toity, fancy-pants instrument like a violin or a cello, or shit, even a piano. But damn can it be sexy as hell, and sometimes there's no more appropriate sound in the world—like when you're fighting some freaky-ass, monster-movie reject.

I ripped into the harmonica, bending notes here—the sharp trill of a blackbird's chirp. Sliding notes there—the pitch failing like a stone, and wailing like a banshee. I worked my lips over the comb ... two-hole drop with a tongue block—2/5 draw and a 3/6 blow. Up and down, up and down: the warbling cry of shrieking tires. The dusty noise of a country road. The crunch of gravel at the crossroads on a dark night. In my mind, I could practically see Robert Johnson with an arm slung around the Devil's shoulders—both of them smiling and tapping along as I played.

Though that little ditty has some pop and pizazz, it can still make a well-adjusted man, with a good career and a loving family, jive right up to the edge of a bridge and jump. It's the most down-and-out blues I know, and I was playing the shit out of it. Hopefully, the Dara-Naric would realize how terrible and pointless its life was and slither off into the dark reaches of the Ether and maybe drown itself to death in a swimming pool worth of alcohol.

The creature responded with another terrible roar and backed away from the portal, even as its tentacles continued their assault on anything within a fifty-foot radius of me—shit, it was working. How about that? Hey, never underestimate the power of the blues. Plus, I had to admit it was kind of cool fighting with my own sound track.

I had the slimy-shit on its heels, so to speak, and now it was time to get the hell out of Dodge before it was too late. I squatted down and pushed off hard, propelling myself upward with a boost of Vis conjured wind. Upward I flew, toward the portal and the crazy-ass Cthulhu monster, the whole while I trumpeted out my gritty blues and burned like a falling star. The combined noise and light was too much for the monstrous creature. It began to retreat and fade into the Ether as I rocketed through the open portal way, which promptly snapped shut behind me with a metallic *hiss-clack*.

I sailed into Harold's warehouse cavern, flying right out of The Pit and toward the metal storage racks nearest the edge. With a hasty effort of will, I redirected the wind construct to buffer my descent—hadn't completely thought through the whole landing part of my escape plan. My ploy worked, and I touched down unscathed and no worse for the wear. Unfortunately, the pressure of the air toppled one of Harold's precious racks—the contents of the shelf fell in a great clamor of tinkles and breaks. Shucks, oh well. Maybe next time Harold will think twice before sending me into the vast Ether to fight an asteroid-sized tentacle monster.

"No!" Harold screamed, scuttling over to the fallen objects, as though they were close comrades who'd been injured on the field of battle. "My poor collection." He rounded on me with a scowl on his face.

"Yes, Harold," I said, "I am fine, thanks for asking ... what's that? How did I fare against the freaky, indestructible, tentacle blob? Great!"

"You survived," he said, "more than I can say for some of my poor collection here." He pointed at a thoroughly shattered blue and white vase which looked dusty and antique. "From the Yung Dynasty—circa 1335—though I suppose it can be replaced," he conceded. "Maybe I should bill you for it. No, no I suppose getting rid of the Dara-Naric is payment enough."

"How generous of you. Now, is the critter gone or what?" I asked.

"Yes, yes. Whatever you did was enough. It has departed back from whence it came."

He flipped me an old coin, a thin brass token, which looked vaguely Romanesque. The figure on each side resembled Mercury, messenger of the gods. Well the Roman gods, at any rate.

"My end of the bargain" he said in explanation. "Hold the coin, channel a little Vis, and give me a ring when you have the details figured out. And please, allow me to show you the way out—wouldn't want you to break anything else."

TWENTY-FIVE

Debrief

My trip back to The Lonely Mountain was uneventful and getting out of the Hub and back to LA proved far easier than the trip in had been. In the alleyway behind Firroth's bar was a metal door with the words: *Santa Paula Exit, Sam's Meats*, spray painted on it in bright red block letters. The door had no lock, no key, and absolutely no need to access the Vis to open it. Figures. Might've been Harold's work—occasionally, he gets contracted out by the Hub's City Council to do necessary infrastructure building.

The door dumped me by the rollaway dumpster, not far from where the Camino was parked. It took me an hour or so to get back to Greg's place. It was full dark when I finally pulled up, but Greg's Ford was still missing from the driveway, which was a little worrisome. There was nothing I could do about it though; Greg would have to put on his big girl pants and take care of himself. He'd be fine—hell, by now, he probably had Morse's and Yraeta's boys doing live-fire line drills. Maybe he even had them digging trenches, filling sandbags, and fortifying bunkers somewhere. Guy's a hard charger. He'd be okay.

I unlocked the front door and made my way into the kitchen, tossed the brown folder from Harold on the table, and decided the fridge needed to be raided. It was eying me like a sorority house filled with open windows. Hey, don't look at me that way, I did a semester in college after the Marine Corps—I know about sororities. Plus, I've seen Animal House like a bajillion times.

My stomach growled its assent, this mission was top priority, people. I found a frosty Coors in the door panel and a tub of Moose Tracks ice cream in the freezer. Beer and ice cream. Maybe not the breakfast of champions, but damn if it didn't sound exactly like what I needed. I grabbed a spoon from a counter drawer, placed my raided loot on the table, and pulled out a chair.

I took a gobble of vanilla-chocolate paradise and chased it with long drink of Rocky Mountain goodness. I could feel my eyes glaze over: joy, rapture, savory, taste-bud bliss. Beer and ice cream, the food and drink of the gods I tell you—ambrosia heisted and mass-produced for us mere mortals. I burrowed my way through another couple mouthfuls before finally dragging the folder on Arjun over for review.

All told, there were maybe two-dozen loose-leaf sheets in the folder. The first page had a glossy color photo of Arjun paper-clipped to The Guild's equivalent of a rap sheet. Birth date, physical description—5' 8" and 150 pounds, slight build—known aliases, known locations, political and religious leanings. The guy had been involved with all kinds of risky and active political groups: the Rashtriya Swayamsevak Sangh, the Bharatiya Janata Party—these were serious Hindi groups that believed in, and worked toward, Hindutva.

There was also a list of known offenses and crimes. That last was a doozy, practically needed its own zip code. Political assassinations, instigating mass riots, mind-control, consorting with demons, illegal weapons trafficking, mass murder. Arjun was a friggin' crusader, no doubt about it. He wanted a religiously pure, reunified India, and he was willing to do bad things to get it.

I compared the list of horrific offenses with the picture clipped to the page. He didn't look like a mad, rogue mage bent on unleashing demons or worse on mankind. He looked like an okay dude. Brown skin, square jaw—covered with a five-o'clock shadow—and hazel-eyes that looked bright and content. He was smiling. If I'd seen him at a bar, I would've bought him a beer.

Behind the cover sheet were a few more glossy photos: Arjun attired in a traditional Indian dhoti, swathed in white and sporting an AK as an accessory piece. Arjun wearing a pair of khakis and a black polo, talking with a man that looked suspiciously like Detective Al. Another photo of a large warehouse—single level, red brick, with boards fastened over the windows and a large tan warehouse attached to the rear. The place looked a little distressed, but would've fit nicely in any of the industrial parks in South LA. Lucky for me, there was an honest to goodness blueprint attached to the photo, complete with an address.

The building was on Alma Ave in Gardena, separated from Compton by the wide snaking concrete river which is the 110. The time stamp on the photo was only a couple of weeks old. I had Arjun—had him dead to rights. I had a blueprint of his friggin' villain lair and I had a way in. Finally, in control.

I heard the front door rattle open, I dropped my hand to my piece.

"Just me," Greg called from the living room. He appeared in the kitchen a moment later, minus shoes, and took the seat across from me. "You can take your hand off your revolver. You're getting twitchy in your old age." He eyed the tub of ice cream and beer for a moment. "What, your junior high sweetheart dump you?"

I stoically took another bite of Moose-y track goodness—I was choosing the high road, not willing to validate his remark with a response. Sliding the folder across the table to him, I pointed at the picture of Arjun with my ice cream streaked spoon.

"Harold came through for us—he got the goods and consented to make the Way. Also, he informed me that your mom left her underwear at his place last night." Who am I kidding? I don't take the high road, not where lewd and wildly inappropriate jokes were possible. I took another slurp of ice cream.

"Mom's ninety-four, Yancy. Not okay," he said, eyes glued to the dossier.

"How did things go with Morse and Yraeta?" I asked.

"Morse is in for sure." He pulled out a cheap, black, disposable cell phone and set it on the table between us. "I'm thinkin' Yraeta's in too—the guy is a killer and he wants his comeuppance. But his goon gave me this. There's one contact in the phone, its direct to Yraeta. He wants to talk with you personally."

I found the pre-programed number and hit the call button. The phone rang twice.

"Mr. Lazarus." The voice was smooth as cream and tinged with the sounds of central Mexico.

"Yeah," I said, "this Yraeta?" I didn't use any title. I wasn't going to play the part of diplomat and I wasn't going to kowtow to him even if I needed his help. He'd tried to kill me. I took another spoonful of ice cream. "So, you gonna play ball or what?" I asked.

"How very disrespectful of you, Mr. Lazarus. Why don't we start over and set some ground rules. No one talks to me that way, not ever." He sounded positively pleasant. "If you talk to me like that again, I will hack you to pieces with a machete, drink your blood, and post your head on a spike. *Comprende Singao?*"

"Talks cheap, clown," I said. "So here's the deal: I don't have time for your bullshit threats. I get that you think you're the meanest thing on the block. But reality check … you're not. Shit, compared to some of the things I've seen today—just today— amigo, you'd be lucky to get a seat at the kiddy table."

I *almost* wanted to call the words back. There are some things you don't say to a guy who has hacked a body to pieces with a machete. It needed to be said, though, because guys like Yraeta—regardless of how many languages they speak—only understand one: violence. If I let him push me around with his threats and posturing, he'd use me up and discard me without a look back.

I needed to let him know I was a threat.

"So here's my counter offer ass-wipe, if you come at me again it's going to take a lot more than a machete to stop me. I'll come for you, *comprende*? And the shit I'll do to you will make those Saw movies look PG."

There was silence on the other end of the line. I hadn't heard the call drop, but I was afraid I had pushed him too far.

"Early this morning," Yraeta finally said, breaking the silence, "a pack of monsters broke into my home, maimed three of my staff, and kidnapped my daughter. She is eleven, her name is Samantha—she goes by Sammy. The creatures left a note … I am to remain uninvolved. If I do, my daughter will eventually be returned to me."

"So you're going to sit out?"

"No," he said. "No one takes what is mine. No one ... I also know men like this kidnapper—he is treacherous. He will kill her, I believe this in my heart ... I want my daughter back. And I want the man who took her *buried*," the last was a whisper more frightening than all his posturing. "You can do this?"

"Yeah, I can do it."

"Then I will ... *play ball*. I will give you anything you require. In regards to what has passed between us, it will remain in the past, yes? Get my daughter. Bury the man who took her."

"Groovy. Greg will be in touch with your guys shortly." I hung up, feeling petty yet satisfied that I'd gotten the last word in.

"Excellent," I said turning to Greg, my fingers steepled, making me feel vaguely like Mr. Burns from the Simpsons. "Time Arjun got a lick of his own medicine."

TWENTY-SIX:

Let's Boogie

Greg and I pulled up to Detective Al's place at ten after six. Ten after six in the *morning,* which naturally meant I was guzzling my way through a 24oz jug of gas station coffee. I was tired as hell, but also amped up like a fighter heading into the ring. I felt a steady throb of nerve wrenching anticipation mixed with shaky-muscle adrenaline, each vying for superiority: like a hyperactive, ADHD, monkey all jacked on shots of Red Bull and speed. Things were about to get intense and I was on the verge of flinging some serious metaphorical monkey poo around.

"Ready?" Greg asked, one hand clutched to the steering wheel, the other cradling a cup of coffee.

"Be ready to boogie." I popped the door and got out into the crisp morning air.

I jogged across the street, trying to look like a normal morning jogger and failing miserably. Who goes out for a run in ratty jeans and a leather coat, not to mention a military-grade flak jacket? Yeah, that's right—I'd gotten a few upgrades, courtesy of Morse. But hey, that's what the glamour's for, right? I cleared my mind and breathed in the Vis, conjuring up the same little probe construct I'd used at Harold's—all wispy parts spirit and air—and sent it forth to feel out the garage, to test for any potential dangers, and search for the presence of Rakshasa.

I suspected most of the Rakshasa would be bunkered down in the nest. Al's Charger sat in the driveway, accompanied by two other vehicles: a white, soft topped Jeep Wrangler, and a sporty, blue, Mazda hatchback. A good tell that someone, or several someone's, had come home to roost. Plus, the sun had risen not long ago and Rakshasa tend to sleep during the day. Now, this isn't like a "vampire" sunlight thing—it's not a hard and fast rule.

Rakshasa are nocturnal predators, and nocturnal predators go back to the den when the sun rises. Common sense. Even supernatural animals have habits and routines they usually abide by.

I was also sure the Rakshasa would still be nesting here despite the fact that I'd discovered their hidey-hole. Again, Rakshasa are predatory creatures. Like most predators, they're highly protective of their territory—think a pack of junkyard dogs guarding their bounty of old cars and abandoned couches—when they make a home, even temporarily, they like to hold onto it. Rakshasa may be hard-hitting, human-eating, shape changing badasses, but they're also predictable in their own way.

At least, I was hoping so.

The only way to know for sure, though, was with the wispy construct I was manipulating toward the detached garage. Well, I guess I could've gone and knocked on the garage door disguised as a pizza man or something, but that probably wouldn't have turned out so well.

My spirit construct brushed up against the outside of the garage and I could feel the presence of warm bodies in there. I also sensed several Vis wards, set in place since my last visit. The wards were weak things not meant to pack much of a punch; they were small-scale deterrents meant to warn away any Rube mortals who wandered by, or give warning to the Rakshasa if some dastardly mage type showed up again.

Excellent. Time to kick the anthill.

I let my probe construct dissipate while simultaneously bringing a wrecking ball of force into play. I was going to crash their slumber party—I was gonna go all big bad wolf on those slumbering, human-eating, piggies. Dastardly indeed.

I attacked, left hand out, palm open, a tight grin cutting my face. A silvered hammer of air and spirit coalesced into shape, rocketing forward like a friggin' scud missile of Vis. A second later, the garage door exploded with a *crack*, a shower of white-painted wood chunks and rusty metal flew inward exposing the garage interior to the soft light of the new day.

Cockroaches—the disgusting little bastards—swarmed out in agitation, a living river of black and brown pouring out into the back yard and driveway. Cockroaches are also creatures of the dark. Night is when the little chitinous buggers venture forth to dig through trashcans and otherwise be creepy and gross; they don't like being exposed to daylight any more than Rakshasa. The Rakshasa were a little slower in their response, fine by me. That first Rakshasa—outside the motel in Las Cruces—had caught me on the john with my pants around my ankles. It was nice to return the favor.

Turnabout is fair play, they say, and damned if I wasn't going to dish out some hardcore turnabout.

The Rakshasa were laying in a literal dog pile, all their rancid, flabby flesh intertwined in a heap of limbs and claws, grayflesh and fangs. They started to stir, to wither and twist in distress, but I wasn't about to give them time to wake up and splash some water in their eyes before we started our game. I conjured up a bit of flame and doused the interior of the garage and the fleeing bugs. Not enough flame to actually set the garage on fire—I didn't want to accidentally burn some poor schlub's house down—but enough to get their attention and befuddle night-adjusted eyes. There's virtually nothing more disorienting than having someone throw on the light and make a bunch of ruckus when you're sound asleep.

I have to imagine it's even worse if you suddenly find yourself on fire.

Some days, being a mage is a very rewarding occupation.

Before the nest could even think about getting their shit together, I drew my pistol and fired into the mass. I was careful to aim only at protruding arms or hands, legs or feet. I wanted to inflict painful and annoying wounds that would seriously piss them off, but which wouldn't be crippling. I wasn't prepared to kill all these baddies here. And I sure as hell didn't want to start a fullfledged war in a residential neighborhood. Some misplaced bullet could easily careen into some innocent kid the next block over.

I wanted to get them sufficiently angry enough to pursue me. Essentially, I was kicking over their sandcastle and then throwing some beach sand in their collective eyes. Now typically, I don't condone bullying—heaven knows I'm usually on the wrong end of that equation—but sometimes being the bully does feel good. Like Scrooge McDuck backstroking through an obscene pile of gold, good.

The Rakshasa were moving now, breaking free of the debris littered confines of the garage, spilling into the backyard in all their full, flabby-ass, Rakshasa glory. I knew they weren't thinking clearly since they didn't even bother to don their human flesh masks.

They were charging toward me, unthinking, full of hate and anger, a herd of red-eyed bulls hot on the trail of some audacious matador. Perfect. In bullfighting, the matador taunts the bull, twirling his cape, and lashing out with sharp, painful javelins, always in reach yet just out of grasp. The bull, understandably, becomes incensed, seeking to gore that damned matador whatever the cost, all the while becoming both wearier and more careless.

It's a dangerous gamble for the matador and there have been many who get the pointy, business end of the bull in the process. *But,* if the matador plays the game right, they can finish the job with a helluva flourish: a dead bull at the end of a single, meticulously placed sword thrust, the *estocada*.

I had a flourish of my own for these evil, fang-toothed, ass-cows. My own version of the *estocada*—assuming I didn't get gored in the process.

On a completely unrelated note, it's better not to ask why I know so much about bullfighting. I've lived a long and ... well, let's say complicated life. Some things are just best left alone.

The Rakshasa were closer now, their long legs eating up the distance between us in a mad dash to take vengeance on me, presumably in a variety of horrible and unsavory ways. Though they were moving at a good clip, it was a disorganized rush. I'd wounded many of their number and not a one of them had thought to grab a gun. I back peddled for the car, pumping a few more rounds into their bodies with a nice compact Walter PPK—a sporty little German-made pistol—which Morse had graciously loaned to me. It barked in my hand, and though I knew it wouldn't do much to hurt the Rakshasa, it did slow them down a little.

I ejected the mag when it ran dry, letting it drop to the ground, while I speed reloaded, pulling a fresh clip from a mag-pouch attached to my flak jacket. What can I say, sometimes it's nice to have friends in low places—you never know when you'll need a favor from a gunrunner. I'm sure my mom would be proud of me, making friends like a real life grown up.

The nearest Rakshasa howled in fury as I got close to Greg's idling car. The thing leapt into the air, its muscles flexing, its fangs flashing.

"DOWN!" hollered Greg from the driver's seat. I let the Walter drop as I ducked, curling into a roll which brought me well out of Greg's line of fire.

Out of the corner of my eye, I could see Greg open up with a 12 gauge pump-action, one of the guns Morse and his guys had been playing with back at the safehouse. *Boof, boof, boof, boof.* The sound was nearly deafening and the impact effect was truly spectacular.

Greg wasn't firing off any ol' rounds, he'd loaded the weapon with an alternating combination of Bolo and Dragon's Breath shells. Bolo rounds are fierce: two large buckshot pellets connected by a thick razor sharp wire; they're designed to spin through the air and carve out huge channel wounds in whatever they hit. Dragon's Breath is an incendiary round, filled with hot burning magnesium pellets—it turns your plain-Jane shottie into a bona fide flamethrower.

Greg's gun alternated between spitting out the fast moving bolos and literally belching flame at the oncoming Rakshasa. The first four or five rounds hit center mass, and the Rakshasa went tumbling tail over teakettle, as though it'd taken a real wallop from a professional linebacker. It was also burning merrily—looked like a grumpy makeshift yuletide log—as it lay unmoving on the street. I knew the fire wouldn't do much in terms of long-term damage, but I still felt all warm and fuzzy inside.

I got to my feet and was sorely tempted to try a hood slide, all Dukes of Hazard style. Then I ran around the front instead of making a giant jackass out of myself.

Probably would have shot myself accidentally had I tried the damn thing, something Greg would never let me live down. It sure would have *looked* badass though.

I got into the passenger seat and glanced out of the window as Greg gave her gas. The Rakshasa were melting into human masks and loading up into their various cars: three in the Charger, two more in the Wrangler, and the last pair—which included the one Greg had set on fire—into the Mazda hatchback. As each pulled out to give chase, Greg put the pedal down, and we roared forward.

Now, I know what you're probably thinking here—Ford Focuses don't *roar* forward.

But we weren't in the Ford Focus, we were riding in a souped-up, midnight-black, 69' Ford Fairlane. This was the car Greg worked on—his hobbyhorse—and it was all fat wheels, slick lines, and over-clocked engine. It could go as fast as the Roadrunner on jet-powered roller skates and it looked good doing it. With that said, the three cars carrying the Rakshasa were gaining on us. We could've lost these suckers in the time it takes to blink a handful of times, but we wanted them to follow—we wanted rage to guide them right into the jaws of our nasty trap. Our final, bull-fighting, sword thrust.

TWENTY-SEVEN:

Bat Outta Hell

I've said it before, anger makes people act in some intensely careless and profoundly stupid ways. Rakshasa may be evil, but they aren't generally stupid. Under normal circumstances, this lot wouldn't have chased me out in an onslaught of gunfire, completely exposed and lacking even the forethought of their flesh masks. Probably, they wouldn't get in a car and chase Greg and I to some undisclosed location, where bad things would happen. But when you spit in someone's eye, bust up their house real good, and set their pet on fire, people do irrational things.

"Buckle up," Greg said as he put the pedal down, zipping south and west along Amherst Drive. Peaceful suburbia cruised by in a flash of single-story houses and green lawns edged with Californian ash—tall thin trees, with great billowing green tops. "Wouldn't want you to get a boo-boo if anything happens. Heaven knows I'd never hear the end of your cryin'."

"Hey, I have an idea," I said as I peeked back over my shoulder. "How about you drive the car and save the standup for someone funny." I did buckle up, even though it annoyed me to do it. Seat belts *do* save lives.

"I am funny," he said as he took a hard left onto North 6th, followed in close succession by a right onto Bethany Road. The maneuver left a long streak of black on the asphalt.

"Yeah," I said, "you're about as funny as *Schindler's List*. Now drive."

More single-family homes zipped by, their glass eyes closed to the world—curtains drawn against the morning light.

Though Greg was pushing the speed, a glance in the rearview mirror showed me that the Rakshasa were keeping pace, all three vehicles still with us. I could feel the tension building in

Greg as he focused on the road, knuckles white against the steering wheel. Car chases are not easy and they never look like they do in the movies.

Probably, you've never been in a car chase, but let me tell you, things happen so friggin' fast it's hard to believe. One moment you're cruising along—everything's buckled down—then *boom* some poor state trooper's scooping up pieces of you with a spatula. A real car chase is like trying to drive while playing hot potato with a basket full of grenades. Intense, and it all seems to happen in the span of a single, adrenaline-filled, heartbeat.

We flew along Bethany for another four blocks. I left Greg to his task while I craned over my shoulder, scanning our tail, making sure the Rakshasa didn't get too close or too far behind. We wanted them to follow, but we also wanted to convince them that we were genuinely trying to get away. It was a damn fine balance.

The tires screeched and my seat belt snapped tight against my chest—

A golden Toyota pickup pulled through the diagonal intersection in front of us: an elderly gent, out for an early morning drive. Greg avoided plowing into the poor guy—though I think we gave him a helluva scare—and got moving again, but the delay cost us priceless seconds. Like I said, car chases are fast and any slip up can have terrible repercussions.

I peeked back at our pursuers and I felt my stomach drop out of the bottom.

I only spotted the Charger and the Wrangler. We'd lost the Mazda.

"We're one short!" I hollered, "I don't have eyes on the Mazda." Greg nodded his assent, but didn't take the time to spare me a glance. His attention was all for the road, the drive, the pedal beneath his foot. The suburban homes gave way to the sprawl of eateries and large shops as we zigged onto North 3rd Street, angling toward the freeway. The buildings transformed into modern stucco things, but only a few shops were open at this early hour. Thank God.

We found the Mazda about ten seconds after pulling onto 3rd Street. The driver—wearing the flesh mask of a middle-aged man with thinning hair—must've taken a side street and outmaneuvered us when we got caught behind the pick-up. Son of a bitch. The hatchback clipped us hard on the right fender, causing our car to hook and weave, all amidst the shriek and crunch of metal and carbon fiber.

"Sonuva bitch," Greg muttered, mirroring my thoughts exactly. Greg swerved left and floored it, trying desperately to put some distance between the crafty Rakshasa and us. "This car is a classic!" He bellowed out the open window. He took one hand off the wheel and flipped the Mazda driver the bird. It was a stupid thing to do and Greg should have known better. But the car was his baby, and no one puts baby in a corner.

On the plus side, at least we weren't going to lose them anytime soon, which seemed a little *bass-akwards* considering this was a get away. Sometimes the only difference between a crazy plan and a genius plan is whether or not it works. Soon enough, we'd find out if our plan fell into the Patton or Custer category.

Greg jockeyed for position with the Mazda. The driver was riding in our blind spot, keeping in tight, scraping paint off the passenger-side fender. Problematic since we needed to take a right and soon. If we tried to take the upcoming turn without first clearing the Mazda, the guy would T-bone us slaughterhouse style.

I hastily rolled down my window, drew in Vis and lobbed a small glowing blob of blue into the roadway behind us. The construct was a hasty piece of work, composed of equal parts air and water. The blob bounced off the ground and into the Mazda's windshield, exploding in a harmless wall of blue mist, which, hopefully, would distract the driver long enough for us to pull away.

Even though the construct was harmless, the driver didn't know that. He threw on the brakes—a knee-jerk response when something collides with your windshield—giving us the edge we needed to break into the lead.

Greg cranked the wheel, pulling us into a hard zag onto Burbank Boulevard, which quickly dumped us onto the 5 South, a rambling mass of concrete and asphalt eight lanes wide.

We took the freeway entrance loop at a speed some might consider dangerous, but Greg handled the thing with aplomb. A moment later our pursuers burst onto the freeway, kicking into high gear with the rumble of engines working hard.

We'd be headed south on the 5 for a while, so I relaxed a little in my seat. Greg could drive the crap out of his Fairlane and out here on the open road there was little worry that the Rakshasa goons would catch us. We had to be slow enough to keep sight of them, true—or rather let them keep sight of us—but we didn't need to let them scuff off any more paint. The real worry out here was not the Rakshasa, but the Fuzz—yeah, you heard right. The *Fuzz*.

Now, Californian's are in the habit of driving fast—most Californian babies pop out of the womb and into the driver's seat. I mean it isn't uncommon to spot someone speeding happily along at eighty or ninety on the 5. High-speed car chases are another thing entirely, though. Four cars, all doing in excess of a buck ten will usually garner some serious notice, even in California. *Usually*.

If I, Joe Blow Vanilla Civilian, saw a crew of cars whizzing passed me at ninety plus, I'd call those jokers in without a second thought. Let's be real for a second here, cars are dangerous business. Car accidents are the fifth leading cause of death in America, which kind of makes sense. Driving basically amounts to strapping a frail, imperfect person into the seat of a two-thousand pound rocket and then setting them loose on the world. Terrifying, and probably the most dangerous thing you'll ever do in your life. Crazy driving kills and cops are damned quick to swoop in like an avenging angel when people go zipping around town all *Gone In Sixty Seconds* style (the original 1974 version mind you).

Greg and I knew this—we aren't the dummies we appear to be on first glance. Greg and I had purposely rigged the game to make sure the odds would be in our favor. First, it was early in the AM, which is the best time to drive in California. There were still plenty of cars out, but not nearly the volume you might expect to see around late morning or midday.

The number of vehicles was further reduced by the glamour wards I'd hastily put in place at the major freeway entrances the night before. They were subtle things which wouldn't last long, but for now, they gently suggested that drivers take another way or even turn around and head home for the day.

Second. It was 6:32 AM, which is, statistically speaking, the absolute best time for some brainless, high speed shenanigans. Technically, there are always cops on patrol at any given time, day or night. Shifts are designed so that there are *always* responders. In reality, however, shift changes have a significant impact on the ability of police to respond. Shift change is the single best time to commit a crime.

Off-going shifts have to finish and file any paper work before signing off for the day—and for traffic cops, accident reports can be time consuming. Usually those reports are written and filed between six and seven, meaning there are fewer cops out patrolling the streets. Likewise, the on-coming shift is usually busy doing morning roll call and daily briefs for that first hour, meaning they, too, are somewhere other than the street. So, my friends, six to seven is the golden window for all things mischievous or nefarious.

Like I said, we're not as brainless as we might first appear … well, Greg's not at least, he's the one that came up with this part of the plan.

We took the 5 to the 110 S, heading toward LA proper, and got off on the Manchester Avenue exit. The drive should've taken twenty minutes. We did it in under ten, all the while keeping our Rakshasa tails in sight, which ought to tell you something about both how fast we were boogieing and how phenomenal Greg is behind the wheel. I drive a lot, and I'm pretty good, but Greg's like NASCAR good.

Our careful forethought also paid off: not a single cop all the way to our exit.

Gosh, sometimes magic really does happen.

We took the ramp at an unnerving speed. When we hit Manchester, Greg brought us into a turn that left the rear end fishtailing like a drunken sailor after a long night on liberty, swaying first left and then right. I could taste the acrid scent of burnt rubber and feared—at least for a second—that our luck had run out. We were only a few blocks from where we needed to be so I figured it was only reasonable that Greg would roll the friggin' car.

After a moment, however, the tires straightened and we were moving forward toward our destination.

The bull's horns gored us all of five seconds later.

TWENTY-EIGHT:

Gored

Greg finally straightened us out from the fishtail and I could literally see the warehouse where our end game ambush waited.

Then there was so much sound filling my ears: the shriek of metal, and squeal of tires, the tinkle of breaking glass. A symphony of individual noises all beautiful and terrible, crowding my ears, pushing out my thoughts, filling up the inside of my head. After a moment, the sound faded and I was in a vacuum. Things were tumbling around the inside of the car, like we'd been tossed into the dryer, but there was no sound.

I looked out the window—it hurt to turn my neck, everything felt so stiff. Things were wrong, somehow. I could see the crunched hood of Detective Al's Charger, but the whole image was inverted. No, that's not right.

Its tires were firmly attached to the ground. Broken car debris littered the street around it in an arch. The sky was up.

Then the picture shifted again, we were on a Tilt-a-Whirl. The sky righted itself and sound crashed back in on me—a breaking wave. The tires hit the ground, rocking the car perceptibly, but not enough to send us into another cartwheel. My seatbelt cranked tight around my chest. It was hard to breathe and I wanted—I *needed*—to have the thing off me. To be out in the air where everything wasn't spinning. Where I'd be able to catch a breath.

There was something wet on my hand. I held up my fingers. Red. Oh shit. That was blood, a good amount too. I urgently searched my body, feeling for wounds. Nothing.

I noticed Greg for the first time. He was slumped over the wheel—there was blood all over his face.

"Sonuvabitch," he muttered weakly. "Sonuvabitch. Someone help." Then he was quiet.

There was glass in my lap. Smoke filled my nostrils with its acrid stink. Someone moving outside, but it wasn't a someone, it was a something. Gray, flabby, and too large.

Shit. The Rakshasa.

I tried to draw in the Vis, but it was tough going, my head felt stuffed full of cotton. I needed to be out of here, I needed to help Greg. I wasn't going to go out like this, punked by a bunch of flunkies. Not when I was so close to the end, to safety. I reached and strained for the source, for power and life and freedom. At last I grabbed hold, and I channeled that power, working without thought or guidance, letting the deeper part of myself reign as my mind tried to reboot.

The car frame twisted around me. Melting and molding, stretching and folding, until I stood free from the wreckage, Greg's limp body thrown over my shoulders in a classic fireman's carry. I didn't have a clue in hell what I'd done. It didn't matter. I was out and so was Greg. My feet moved, my intuition guiding each step. Adrenaline and endorphins mixed and mingled with the Vis pumping through my system, lending me strength and agility despite my pain and exhaustion.

It occurred to me that Greg had once saved me, just like this. I guess it goes to show that if you know someone long enough, everything comes round full circle.

The three Rakshasa from the Charger were pursuing me on foot … I could hear their heavy footfalls, feel the rumble of the impact through my Vis heightened senses. Two more cars emerged into Manchester Street and though I didn't look back, I knew it was the Wrangler and the Mazda. No time to think about them, no time to think at all—I was in the zone, my body had co-opted the pilot seat and I was sprinting, dammit. Sprinting through a throbbing ass-cheek, an aching body, a nauseating headache, and with Greg sprawled supine across my shoulders.

I was racing against a bunch of gibbering, fanged, people-eating freaks. And I was winning.

I could see my goal ahead and on the right, not but fifty yards and closing, a few scant spaces down from the intersection of Manchester and Avalon. The building was nothing special. It didn't look like much of a safehouse: a plain, squat, tired looking structure of unremarkable tan brick. One more warehouse nestled amongst a road full of other unremarkable warehouses.

A chain-link fence, wrapped about the top with barbed wire, surrounded the perimeter. The barbed wire looked like an unnecessary precaution—there were no cars out front to protect, or shipping vehicles ready to ferry their wares. The building didn't precisely look run down or abandoned, more like currently uninhabited.

There was no reason to suspect this building was any more than it seemed.

I rounded the corner, the screech of tires followed fast on my heels—the Rakshasa were gaining ground. I didn't spare a moment to look back—I didn't have a moment to look back—they were so close now, I could feel them through their terrible footfalls on the pavement. Even with the boost from adrenaline and the Vis, they were gaining on me. There was no way I could beat these things in a friggin' race, not over the long haul. Even after setting them on fire and pumping them full of holes, they *still* had the physical advantage on me, and they had the advantage in spades. I'd surprised them and gotten a good head start—I'd cheated—but I wasn't sure it was going to be enough.

Their eyes were on my back. The heavy panting noises of a large animal in pursuit filled my ears. The *thud-thud-thud* of rapidly closing foot falls. The musky stink of them filled my nostrils.

The chain-link fence was fifteen feet away, maybe ten.

God, they were going to get me.

In my mind I could see a clawed hand reaching out for my neck, eager to sink talons deep into my flesh. I pushed the image away, focusing instead on the building ahead of me.

A chorus of yawls and yips followed me—it was a triumphant noise, the trumpet of a pack of hyenas that has finally run a weak and wounded prey to ground.

With a huff, I projected a thin beam of force, just strong enough to push the swinging chain-link gates inward. I passed the entrance and swerved right, making sure the fence was at my back. Angling for the front door. Close now. But my legs were shaking and chattering under the effort. Tires screeched somewhere behind me, followed in quick order by the clamor of car doors being slammed and the rattle of bodies scaling the surrounding fence.

I ran full blast into the front door, shouldering the thing open with ease—recently oiled.

And left intentionally open for me.

TWENTY-NINE:

Gunageddon

I ducked left, Greg still slung unmoving across my shoulders, scurrying along the inside of the wall, eager to remove myself from the veritable ocean of gun muzzles, all trained on the entryway. At some point, the front area of this building had probably housed a reception desk and shipping offices. But the interior had been gutted, so now only a single large room remained. The front door let into an empty fifty foot circle of space, encased by heavy-duty razor wire: a perfectly designed killing field.

On the other side of the razor wire barrier was a not-so-small army of heavily armed men—maybe fifty, all told—from both Morse's and Yraeta's crews. The men, and a spattering of women too, were arrayed behind fortified sandbags and black iron monstrosities called Czech Hedgehogs, which looked like a giant set of jacks. The whole scene could've been ripped straight out of a World War II beach invasion flick. Only with more leather and tattoos. Kind of the biker meets mobster version of D-Day.

Now, when I say the goons were heavily armed, I feel like that doesn't quite do it justice. There were five different Ma-Duce—colossal .50 caliber, Browning machine guns for all you non-initiates—firing positions scattered around the room, including two built on elevated metal platforms in the rear of the room. There were twice as many 240G hidey-holes, plus everybody and their leather-clad brother seemed to be toting an Uzi, M-4, or AK.

To top it all off, the smaller caliber rounds had been treated with Fipronil—the potent pesticide Greg and I used during our last run in with the Rakshasa.

This much firepower was a daunting, terrifying thing even if it wasn't currently aimed at me. If you've never seen the damage a Ma-Duce can do, just imagine demolished buildings, fiery helicopters crashes, or any movie ever directed by Michel Bay.

These are the weapons used to topple friggin' governments. Even Rakshasa didn't stand a chance against firepower like this. Unfortunately, that also meant the building walls wouldn't fare much better. I'd pressured Yraeta into having some eight-inch steel-plate welded to the building's preexisting interior walls—I didn't want to see one of those fifty-cal rounds punching through the concrete and into a RTD bus full of retirees.

One of the most important weapon rules is to not only know your target, but also what lies behind your target.

Thankfully, the steel walls would contain most of the destruction. If, on the off chance a round did get loose, this section of town was mostly industrial and Yraeta owned the whole block—storage and shipping for drugs and weapons—including the handful of cops responsible for patrolling the area. Each one in his pocket. We wouldn't have a lick of trouble from the authorities despite the fact that we were about to kick off the Gunageddon.

I scuttled with Greg all the way to the far wall, hooked right passed a small open spot in the razor wire, and headed along a narrow walkway leading to the back. We'd covered about half the distance when the Rakshasa burst in through the front door en masse, the whole lot of them mad as a pack of pit bulls with rabies. The cacophony of gunfire resounding off the steel interior was literally deafening, at least for a moment. I quickly wove a small construct of super dense air for Greg and I—basically a set of ear buds, though that didn't do a damn thing for the ringing already in my ears.

I had places to be, but I couldn't resist the impulse to stop and watch retribution in action, even if only for a minute. I mean seriously, how often do you get an opportunity to see a pack of legendary Indian monsters get all exploded-like by a bunch of Rube goons wielding fifty-cals?

Rounds the size of small Bratwursts collided into flabby gray skin with terrible power—huge pieces of meat soared through the air. The fifty-cal's and 240s were like Great Whites rending muscle and bone in great ferocious bites. The smaller caliber guns let loose in the staccato rhythm of measured fire, adding their damage like a school of piranhas swimming amongst their sharky brethren.

The first few Rakshasa to enter collapsed to the floor under the sheer weight of the lead poured into their flesh. Blood and gore stained the concrete in shades of inky black and crimson red. One Rakshasa bound high into the air—desperate for escape—leaping the razor wire, only to take a belly full of 240 rounds. It spiraled down onto one of the black Hedgehogs below, crashing like a meteor, impaled through the chest upon one of the protruding metal barbs.

Like watching a giant wood chipper in action: relentless, bloody, with nothing larger than a quarter left intact.

I wanted to celebrate but didn't—that would be for later, if I survived what was to come.

I got moving again, now only shuffling along toward a small door set in the corner of the back wall, starting to feel the fatigue, even through the buffer of Vis surrounding me.

The room behind was the warehouse proper: tables, ladders and shelving—filled with an assortment of crates and boxes—lined the walls. Harsh fluorescent lighting flooded the space, illuminating ten more men, each decked out in black leather or Kevlar, each carrying sleek, matte-black, weapons. These guys were the last line of defense, meant to protect me should the Rakshasa somehow manage to force their way through.

Morse and H & R Block were among them, as well as McGoon—the thug in the nice suit, who'd first approached me in Nick's Smoke House back in the Big Easy. Man did that feel like a lifetime ago. I was actually glad I'd decided not to kill him way back when—he looked dangerous as hell, all decked out in black BDU's with a whole friggin' armory strapped about his person.

Morse noticed Greg slung over my shoulder and hurried across the room, helping me lower him onto the floor.

"What happened?" He pulled a hanky from his back pocket and carefully pressed it onto the jagged wound across Greg's scalp.

"Shit-eating things rolled us just pass the Manchester exit—I don't know how they got around us like that."

"Doesn't matter," H & R said in precise clipped tones, "it's done, and you two got the creatures into the trap. That's what's important."

"Move the pressure dressing," I said to Morse.

He looked at me askew, like maybe I should qualify for the biggest idiot of the year award. "I've got to stop the bleeding," he said. "The wound looks superficial, but he's lost a lot of blood."

"I'm gonna fix him up before I split," I said, "not going to let him bleed out here."

He looked confused but complied, lifting the rag away from Greg's head. Morse was right, the wound didn't look too deep, though I could see a small white stretch of bone beneath. I placed my hands on either side of Greg's head and drew from the Vis. Healing is not my strong suit and it takes a ton of juice for me to patch up even the simplest of wounds.

Since I was about to go metaphorically bitch-slap Arjun in the grill and challenge him to a magi duel, I probably shouldn't have been wasting the energy to do this working. But I'd never forgive myself if Greg bled out and I could've done something.

I wove a delicate lace work of air and water, earth and fire, traces of metal and hints of his spirit, each intertwining with one another, a braided mesh of power. A complex blanket of golden lines—shimmering and shifting through a kaleidoscope of patterns—settled into Greg's skin, pulsing and glowing faintly from beneath. A full minute passed and nothing happened, but I kept pumping energy into the construct.

Sweat droplets sprouted on my brow and sent wet trails streaking down my face. My eyes stung from perspiration.

Slowly, slowly Greg's skin knit itself back together, thin strands of flesh binding one side of the gash to the other, until only a thin pink scar remained.

I let the weave go, though I held onto the Vis raging in my body. The power flowing through me was about the only thing keeping me going, and I was afraid that if I let go I wouldn't be able to grab hold of the power again.

Now, I know what you're probably thinking: hey, you can heal injuries? The hell? Why don't you patch yourself up and then hop on over to scuffle with Arjun, all good as new like? Trust me, if it were that easy I'd be all over it like flies on stink. Using the Vis isn't an instant fix to everything that ails you, let me tell you— it is tough, costly, and there are rules. Healing is some serious heavy-duty lifting, which makes sense considering how intensely complicated and intricate the human body is. Your body isn't some Honda you can swing on down by the auto-shop and get a tune up for.

It's a real mystery, a miracle really, and it takes a lot of raw energy and talent to fix 'er up.

First off, I don't have much talent in the way of healing— what I'd done for Greg was about the extent of my abilities. Second, not everything can be healed, including most major diseases, long-term injuries, and, of course, death. In fact, there are more things that *cannot* be healed than the other way around. The only guy I know of that could heal *everything*—including death— was Jesus, and he's like *Jesus*.

Lastly, and this is a big one, mind you, you cannot heal yourself, unless, again, you're friggin' Jesus.

Even if I had a major healing talent, which I don't, I couldn't patch up my scrapes, breaks, and bullet holes any more than I could lift myself off the ground using brute strength. If you're a strong guy or gal maybe you can pick up more than your own body weight. No matter what you do, however, you'll never be able to pick yourself up. Healing's like that.

"It's obvious that Mr. Chandler cannot accompany you as back up," said H & R as I staggered to my feet. "Either Mr. Morse or I should go with, as insurance."

Greg had been my second, and the only guy in the whole group I trusted to get my back. But he was going to be done for a while. Going in alone wasn't a good option—even if I didn't trust Morse or H & R.

Better not to go it alone.

"Alright." I tapped my chin in thought. Neither of these men were exactly saints and I wanted to pick the guy least likely to shoot me in the back after I finished Arjun off.

"You," I pointed at H & R, "I wouldn't trust to feed my cat—if I had a cat. Also, I don't think you could fight your way free of a wet bag even if you had a personal coach and a machete.

Saddle up Morse, you're riding shotgun on this one." He nodded in agreement and handed me a compact M-4 and a few nasty little trinkets, which I shoved into my coat pocket. "Hey Meathead," I said to H & R's thug, the guy from the Big Easy. "You wanna get in on this and earn your keep?"

He nodded and his face broke into a big ugly grin, which would probably send his mother running away in terror. Hopefully by having both Morse and McGoon in tow, each would keep the other in check.

In the center of the room lay a perfect circle, inscribed with orange spray paint. The inside of the circle was covered with runes and sigils I didn't recognize, old and ancient things with a power all their own. The circle was Harold's creation and my one-way ticket to evil-mage-ass-kicking town.

"Let's do this." I stepped into the circle with Morse and McGoon right on my heels. I fumbled around in my pocket for a moment, searching for the old Roman coin Harold had given me. I palmed the coin and trickled the tiniest weave of spirit into it.

A doorway, six by four-feet and deepest black, materialized before us as smooth and quick as an eye-blink. Say what you will about Harold—Heaven knows I've said plenty, most of it negative—but he does have a talent with Ways.

"Ready?" I asked looking back toward my posse—yeah that's right, I have a posse—who both nodded solemnly. We stepped into the black, which enclosed itself around us like a fist.

It was time to go punch Arjun's face in. Let the ass-kickery commence.

THIRTY:

Beat Down

I conjured up a fist-sized globe of soft-glowing blue light, which hung a few inches above my outstretched palm. It did effectively zero to dispel the blackness surrounding us, but I thought it might bring some comfort to Morse and McGoon—the Ether's creepy as hell. There wasn't anything to uncover, of course, no walkway or buildings, no cars or people, no scenery of any kind.

"What is this place?" Morse whispered, his voice flat yet too loud for the space.

"Don't worry about what this place is. Just keep walking and keep quiet. We don't want to attract anything that swims in these dark waters." I suppressed a shudder as I recalled my encounter with the Dara-Naric.

We trudged on for maybe another ten minutes, though it was hard to tell in the blank and unchanging landscape. The longer we lingered in the Way, the more I sensed we were being watched by some unseen observer. Nothing to do, but continue onward.

Eventually, I felt a shift in the atmosphere even though there was no perceptible change in the Way—it looked exactly as it had when we first entered, but it wasn't.

The coin was heavy in my pocket and too warm against my leg. The air also felt less heavy, less dense, and the blackness surrounding our intrepid party also appeared to be less complete—maybe that last one was my imagination though.

"Alright," I said, "this is it. Everybody get their shit together—game faces on, no mistakes. Right?" Neither Morse nor McGoon spoke, talking in the Way seemed borderline sacrilegious, but they nodded their understanding. "On three."

I let the ball of light dissipate, brought my M-16 up into position, counted to three with my fingers, and opened the Way with the coin.

Another door revolved into place before us, unnaturally bright in this forever-night place. The doorway looked out on the interior of a plain warehouse facility: an old dusty forklift lingered in one corner, while rows and rows of empty steel racks ran off in either direction. A large space in the center of the massive room had been fashioned into impromptu living quarters, complete with a twin-sized bed, a simple rug of Indian origin, a footlocker, and a cheap particleboard desk covered in assorted papers.

Arjun was sitting at the desk, his back conveniently facing us when the portal from the Way sprang into being. He swiveled toward us in his desk chair, a look of panic cavorting across his features, distorting his lips into a snarl. He tapped into the Vis, gathering raw energy into a shield to defend against bullets or other offensive Vis constructs. It was a smart, solid play, exactly the kind of thing any good mage would do under similar circumstances.

Instead of opening up on the guy or unleashing a wave of flame, I tossed a flash-bang into the room—a small grenade which makes a lot of noise and causes temporary light blindness. Arjun's hasty shield would stop incoming projectiles, but it wouldn't do dick against a brilliant blast of light. Most magi aren't prepared to tangle with Rube weaponry—mostly, they tend to think in terms of Vis constructs, ritual workings, or supernatural goons. Rarely, if ever, do they take into account things like physical combat or the latest in ingenious, military-grade, ass-smiting technology.

Since I'm a mage, they expect me to swing with my best energy punch. But a flash-bang? Never.

I covered my eyes, guarding against the light.

Arjun screeched as the bomb detonated. I also heard the squeal of a small girl—a high-pitch, terrified sound followed by racking sobs. She was the other reason I'd chosen the flash-bang over a typical grenade or just going in all guns a-blazin,' Rambo style. An urban assault is a tricky bit of work. There's a lot that can go wrong, particularly when you're stuck working in a wide-open space like a warehouse, with possible unknown assailants, and hostages. It would've been easy for someone to accidentally peg the little girl by mistake.

There was no chance a flash-bang would do her harm, though it would be scary as a shark with legs to an eleven-year-old.

I opened my eyes and moved into the room. The girl was off to the right, chained by her wrists to one of the abandoned metal storage shelves. She was shivering and crying. I could feel her sobs resonate in my chest like a knife wound—Arjun was a fucking grade-A monster for taking her. Some things you don't do, some things are never worth the price paid to achieve them. Never. But Arjun seemed like an *ends justify the means* kind of guy.

Morse followed me out of the portal, cutting left and back, while McGoon broke right. They were supposed to clear the room of any potential threats while also providing me plenty of space to deal with Arjun. They were back-up—in case things went south— but if they stayed in too close they'd be more of a liability for me than an asset. Mage duels can get out of hand quick; they tend to have a large kill radius for anyone unfortunate enough to be caught too close. If Morse and McGoon were clinging to my back like a couple of wide-eyed schoolgirls on the first day of class, I'd have to divide my attention to keep from harming them.

I flipped the safety off my M-4 and squeezed off a few shots at Arjun, walking forward in the odd, gating, heel-toe movement, which allowed me to keep the rifle barrel on target, even while moving. I dumped fifteen rounds, but they didn't even come close to touching him. His shield was like nothing I'd ever seen before—instead of rebuffing the rounds, or disintegrating them like my shield would, Arjun created a bubble of silver-glowing magnetic force. The field snatched the rounds out of the air, sending them into a loose orbit around him. Tiny copper planets rotating around a human-shaped sun.

Arjun smiled, his grin was a real *screw you.*

The bullets spun free and fired out of circuit, hurtling at me with a velocity even the M-4 couldn't have matched.

Damn.

Cool trick.

I'd never thought about doing something like that: metal and magnetism aren't my strongest suits, but the weave didn't look too terribly complicated. If I lived through this, I thought I could probably duplicate the construct with only a little practice.

I tossed my rifle aside—I could see it would hinder more than help against a talent like Arjun—and pulled up my friction shield. The shield shredded the bullets, but I didn't pay them any mind.

I darted left, away from the girl, and in toward Arjun. Wanted to make sure he didn't accidentally hit her during the course of the duel. Plus, I figured getting in closer would grant me a greater advantage. I'm not much bigger than Arjun, but I've been in a shit-ton of fights—I could probably smack the crazy out of his smarmy-ass if I got close enough.

The ground tore free beneath me.

I jumped up and right, just in time to see a chunk of concrete dissolve in a pit of green-glowing sludge. I lashed out with my hand, a thigh-thick lance of flame washed over Arjun. The flame passed right through his middle and I wanted to scream in triumph. My victory celebration was premature, however—the flame didn't engulf him as it should have with a direct hit like that, but rather disappeared *into* him.

A craggily barrage of ice spikes—about a dozen in all and each the size of a chop-stick—torpedoed at me from the left. An illusion. Arjun had created an illusionary simulacrum of himself, while maneuvering to my side. It never rains, it pours—and usually, for me, it becomes a torrential downpour of shit. I brought up a blue dome of solid energy. The spikes—save one—exploded on impact into a shower of crystalline ice confetti. Hadn't quite been quick enough, though. That first spike had punched two inches into my left calf before I'd gotten the shield in place.

"Ass-faced-ice-porcupine!" I shouted as I went down. Don't ask me why—sometimes the brain can come up with some wonky stuff when the pressure's on. Let's face it, all my smart-ass jokes can't be comic gold. I'm only human.

I left the ice spike in place, if I melted the thing away it could leave me bleeding out on the floor. So instead, I pumped more energy into the little construct protruding from my leg. The cold was a sharp bite in my flesh, a railroad spike of pain, but in seconds my calf went numb. Not a good long-term solution, but it would keep me in the rumble. I stumbled back to my feet—my numb leg made it tough going—and hobbled back toward Arjun.

"I am the better mage!" he yelled as he sent another three waves of ice quills at me.

"Maybe so." The quills shattered on my shield. "But I've never been good at quitting—I've been smoking since sixteen." I heated the concrete beneath his feet, fusing the soles of his shoes to the floor, while simultaneously calling up another searing wave of flame, aimed center mass. He tried to dash out of the way, but failed, frustration evident as he realized what I had done to his loafers. Tricky. A shimmering shield of artic ice formed in a half circled around him, meeting the flame with a terrible hiss and a gush of steam.

"*Gladium potestatis*!" I screamed, conjuring my sword into life with a burst of azure-light, lumbering through the vapor, hacking wildly at the space I'd last seen Arjun.

A javelin of wind hit me in the side like a hammer blow, hurling me five feet and disbanding the thick haze.

I scrambled to regain my footing, bringing my sword up to the ready—*chudan*—searching for Arjun. A flurry of green whips, each the width of a finger, lashed out of empty air, another of Arjun's illusions disappearing with the strike.

I interposed my blade in time to deflect the whip strike, but the attack had been close and well played. Arjun was about eight feet off; in one outstretched hand he held a weapon of pale sickly green flame. The whip was inordinately long—nine sinuous cords jutted from the end, a cat o' nine-tails. Hadn't expected Arjun to have this kind of trick up his sleeve. I'd wrongly assumed that he wouldn't be used to going toe-to-toe with a real live opponent like this. Sometimes it seems like I get everything wrong.

"I admire you, Yancy," he said, breathing hard. "So much dedication and determination of will. Truly admirable."

"That's a one way street." I circled right. Needed to be closer—as things stood, there was too much distance between us for me to make a clean strike. "I've got no admiration for you. A little respect maybe, but no admiration. I don't get you, Arjun. I don't get you. You don't seem so bad—why do this? What'd you gain?"

I struck low with a gust of air, not expecting or waiting for an answer. Charging in on the heels of my narrow jet stream, I dropped my sword low and swept my blade diagonally upward. Arjun struck back, his whip caught my sword-edge with one length, while another shot toward my face with a will of its own. I redirected my wind gust, narrowly avoiding the strike, lurching back a few steps and out of the reach of Arjun's weapon.

"You can't win. This is end game," he said. "I will free the Daitya, who is but the harbinger of the invasion—he will kill and slay, gathering enough Vim to open a permanent Way for his ilk. They, in turn, will spread mayhem and death across this land until they are able to free their Ancient Master, Vritra. Vritra will consume this continent, spread a pox upon your people, and, in return, Vritra will deliver me India and power over those fools in The Guild."

I dipped a little nearer—I *needed* to close the distance. His whip struck like a friggin' cobra, a live and sentient thing, attacking the second I drew within reach. Each length moved independently, each on a slightly different trajectory, pushing my abilities to their utmost limit: an overhand block, a lunging block, a wave-counter and a dive, a furious riposte.

I gave Arjun some distance. This fight was taking a toll on him as well, he looked relieved to have a little breathing room.

"Okay," I said, panting. "Let me see if I have this right. Your plan is to release the supernatural Legion of Doom, so that they can what—get their boss out of the clink? Then half the world burns, but you get India? Arjun, if you're after Hindutva, or whatever, I'm not sure you've thought this thing all the way through. This seems like an awfully screwy way to bring about world peace or India's new golden age."

He feinted right, dodged left, and came at me with his whip. I was outside his effective radius, but the attack had been a distraction. The real threat was the wall of cancer-green flame sprouting up from the floor to my right, a terrible inferno that would roast me like a spitted-pig if I misstepped. I forced a quick construct of air into place, smothering the flame and robbing it of the oxygen it needed to survive.

We circled, first left then right, a slow deliberate dance, giving us both a chance to catch some air.

"It's hard for an unbeliever such as you to understand the complexities of the events unfolding this day," he said. "Nearly impossible to understand why this tragedy *must* play out in the broken lives of men and women, children and innocents. But it must be so. Even you Westerners understand that sometimes the forest must first burn before it can regrow into something healthy and whole. All I have done here is burn down the clutter on the forest floor—I started the cleansing with riff-raff: prostitutes, drug dealers, gunrunners. They will not be missed. Did not God flood the earth of all but a handful of righteous men and women so that humanity might start again, fresh? This is no different!"

"You're not God!" I shouted. "You've got no right to pick and choose!"

"I have the power, thus I have the right! I will be God," he shouted, sprinting forward to strike at my flank, all nine-tails of his whip flying at me. I couldn't deflect so many incoming threats, not with my sword. I let the construct evaporate and called my shimmering blue dome of power into being, catching the fiery lengths along its surface—

A crack of power, as thunderous as a gun blast, resounded through the air on impact. Instead of falling limply aside, as any normal whip would, Arjun's weapon twisted and writhed, wriggling along the surface of my shield. Each section exploring my domed working, like some terrible multi-headed hydra.

Damn, the guy had more tricks in his bag than a traveling sideshow magician.

His weapon exerted a tremendous weight on my barrier, a hairsbreath more and I wouldn't be able to hold the defense. My shield flickered and faded in places, losing the energy it needed to resist the attacks.

Arjun's wall of jade-fire sprung up once more, encircling me, pushing against my domed defense on every side, sending a terrible wave of heat coursing through the thin protective barrier. Son of a bitch. There was no way I could hold out for long under that kind of stress. The combined pressure of the probing whip and the firewall was too great a strain on my fragile and overworked shield—it wasn't meant to withstand this kind of assault and I didn't have the reserve of will for it.

Time to roll the dice and play a little fast and loose.

I gathered air around me, compressing more and more oxygen molecules within the confines of my faintly glowing dome. The stress mounted and mounted, I could feel the weight of the air strain against my eardrums—I'd manufactured my own hyperbaric chamber. At last, when I knew the chamber must either burst or crush me, I collapsed the defense outright, propelling the air outward in all directions. The explosion created a vacuum that momentarily stole my breath, but which also robbed the life from the surrounding wall of flame and Arjun's whip. Both promptly sputtered and died.

The subsequent sonic boom knocked Arjun back a step and hurled me in his direction. Fine by me. I hit him around the center like 'Mean Joe' Greene—four-time Super Bowl champion, defensive lineman for the Steelers—and we both collapsed to the floor in a heap. I reached into my pocket and fumbled out my last surprise, courtesy of Morse: a can of military-grade OC spray, the shit could put down a charging bear. I sprayed a full pump right into Arjun's eyes, nose and mouth. Of course, being in such close proximity meant I dosed myself too, but that was okay.

OC spray kind of feels like having your face and lungs scraped away by an industrial-grade sander. You can't breathe or see, any exposed flesh swells and distorts, and it feels like drowning and burning all at once. The natural response to getting doused by OC is to curl up into the fetal position and cry for a couple of days. Except you try not to cry because crying makes the OC spray burn worse—it's oil based and *any* water serves to reactivate the chemical agent. Imagine having your face covered in honey and then dipped in a fire-ant hill. Now you're there.

Still, I was okay with being sprayed. Not because it didn't hurt—it hurt worse than a Muay-Thai kick to the groin—but because it's a pain I'm familiar with. I've been blasted in the face with OC plenty of times, so I knew what to expect, I knew how my body would respond, which meant I could be relatively calm even in the midst of the terrible, sand-paper, fire-ant, groin-kicking pain.

I could work through that shit. Not so for poor Arjun.

He wailed and screeched, flailing about wildly, catching my face and chest with a few wild, but ineffective, swings. I squinted my eyes and beat him, landing carefully placed blows to his ribs, neck, and face.

Dammit! I wanted to scratch my skin off, but I wanted to put this mess to rest even more.

Arjun's writhing arms deflected many of the blows, but I still landed some solid hits, which had him pleading for me to stop. I didn't.

Machine gun fire erupted from back in the warehouse, sharp and echoing in the cavernous room.

"In the rafters," Morse yelled from a distance, followed by the bark of gunfire.

"I got eyes on!" McGoon hollered from somewhere else. "It's on the move, heading straight for you."

I didn't have a clue what was happening—it was hard to think through the pain and swelling which had invaded my face and throat. Couldn't worry about Morse and McGoon. Even if Arjun did have reinforcements on the way, they weren't my immediate concern: obliterating Arjun was. If he did have goons incoming, they'd probably kill me dead, but not before I beat him into a lumpy pile of meat. Hopefully.

Body, *thwack*, body, *thwack*, face, *thump*.

Repeat.

Body, *thwack*—for all the broken bodies of women and kids.

Body, *thwack*—for all the ruined lives.

Face, *thump*—for the hell and agony he'd put me through, put my friends through.

Blood covered his face, my knuckles. He was still moaning, but his fitful struggling had slowed significantly.

The knife sank into my lower back, right beneath the edge of my bunched up jacket. I howled like a banshee with a loudspeaker and pitched over to the side, clawing for the handle, frantic to have the excruciating sting gone. A gray, clawed hand wrapped around my throat and pitched me some five feet to the side. I landed with a dull *thud*, my hands still scrambling at my back.

It was a single Rakshasa, wearing black fatigue pants, with a sheath full of ninja kunai-knives strapped to its belt. The same no-good, ass-clown from the motel—the one who'd gotten the jump on me that first time and had thrown me through a window. Damn, I was really hoping this one had been sliced up by one of those fifty-cal gunners. Life's not fair though, not by half, so it made sense that this jerk would be the only Rakshasa of the bunch to survive and that he'd be the one to punch my ticket. Asstastic.

He scooped Arjun up in protective arms and rushed him to the bed, laying him down gently, reverently even.

"Okay, Boss?" it asked with a voice ill-adept for human speech.

"The basin of water, at the foot of the bed. Get it." Arjun said, swinging his legs over the edge of the thin mattress and tentatively sitting up. The Rakshasa hurried to comply. Arjun splashed a little water on his face, trying to clear the blood and OC from his eyes. He doubled back over with a shriek, hands rubbing at his face in near panic.

I chuckled, even half-dead with a knife sticking out of my back. Small victories.

"Enough!" He yelled. "We end this here. Have you secured the intruders?"

"Yeah, Boss," the Rakshasa said, "Both of 'em are unconscious. Alive. Figured you might want to feed 'em to the Daitya."

"Good. Get the ritual instruments ready—and if the mage moves a *muscle*," he hissed the word, "I want him dead—you hear that Lazarus!? Dead!" Apparently, someone was a little grumpy-pants about the whole OC spray thing.

I grunted my acknowledgment, but it wasn't like I was going anywhere. I was done. Arjun moved over near the girl and into a large and elaborate summing circle, painted on the ground and surrounded with unlit candles.

"I'm going to kill her now, Lazarus. I'm going to sacrifice her, open the portal, and let the Daitya consume you and your accomplices. With your life force in him, he will surely have enough power to maintain his form on our plane indefinitely."

"Must have suffered some brain trauma in our scuffle," I said through clenched teeth, "it's only Monday, jackass. You've got a week before you can invite Big and Ugly over for your next shindig." I laid my head down. It hurt to talk. To breathe. To live.

"You are an ignorant child." He took a ceremonial knife—an old wood-handled thing with a stone blade—from the returning Rakshasa. "I can summon the Daitya whenever I choose, assuming I am willing to pay the price."

News to me.

"Granting the Daitya access to our world is not easy, Lazarus. The portal requires sacrifice: either seven unblemished, one-year-old, male lambs—one each day at sun's set—or a single, unblemished child."

"So you could've been sending this thing out daily?" I asked. "The hell, man? Why didn't you?"

"I'm not a monster—I don't *like* to kill," he said, exasperated and tired.

"You're kidding right? You're going to help a friggin' plague-god break free—he'll murder millions."

"Yes, but I don't like to do the killing myself."

"Not man enough to pull the trigger?" I asked, equal parts scorn and exhaustion in my voice.

"No," he said without hesitation. "Not if I don't have to. Most civilians are fine with soldiers killing the enemies of their nation, yet most would not like to pull the trigger themselves. Many people aren't even comfortable killing animals, but have no qualms about eating steak or poultry. I am no different—save that I will do what I must. I will burn down the world in order to start again, in order to save it."

He took off his blood-drenched shirt and stepped into the circle. With a small effort of will, he set the myriad of candles around him ablaze and then drew the stone knife along the inside of his left arm. The cut was not long or deep, but blood welled under the pressure of the old, pitted blade. He shook the crimson from the tip of the knife into an ancient bronze cup, no larger than a coffee mug, sitting on the concrete floor. I could feel the thrum of energy and tension filling the air. He was using himself, his blood, as the anchor and control for the gateway.

The girl's blood would serve as the key to open the lock.

The Rakshasa moved into position next to Arjun, it had my M-16 pointed right at me.

"It's over," Arjun said. "Now lie still and make peace with your gods. Take some solace, though, I will make the end quick for you. You fought well despite the fact that you are terribly misguided." He turned and looked at the Rakshasa, "If any of them move—Lazarus or the others—kill them without prejudice." He turned back to face the girl. "I'm sorry," he said to her and then began to chant, a slow, slightly off-key mantra in some long-forgotten tongue.

THIRTY-ONE:

End Game

I was done, I knew it in my heart—Arjun had played a better hand, and for me the fat ol' Blues Man was about to trumpet his last note. I could feel blood seeping out of the knife wound in my back—there wasn't a pool by any means, but certainly enough to concern me. Also, it was starting to get cold and my legs felt too heavy. I wasn't ready to die here, I wasn't ready to go on to whatever came next. My heart was beating heavy in my chest and tears ran down my cheeks.

There was a lot I hadn't done, people I'd never had a chance to say good-bye to.

My sons were still out there. My grandkids. All probably thought I was long dead. Still, I would've liked to see them again. I always suspected it would end more or less like this for me—a lonely and violent death. I'd accepted that reality. But there's an ocean worth of difference between accepting something rationally and staring that ugly, shit-kicking truth in the face.

I knew from the beginning that it was a mistake to get involved in this ordeal. Knew it wouldn't end well for a whole lot of people—me, right smack-dab, at the top of the list.

I'm not a hero, I never wanted to be. All I wanted was to play my music, throw down a little action on a game of poker once in a while, and be mostly alone.

Instead, I was bleeding out on the floor while a little girl cowered in the corner—her face dirty and tear-streaked, her knee-highs covered in warehouse filth, her arms curled around her coltish legs. Instead, I had a little girl who was about to be murdered. An eleven-year-old named Samantha who went by Sammy.

If I didn't stop Arjun a bunch of other good people would die too, but those people were far away, while Sammy was sitting right in front of me. Crying.

Like Mick Jagger said so long ago, *you can't always get what you want*. Too true, brother. Too true. And if I was going to go out ... well, dammit, at least I could try to give that little girl a chance. I even had a plan, sort of. A long shot which might stop Arjun and maybe save the girl.

She would get a fucking chance, even if it cost me everything.

I hadn't ever let go of the Vis, even though the flow feeding into me was a weak thing, a trickle of power. That wouldn't do though, I needed more. I let myself go, let myself draw more deeply than I should have, especially in my weak state, knowing I could easily burn myself out and lose the ability to touch the Vis. I reassured the gibbering voice of caution in my head that I was going to die, so it wasn't worth worrying about. The power I was holding was substantial, but there was so much juju floating around in the air, Arjun would never notice.

If you're diddy boppin' along the road on some warm still day, you might notice a strong gust of wind. You sure as shit won't notice that same breeze if there's a friggin' tornado roaring by a block over. Arjun was calling up a tornado.

But I couldn't throw some quick-and-dirty, last-ditch-effort, construct at him. Whatever else he may have been, he was a damn good mage, operating from a place of strength, and he'd have a defense up for just about anything. He had my measure. He might not be able to feel my power, but if a new and different construct sprang into being, he'd sense it from a mile off and swat it down like a gnat.

But he wouldn't notice a construct almost identical to his own. Weaving a construct with the same resonance pattern as his would be like hiding a smaller shadow inside of a much larger one.

I focused my flagging will, spinning hundreds of razor-thin strands of radiant heat into a rough lattice square, overlaid and woven through with streams of air, and knots of earthen power. The structure was invisible to the unaided human eye, but it would have vaguely resembled a medieval castle gate—a door—which is what it was. Arjun was opening a gateway, so I decided I would open one too. I constructed mine strand by strand about a foot below his feet, right between him and the Rakshasa, hidden beneath the concrete floor of the warehouse.

Remember, I'm not exactly the best at opening portals—big kablooey, lots of fire, black hole of doom into another dimension. I'm no Harold the Mange. When I rip open a gateway it gets messy and dangerous, and all the more so now because I didn't know where this place overlapped with Outworld. Whatever. A big kablooey was just what I needed right about now. And hey, I'm a gambler, I've taken plenty of long shot bets in my days, what was one more? Good to know I could go out being true to myself—maybe I hadn't avoided being inanely heroic, but at least I could still go out playing the ponies.

Arjun's chanting took on a new rhythm, the words coming faster and faster, his pitch rising in fanatic zeal, the knife in his hand hooking and slashing in well-rehearsed and practiced movements. Terrible strain filled the air. The crackling pressure which proceeds a momentous lightning storm or some unspeakable act of Mother Nature.

With the Vis filling me, I could see his construct: easily twice the size of what I had made and far more intricate and beautiful. Arjun's portal resembled the entrance to Notre Dame, while mine, by comparison, vaguely resembled the cave-dwelling entrance of some ancient and especially dense Neanderthal.

I drew still more deeply from the Vis, letting that power flow out of me and into my grubby portal, my body a conduit and little more.

"Please, mister," the little girl whimpered. Arjun stepped closer to the edge of the circle, rising the knife high above his head in a two-fisted hold, readying himself for the killing blow. "Please don't do this, *pleasepleaseplease* ..." Heaving sobs racked her frail form, she drew her knees even more tightly against her body.

Arjun never stopped chanting, but I could see an apology in his face, regret in his eyes. He was going to kill her—his arms were unwavering as he held the knife waiting to sink it home—but he didn't want to. To him this was a death of necessity, but nothing more. In that moment, I could almost understand him. His was a unique brand of crazy, but maybe once upon a time, in a place called Nam, I'd taken a sip of that brew. So I could get it. Almost.

The knife plunged downward, a lightning strike, but not faster than my thoughts. In the moment I saw his hand move, I simply let my gateway unravel. I curled myself into a ball, though I didn't have the strength to roll my back toward the blast area. I was way too close to the gateway for comfort.

I had enough power left to form a single defensive shield: the shimmering blue working—meant to absorb the blast impact and deflect incoming debris—sprang into life. I could see Sammy's face tinged blue by the shield surrounding her. She'd be okay, and for me ... well, I'd have a great seat for the fireworks.

The explosion rocked the room, concrete and stone flying through the air in a spray of deadly shrapnel. Huge clods of dirt and rock filled the air, a cloud of smaller projectiles swept through the room like a sandstorm. Little jagged pieces of stone bit into my exposed skin like a swarm of horseflies. Huge chunks of floor smacked into my ribs, chest, and face—the latter resulting in a busted lip and right eyebrow. If I did survive my own attack, I'd have the mother of all shiners to show for it—and I'd be responsible. I wouldn't even be able to say *you should see the other guy*, because I would be the other guy.

Arjun let out a startled squawk and the Rakshasa uttered a harsh bark as the blast lifted them into the air. Hadn't been ready for my exploding floor trick, I was sure. A large chunk of concrete—maybe a couple hundred pounds or so—landed on Arjun's stomach with a thick meaty, *squish*, effectively pinning him to the floor. If the blast hadn't killed him, it wouldn't be long before the stone did.

The Rakshasa lost one gray-skinned leg in the explosion, but the detonation still hadn't killed it. The son of a bitch should have been the consistency of pudding—shit, but those things are tough. It was okay. I hadn't counted on the explosion doing all the heavy lifting anyways. Best not to put all your eggs into one basket, as they say.

The floor imploded with a great *whoof*—the temporary gateway I'd created inhaled the particulate cloud swirling about the air in a terrible tornado of motion. It also inhaled the Rakshasa, who'd landed a few feet away from the epicenter of the vortex. The thing clawed and fought to keep from falling into the abyss, but it was a useless effort. Rakshasa may be as tough as a gang of Tijuana Federales on a power trip, but they don't weigh that much more than a couple of full-grown men.

The Rakshasa was too close to the portal and didn't have the mass to keep its feet—err, well, *foot* technically. It let out one last terrible howl as it vanished through the portal and disappeared, hopefully into some dark and terrible region of the Ways where it would die in some utterly unfortunate and amusing way. Maybe food for a Dara-Naric.

Arjun had been thrown clear of the gravitational pull of the opening and the two-hundred-pound boulder nailing his ass to the ground like a giant paperweight helped him stay firmly put. I, on the other hand, wasn't so lucky. I hadn't been nearly as close as Arjun or the Rakshasa—evident by the fact that I was still breathing and had all my limbs intact and what have you—but I could feel my body slowly sliding toward the portal.

With a groan, I rolled onto my belly, sprawling out in order to create more surface friction and hopefully find something to grab hold of. I only needed to hang on for another twenty seconds, tops, then the portal would stabilize and shut down. My belly-flop maneuver definitely bought me a few seconds, but I didn't think it would be enough. I weakly floundered about with my arms and knees, digging in with the toes of my boots, frantically trying to low crawl my way to safety. The effort was enormous, the pain in my back a throbbing fire running up and down my spine, the ice spike in my leg a lancing jolt of frozen hell.

A crushing weight landed on top of me, avoiding the knife by a few inches, but creating a wave of pain so intense it was hard to think. McGoon had thrown his weight onto me and together our combined mass halted the slide. Five or so seconds later, a sharp whip crack in the air told me the portal had stabilized. It would close down shortly. Yraeta's goon had saved my life, how about that? I found myself acutely aware that had I killed him back in that alleyway in New Orleans I might well be dead now. The irony was not lost on me.

The thug rolled off me after the threat passed. I guess you can't always get what you want, but sometimes you do get what you need.

"Don't worry, buddy," he growled in my ear. "We'll get you out of here, get you patched up. It'll be okay. You take it easy now, buddy."

My eyes tracked to where Arjun lay. Morse was standing over him like the Reaper of Death himself, a Glock pointed right at his face. Morse turned his gaze to Yraeta's daughter, no longer obscured by my blue force shield.

"Close your eyes, sweetie. I don't want you to see this. Then we'll take you home to your mommy and daddy. Okay?" She didn't nod or smile, but she did take her hands away from her scabbed knees and pressed them tightly against her eyes. I would've thanked Morse for it if I could have moved or spoken.

"This is for Danny and Jodi," Morse said to Arjun. "For Hawk and Jamie, Boston Paul and Big Rob, for Skinner and Angie, and for the mother-fuckin' Saints, bitch." He pulled the trigger twice, a quick double tap, which left no doubt in my mind about Arjun's fate.

Some part of me took satisfaction in the outcome, but only a small part. I wanted to hate Arjun, but I couldn't, not now. He was a bad guy, no doubt, but not the villain I'd made him out to be in my mind. No one casts themselves as the monster in their own story. Arjun had died trying to do the right thing, even if he'd lost sight of what was *actually* right a long, long way back. He needed killing like a psychotic tiger on steroids needs killing.

I didn't relish his death. I'd seen enough bloodshed to last me a good long while a small part of me wished things could have turned out differently.

You can't always get what you want.

I closed my eyes, too tired to do anything else, too tired to care anymore.

THIRTY-TWO:

R & R

I woke up on a squeaky, spring-filled, twin mattress in a small bedroom with a generic painting of a sailboat on the adjacent wall. Soft light trickled in through the curtained window: early evening, though I didn't know which day. The nightstand next to me held a glass of water with a bendy straw and a small plate full of saltines. My stomach promptly informed me it was both angry and hungry, but I couldn't muster the motivation to sit up and eat.

Everything hurt, everything: my face, back, ass, arms and legs—my left calf was screaming like a lunatic in a padded cell. I kind of felt like screaming too.

I wasn't dead, I hurt way too much for that—plus, I imagine Heaven has to have a better waiting room. And if I were in Hell … well, surely upper management would be a little more imaginative.

It was just Greg's spare bedroom and I was alive and recovering, which was a good thing. Except it didn't feel good, everything hurt so much that being dead might've been the better option. Though I've heard Hell isn't exactly all sunshine and picnic baskets either.

I rummaged around on the night table and fumbled the water glass to my mouth, taking a few small sips through the straw. My throat was awfully dry and the water felt cool, soothing. I made quite the racket doing it and spilled about half the glass onto my chest and sheets. Friggin' coordination was toast.

"You're awake." Greg came into the room and took a seat on an uncomfortable looking rocking chair in the corner.

"Yeah I'm awake. How could you possibly expect me to sleep on this mattress? Did you steal this thing from the singles barracks when you retired?"

"See you haven't lost any of your charm," he replied. "I was hoping for some slight brain damage—maybe something in the way of a good lobotomy ... How're you feeling? I've got some Vicodin or Percocet for you if you need to take the edge off."

"Sweet, sweet, dear man," I said, "surely you are an angel of mercy. Maybe this *is* Heaven—Vicodin, please, lots of Vicodin." He got up from his chair, which squeaked on the floorboards, left the room, and came back a few minutes later with an orange prescription bottle in hand.

"They're five hundred milligrams each. You want three?"

I nodded my head and regretted it. "Before I get all doped up and loopy. How's Sammy—did she make it out alright?"

He snorted.

"Yeah, she's fine—scared and shaken up, but fine. Practically in love with you, I'd wager. Morse and Sanderson—"

"Who's Sanderson?" I asked.

"The big guy from Yraeta's crew—the one who saved your life."

"Aw, McGoon. Sanderson, really? Such a plain name for such a giant, ugly, bag of meat. I'll have to send him a thank you card. Okay, okay, I'm tracking. Go on."

"I was saying, Morse and *McGoon* are fine too, they saw the whole thing. Saw you blow up Arjun and the Rakshasa and save the girl. I think the whole bunch of 'em are going to join the Yancy Lazarus Fan Club. Makes me just about sick."

"Gee, Greg, don't sugar coat anything now. Why don't you tell me how you really feel?"

"Don't even get me started," he said. "The whole lot of 'em are all gushy about you. Morse said you're welcome to stop by The Full House anytime—they'll always have a seat open for you at the card table if you're interested. His words."

"And Yraeta?" I asked.

"Says he's in your debt—like I said, that little girl is in love with you. Wouldn't be surprised if she gets an action-hero poster of you on her wall."

"How about you, Greg? You doing okay? Head healing up alright?"

"I'm fine, princess." He subconsciously ran a finger over the faint pink scar on his head. "No need to worry about me ... but, thanks for saving me. Next time, though, how about you work your damn hoodoo so the car just doesn't hit us, huh? It's gonna take me a year to get the Fairlane back up and runnin'."

"You're welcome, Greg."

"Eat a few crackers," he said, "take the Valium, and sleep more. I'll be back to check on you later. Need anything else, your highness?"

"Yeah," I said. "When you go out can you grab me some ribs? From Frank's, too. I don't want any cheap stuff. And I could use a little music, I'm thinking 'Sitting on the Dock of the Bay.'"

He rendered me a mock bow, a serf before his liege, before walking out.

A few minutes later, Otis Redding's smoky, mellow voice filled the house—Greg was playing the actual LP, not some CD or YouTube clip. Genuine vinyl. I sipped my water, downed my pills, and let the music pull me out into the waters of rest—alone at last with some good tunes. About time.

Special Thanks

I'd like to thank my wife, Jeanette, and daughter, Lucy. A special thanks to my parents, Greg and Lori. A quick shout out to my brother Aron and his whole brood—Eve, Brook, Grace, and Collin. Brit, probably you'll never read this, but I love you too. Thank you to my editor, Tracy Stengel, and to all of the Beta readers, especially Brenna and Ashley, who made this book possible.

—James A. Hunter, January 2015

About the Author

Hey all, my name is James Hunter and I'm a writer, among other things. So just a little about me: I'm a former Marine Corps Sergeant, combat veteran, and pirate hunter (seriously). I'm also a member of The Royal Order of the Shellback—'cause that's a real thing. And, a space-ship captain, can't forget that.

Okay … the last one is only in my imagination.

Currently, I work as a missionary and international aid worker with my wife and young daughter in Bangkok, Thailand. When I'm not working, writing, or spending time with family, I occasionally eat and sleep.

Books, Mailing List, and Reviews

If you enjoyed reading about Yancy and want to stay in the loop about the latest book releases, awesomesauce promotional deals, and upcoming book giveaways be sure to subscribe to my email list at www.JamesAHunter.wordpress.com

Word-of-mouth and book reviews are crazy helpful for the success of any writer. If you *really* enjoyed reading about Yancy, please consider leaving a short review at either Amazon or Goodreads—just a couple of lines about your overall reading experience. Thank you in advance.